Mary Sakitty
515 Garden Ave.
Manistique, Mich.

THE TROUBLE IN THOR

THE TROUBLE
IN THOR

by Jo Valentine

Coward-McCann, Inc.
New York

CHAPTER ONE

THE day we are born somebody fastens a diaper on us with a safety pin. From that time forward we do not live without steel.

The gadgets we have in our houses, our cars, iceboxes, and the machines that build the roads for the cars to run on, and the machines the farmer uses to grow the food we keep in the iceboxes, and the machines that make the machines . . . besides the buildings, railroads, bridges, tunnels, the warships and the guns . . . take steel.

So the mills blaze and the metal boils and the steel comes rolling out.

But steel takes iron.

So, before that, down the lakes must come the long flat ore boats in slow parade, low-lying, and hard to see from shore except by the smear of their smoke against the sky, carrying with stately persistence the raw ore.

Yet, before that, those vessels must lie against a dock, to receive the noisy burden that roars down out of the bellies of the ore cars. And the ore trains must, before that, have banged and rattled through the countryside, around the hills, past the little lakes, through the woods, of the north country.

And those cars have passed, before that, below the trestles or beside the great loaders, to receive the ore from the stock pile which is an artificial ridge of the broken stuff, lying on the surface of the ground.

That is not the beginning either.

Now, on the Mesabi they strip the earth away and expose the ore body. But, on the Menominee range, this broken ore has to come up on a small carrier, a buckety elevator . . . a skip, they call it . . . load by puny load, a swift and narrow

1

way out of a deep place. And the ore got into that skip by sliding there on cunningly tilted chutes, themselves only part of a honeycomb, a system, a thing called a mine, burrowed and built and working under the ground.

In the very beginning the ore body lay, one with the rock, hidden below the forest, meadow and lake, unknown. Men hunted it. They drilled until they found it. They dug down. They broke it with dynamite. They knocked it away from its solid home and lifted it out of the ground.

These are mining men, and what they do seems almost impossible, but they do it anyway.

Thor, Michigan, was a mining town. There was no other reason whatsoever for its existence. Yet if you had ridden through it, in the year 1920, you might not have guessed this to be so. It was a pretty little town in those days.

The Upper Peninsula of Michigan, near the Wisconsin border, is hilly and woodsy and smells of pine. Lakes, pond-size or larger, or lying in groups and chains linked together around enchanting little islands and promontories, would look from the air as if they had been punched boldly out of very thick stuff, for the trees there reach to the edge of the water and the water often lies, deep and smiling, reflecting the shore almost as much as the sky. There are, in this country, some rolling spaces where the forests have burned or been cut away, and only a low brush covers the land (although the seedlings hide in the grasses). There are marshes too, choked with the vertical reeds and cattails growing like a cluster of exclamation points. There are rivers: the Menominee, the Niagara, the Sturgeon, and they fall sometimes over the basic ledges. But the land dips and rolls and the road curls sweetly through it, for there are no great mountains and it is all softened and feathered by the forests. It is not farm country. It looks like a place for campers and fishermen, a place to play. It does not look like a violent land.

Had someone thrown a handful of buildings from the sky, they might have fallen, by chance and gravity, exactly in the pattern of the town of Thor. The biggest ones would have rolled to the bottom of the little valley. The rest would have caught, scattering on the gentler slopes, thinning as the hills rose to the north and west, dribbling off through the flat mouth of the valley eastward, except for one little knot of them accumulated there. And, of course, the curving rim of Thor Lake would bite off the same clear and decisive end to the southwest section of the settlement.

Yet there were man-cut corners, a few of them, and some squares.

Of course, if you had come down the road from the northwest you would have passed, on your left, one scalped hillside where, ranged on the bare ground along a steep and crooked side road, there was a terraced series of stern and utilitarian looking buildings. This was West Thor Mine. The shafthouse, at the bottom, would have told you.

But then the road would drift on between woodsy banks for a mile or more before, coming softly down a long hill, you would begin to see the dwellings thickening along the way. At the bottom of the hill the road bent slightly to the left around the little white Methodist Church, then ran a short straight block to a true corner. Here, on a dusty plaza, stood the town hall of naked yellow brick, unshaded, unplanted. The main road did not run before it but turned right and passed two school houses instead. One was a big, buxom, Victorian-looking wooden grade school. The other was a smaller, neater, newer high school which bore, absurdly and pretentiously, on each corner of its portico, three fat concrete Ionic pillars. The schools stood in a green yard with the bare playground hidden behind them, and it was pretty.

At the foot of this second short block, facing straight up the middle of the street, lay the low brooding mass of the Company offices and the general store. The road turned again before it—to left and the east. But, by this time, you have been through the main part of Thor. This was its heart. A town hall, two schools and the Company buildings, and this was all the business section there was, too, except for a lone butcher shop inconspicuously apart, not even on the main road at all.

When the road turned and went east past the depot it was finished with right angles for awhile. It drifted off on a southerly slant across a small bridge over a railroad cut, and finally through a separate cluster of houses called East Thor,

3

which huddled around the ankles of a big Catholic Church. East Thor Mine was not easily seen from the road. You might spy the shafthouse lofting itself above the trees but probably you wouldn't have noticed it.

So you would think of the quaintly turning main street, so refreshingly *not* straight, and *not* lined with false fronts, but running under tall trees in that quick Z, and you would remember the uncommercial look of the place, its coziness and its charm, its fresh green in summer, or the unsoiled white of its heavy and enduring winter coat of snow. Charming, you would think. Such a pretty village!

But if you stayed, you would soon know it was not like ordinary pretty villages. It had other sounds. There would be, of course, the long roar of the ore trains banging through on their track that cut the town's south edge so briefly and abruptly and then ran away between the lake and the town. Or, in the night especially, you would hear the hiss and rattle and long, loud, snorting sighs of the steam shovels loading ore. And there were the whistles hooting the changing shifts—blowing time (all day, all night).

And if you were to walk past the Sunday school picnic grounds—up the slope, northward, on the slippery brown of the pine needles, looking for trilliums or the shy arbutus in the spring—you might hear through the soles of your feet the deep thud of dynamite.

You would begin to see things. You would see the great pipe lines, tarred and black, running through woods and fields. You would see the men going to work in the evening, carrying their full dinner pails for their midnight meal, when, in the ordinary village, the day's work would have been over and the cows come home.

Even so, perhaps you would not know that this was a violent place; that under the pretty little town each day, each night, there was risk, and bold struggle, and sometimes death, and always danger.

The Northwestern train, carrying the mail from points south, was on time. Therefore, at a quarter after eleven in the morning, Cyril Varker rose from his desk and reached for his hat and his canvas bag. The bag belonged to the Com-

4

pany, of course. Yet it was his, for Cyril clung fiercely to this chore. Younger clerks, subordinate to him, would have been glad to frisk freely up the street to the post office during office hours but, although Cyril had risen to be assistant head bookkeeper, he had never relinquished this morning task.

It pleased him to go.

The Company offices had a special, a holy smell of polished wood and paper, a smell that existed only here in the whole town.

Passing through the two wooden gates in the two spindled barriers that split the offices into sections of varying importance, running from the lowly help near the street door back toward the inner keep where Mr. McKeever, the superintendent, sat in his private room, Cyril emerged into sunny July, knowing that the scent of this place traveled with him on this mission.

He was a thin and somewhat twisted man in his thirties who walked with a slight tossing of the foot on the ankle and bent very slightly backward from the hips, as a man might walk who must trundle a paunch ahead of him. Cyril, however, had no paunch; only his sharp hip bones thrust forward in this odd posture. He also carried one shoulder some inches higher than the other, and so there was a twisted look to him. Because he carried his head bent down, he always looked up to see; his brow was perpetually furrowed and his eyes stretched wide open. The thin face showed its bones and had no color, but his hair, although it already had to be arranged carefully to cover all of his head, was a rusty red.

He didn't look well. He never had. He never would.

He turned to the left on the wide pavement in front of the store and then he turned right, crossed the dusty track that led down to the warehouse, and started up the street passing the doctor's office which was set back from the sidewalk as if the shabby gray frame building hid in the schoolyard corner.

Walking in the intermittent shade past the schools and their deserted grounds, all empty and silent in July, Cyril received the brisk heat of the day. He didn't love nature, not he. He loved nothing. But his mind worked. The thoughts

5

ran in his head. They never stopped, never in his waking hours. And he kept watching with those wide eyes strained to see up past the bony ridge of his own skull, and there was little he did not see or, having seen, think about.

At the end of the block he had to cross catty-corner to get to the post office which was in the town hall. It was the only part of the two story building in daily use. The remainder of the ground floor was taken up by a big lobby with double stairs on the west and, on the east, by a warren of queer little rooms with a stairway connection to the stage. The post office, facing south, was in the middle.

The hall, the one room upstairs, was a theater, a ballroom and a gymnasium. Everything happened there. Children in cheesecloth piped their operettas on the same stage from which some of them, in time, would be graduated from high school in solemn exercises. Meantime they screamed for the team at basketball games when the stage became the home bleachers and the hated partisans of the enemy howled in the balcony. Here were given the class plays after the long enchanting prelude of play practice . . . when much courting and intrigue was possible on the fire escape at the back of the building and down those back stairs.

Here also came, when it did come, the outside world—the Chautauqua, lecturers, stock companies and minstrel shows.

And here were held all the dances in Thor. Then glamor, manufactured out of music and crepe paper, perfume and desire, rendered perfectly invisible the black foul lines painted on the floor. The girls' thin slippers, sliding, forgot how they had stamped for a hero's winning toss, and the boys remembered the sweat and the effort as if it had all been in another place. Then, on the theater seats now pushed —they were very pushable, those seats—into a three-sided square, the ladies and girls sat chattering to each other in the intervals, appearing perfectly indifferent to the fact that the male sex had vanished from the room. But when the orchestra on stage sailed into the next number every female heart jumped at least a little. For then, suddenly, the whole wall of the lobby burst open letting in clouds of tobacco smoke and hordes of men and boys who streaked in all directions, each to a lady before whom he stood and muttered,

6

"Dance?" It was the moment of judgment; success or failure, triumph or despair. It was terrible. And it happened to every female sixteen times during the evening, or seventeen if there was an encore. But that was the way they did it in Thor. No programs. No promises. Only the sudden, swift, sentence: Now.

You danced or you sat.

Cyril Varker didn't dance but he used to go. He used to stand in the smoky lobby and listen to everything with his head held crooked to look up sideways. And every time the music started and the men erupted, as was their habit, each after his first choice, veering cannily if he saw he had lost it, Cyril felt a boom of mirth in his stomach, although he kept from laughing. He believed that he alone in Thor, having no part in the drama and no personal anxiety to choose or be chosen, could see how funny the custom was.

He went to everything. It pleased him to watch.

Now he entered the post office, chewing thought sourly. He knew, he felt, that in Thor he was socially displaced. In a sense he had displaced himself. For the place open to him and his twisted body, in a two-sexed world, was too humble for his taste. He had taken himself apart from all competition of that kind. He had devised a more or less secret source of fun and power, which was enough.

Besides, there was this habit of watching and thinking which he enjoyed, and moments, in the course of his work, which he relished very much. Payday, for instance. And getting the Company's mail. In these moments Cyril *was* placed. In them he represented the Company and the Company was, of course, power, and nakedly known.

The post office was a room about twenty-five feet long and half as wide, with the east end a barrier of mailboxes built around the window. Behind that barrier now, vinegary little Mrs. Fielding and her two sleek, fat daughters were sorting as fast and furiously as they could. The window remained closed, the public must wait. Cyril walked diagonally across the bare floor on which he knew were drawn invisible zones. He went to lean in his own spot, the junction between the mailboxes and the candy counter where he was privileged, by power, to hand his empty bag over the glass and receive

7

his full one without being obliged to wait in line at the window.

He leaned there. What a one he was for seeing patterns. He knew the social pattern of Thor itself most sensitively, for one who was not included in the figure. The town was feudal. Perfectly feudal. Economically feudal, as a Company town is bound to be. But socially, in the sense of the Four Hundred, the *creme de la creme*, and who was invited to what—in that sense of society—it was rigidly feudal, too.

Socially then, Mr. McKeever, the superintendent, was the king, and his wife was the queen. And that was plain and final. Now around the throne, like a set of barons, were the aristocrats. Men took rank by their jobs. Although it was not altogether how much money a man made, it was his training and his authority. It was his prestige. It was rank. The mining engineer, the chief engineer, their closest assistants, the manager of the office and of the store, the doctor, of course, and the superintendent of schools; such as these, heads of things and high sub-heads, these were the nobility. Wives took rank according to the husband's position, and that was very nearly plain and final too.

But, mused Cyril, certain matters of national origin and religion entered into the pattern and complicated it. There was a separate structure of society among the Cornish people. Captain Trezona, for instance, as head of underground activity in both mines, ranked high in the authority and importance of his work. Yet he kept, after hours, to his own circle—to the Methodist socials and the church doings, and a few family gatherings. Of course his piety forbade him the theater and the dance, and his wife did not play auction bridge at all, or any other game with the wicked court cards —the red hearts, the black spades—and so never with the ladies club every eighth Wednesday.

Then, too, there was the priest, Father Martin, who most certainly ranked as the head of something, for the Catholic Church was far larger, far stronger, far richer, than the tiny Episcopal Chapel, or even the staunch and close-knit Methodists themselves. Yet Father Martin belonged to a separate figure in the pattern. *He* did not hobnob out of hours with the high moguls.

8

Nor, for the most part, did his parishioners. The foreign-born, the Italians, the Poles, however graded and differentiated their skills and their jobs, were not socially eligible. If they did not seem to realize what splendors they were denied, but rather pitied the cold Protestants in their bleak pews and rather preferred the glory of God in the mass to Mrs. McKeever's parlor, this was beside the point. Somebody had to be excluded. In a feudal system somebody has to be a serf.

Cyril enjoyed the lick of amusement in his mind. . . .

He glanced about him. Patterns, oh yes. He wondered if the young men and boys who gathered this morning, as they always did gather in the zone between the stationery end of the counter and the posters on the back wall, knew why. There were five or six of them waiting there now, and out of the group rose a male buzz of scuffling feet and suppressed guffaws. Why *there?* Cyril wondered. Because they were animal-shy and could easily escape by the door, there, if necessary?

And why was it the rule for females that they must wait for the mail in the zone along the two barred windows? Was it safer or more respectable there? Children, of course, pushed noses on the glass between them and the candy. This was direct and natural. Members of the *haut monde*, he reflected, waited before the mailboxes, for it was they who rented them.

Cyril sucked his cheek.

One of the young men in the far corner met his eye. He was not a very tall young man, and on the slender side. His mouth and teeth were almost girlishly pretty. When he grinned—and grin was the right word for the true merriment, the rollicking quality of his smile—grooves appeared like dimples in his lean cheeks. But his cheekbones were high and prominent; the total cast of his face was gaunt.

He seemed to be a shy boy. He did not put himself forward in the group to be their leader or anyone of special importance. But just the same, the rowdies, the rough young egos, the bursting pushing young men deferred to this one. In a half-furtive way they watched his reaction. They did not court his attention quite openly. They almost—but not

9

quite—showed off before him; not because he was clever or strong or admirable in their eyes, but because in some mysterious way he simply charmed them.

His name was Wesley Trezona and now, silent in the shuffling group, he turned his head and looked at Cyril Varker.

And Cyril Varker, silent in his corner of the post office, sent an eye-beam back. It was private, secret, and threatening. It went over other heads to its mark, to warn and remind. In Cyril's concave breast rose a sweet rage of power, his own, his personal power. He felt, crackling in his head like kindling catching fire, the impulse to smash. So his glance was cold, vicious, unmerciful. It took effect in a convulsion of the young man's throat and a rapid shift of his eyes.

Cyril was pleased. It pleased him very much to have frightened Wesley Trezona.

Mrs. Dr. Hodge came in holding, as usual, her head so high that she could not possibly have seen past her jutting bosom to where her feet were falling. She gave Cyril a medium-grade nod and sailed up to Mrs. Gilchrist. The ladies fell to conversing in genteel voices punctuated with the high hooting that was not really laughter at all. It was the same sound that used to rise out of a ladies' club afternoon and paralyze whatever male was the husband of that Wednesday's hostess, who had to come home to supper to find his house swarming with furs and feathers and all the best china salad-smeared, who must suffer himself to be hooted at by each departing lady and then eat in lonesome heartiness beside an exhausted wife who picked at her food, pale with her memories.

No, the sound was not laughter. There was no mirth in it. Cyril, listening, decided that it must be a social signal of some kind, and what it signaled he struggled to define in his mind. He noted that the shufflers in the corner were pretending to just miss resisting the temptation to hoot, too. Pretending because they never would hoot where the ladies could hear them, even though, were they to do so, the ladies would never admit to having heard them at all.

Cyril's mouth twisted. In what weird mixture of contempt and respect did human beings hold each other? No two classes, mused Cyril, could be much farther apart in their total conception of what life is than these young rowdies and those matrons.

The boys in the corner became as quiet as mice.

Cyril gnawed his lip. His sister, Madeline, had come into the post office.

Her hand sent him a little flip of recognition and he blinked his pale eyes. Cyril hid his sigh. He watched her walk to the zone proper for her. He noted the quality of the nod she drew from Mrs. Dr. Hodge . . . gracious, condescending . . . from Mrs. Gilchrist . . . aloof and slyly interested. He noted the quality of the greeting she drew from the other women and girls—quick smiles put on and snatched off the faces.

He watched his sister Madeline compose herself to wait meekly, dressed in a decent dark dress, not running over for the mail in a house-dress as some had, but hatless, and ungloved—as Mrs. Hodge and Mrs. Gilchrist were not.

He thought bitterly, she'll never make it. Never.

It was not because her husband, Arthur Cole, worked underground. Arthur was an uncertain quantity. Anything could become of him. He was not Catholic, not foreign-born, and he had some education, and he was restless. He had a drive. Arthur might one day acquire rank or even become eligible without it. But Madeline never.

And yet she was educated and quite well, too. Cyril had seen to that himself. And she had been a schoolteacher, which in those days was a respected profession and conferred prestige. Nor was her beauty the flaw, for Marianne Gilchrist herself was a handsome woman, dark-haired, blue-eyed, with a narrow oval face, good nose, fine figure, and *she* ranked.

But Madeline's figure, curved and compact, poised beautifully on her beautiful legs, was designed for one thing only. The whole post office knew it. Madeline's pretty fragrant torso was made to fit in a man's arms. And had. And would, if it could.

The males in their corner knew this. Mrs. Gilchrist knew this. Mrs. Dr. Hodge knew this.

11

I know it, thought Cyril. He used to tease his little sister, saying he got the best of the brains and she the best of the bodies out of the mating of their two parents. Yet Madeline wasn't stupid. Her eyes were particularly fine, large and gray, set well in the creamy skin of her lovely face. Madeline was —Cyril ground his teeth—not stupid, but a little fool, just the same.

He didn't love her, not he. But she was his charge, for their parents were long dead, and he was annoyed with her, as usual, and for her, too. It annoyed him *now* to see the ladies' backs edge around.

He thought angrily, she has personal power and her kind they can't abide. They are afraid of her so they won't let her in. Let her stand as meek as she may, she'll never make it. And all the while his knowledge persisted; she was not meek; she no more sought a meek place in the pattern than he did.

The males in the corner began to mill and move again, and their eyes moved, but not far away from Madeline Cole. It was twenty minutes of twelve. Some difference in the bustle behind the mailbox barrier made it plain to those waiting that the mail was nearly all sorted. Out of the quite considerable crowd that had accumulated, the women began to form a tentative line before the window.

Outside, Henry Duncane drove his Stearns-Knight into the plaza, set the brakes, killed the engine, opened the door, and was out and up the post office steps, as if this was all one rhythmic motion. He was new in Thor—having been the Company's chief engineer for less than a year—and he was young. He came into the post office as he did everything else, decisively, with a verve. His solid footsteps rang on the floor. One gulp of the atmosphere told him that the mail was all sorted except the second class matter, and everyone in the post office knew at once that he did not intend to wait for that. He crossed the crowded room in a straight line, finding no one that he needed to dodge, for people melted out of his path. Mrs. Dr. Hodge smiled sunnily and Mrs. Gilchrist's neck took a swanlike arching. Madeline, too, altered the angle of her head.

Henry Duncane said "Good morning," once for them all,

in his uniquely clear voice. He said, "Varker," to Cyril, and Cyril responded, "Mr. Duncane."

Henry's hand flipped open mailbox two-six-six, which he never bothered to lock, clearheadedly knowing that the combinations were not really secret, and never would be. He took out his letters and began to examine them, slipping each behind the rest rapidly.

Mrs. Gilchrist stepped near him and put her gloves sweetly on his arm.

"And how's dear Elizabeth today?" she said in a discreetly lowered voice.

Duncane did not look up, but he answered, "Elizabeth's well, thank you." Such was the carrying quality of his voice that everyone else in the post office seemed to have been speaking all this while with mush in his mouth.

Mrs. Gilchrist mumbled something, and Duncane in his turn said, "She would be glad to see you."

Only now, having slipped the last letter to the bottom of his pile, he looked up and smiled at her.

But this was all the smiling and all the chitchat there was going to be. He put his mail in his pocket, touched his hat, and turned and walked out, finding his way cleared as before, having accomplished what he came for with such neatness and dispatch that all the others seemed to be drifting dolts, shabbily at the mercy of outside forces, as if only Henry Duncane had control of the world he lived in.

Now the window crashed open—for Mrs. Fielding put a certain amount of dramatic feeling into her work—and the line shuffled obediently into position. The ladies' gloved hands began to fiddle with combinations on their private boxes. Something touched Cyril's sleeve, and he turned to receive from pink Maude Fielding a beaming smile and his mail bag, kept by the timing of this event from observing what he wished to observe.

He took the full bag and surrendered the empty.

He walked out of the post office, dodging around the end of the line which did not shift quite quickly enough out of his path. Nevertheless he heard and resented, in his own footsteps, a mere echoing, a feebler and somewhat degrading imitation of Henry Duncane.

CHAPTER TWO

ELIZABETH MEADOWS DUNCANE stood in the dining room, looking at her table as it was set for a noon dinner. It was all wrong. She thought: There's no use, there *is* no use.

Her lower lip had developed, lately, a little nervous quiver not in her control. It quivered now. She put her hands on the back of a chair and rested her weight against them to relieve the aching of her back. She thought: What a hag I feel, what an old, old, old woman, aching and dragging, and now this silly twitching at the mouth. I must remember I am only twenty-four, and I'm healthy. I *am* healthy. All that ails me is the baby. It's natural. It *is* natural.

These incantations did not help much. She wished it were safely over.

Then she braced her back. "That will do, Libby," she said to herself in her mother's voice, and she looked again at the dining-room table through her mother's eyes.

The white cloth was old and mended. It had been given to Libby as old linen to be put away and used for fine rags. How in the world had that girl dug it out? The silver was not Libby's wedding-present best, but a mixture of three patterns, which was all right for everyday, but it needn't have been thrown on sloppily with the forks pointing in and the knives out. The two napkins were not even alike and the flowers in the center bowl needed changing.

Libby could imagine her mother's quick eyes noting all this, and her mother's quick hands transforming the table and the whole big room into something neat and cozy, orderly and charming, with the swift magic of her experience. For it wasn't a question of money—it wasn't because she

14

and Henry didn't have things. It *was* a question of skill, of an art, really.

She began to straighten a fork and then she took her hand away. "Celestina," she called.

Celestina answered from the kitchen. "Yeh?" She would not say "Yes, ma'am." She would not even say "Yes." The "s" was always lost and left off.

"Will you come here, please." Libby's voice promised sharpness.

Celestina came through the door with a big spoon in her hand. Her heavy black hair made an insubordinate mass of curls around her gypsy face. "I'm fixing gravy," she said defensively, her amber eyes dull. Libby already knew that when Celestina's eyes looked as if they were dusty and did not shine, Celestina was in no mood to listen to instruction.

"Well, you'd better keep an eye on it, then," Libby was forced to say. "Don't . . ." But she didn't continue. No use. The gravy would be greasy and have white lumps in it.

The worst of it was that Libby herself did not know how to avoid this. Celestina was a terrible cook, but Libby was not much of a cook either. The difference between us, thought Libby, is just that I at least know what food ought to be. She tried to lift the weight of her discouragement by being fair. How could Celestina know, after all? Libby reminded herself. An ignorant little Italian girl only sixteen years old. You have to train them. Everybody says so. When mother comes, I'll make her teach me. Then I can teach Celestina when this is over, safely over.

She held her lip steady with her teeth, put the table silver neatly parallel, and nipped out some of the shabbier blossoms from the centerpiece. She narrowed her eyes and, pumping hard with her imagination, she decided it would do. It would have to do.

She went into the sitting room, but she did not sit down. Henry would be home soon and it was difficult to struggle up again. So she leaned against the wall and pushed wearily at her fair hair. Very fair, very fine hair she had. Somebody had once called it white gold. A boy, a date, long ago, before Henry Duncane (who was not a boy, but an exciting man)

15

had appeared and swept her off all breathless with her sudden bridehood, to this far place.

Ah, but it was far! She came from Connecticut, from a long line of quiet people who had never aspired to be anything but simple and decent but who had, in the course of three hundred years, become perhaps less simple than they imagined. Libby was late-flowering. In some ways, at twenty-four, she was younger than young Celestina. And, in some ways, Celestina would never be as mature as Libby was already.

For Libby had enough detachment to know that she was being harmfully sorry for herself, and she had insight into some of the causes. In those days a pregnant woman did not run around town in a cute pair of specially designed slacks and a gaudy smock. Libby had been secluded in the big house for months. This was only decent. She didn't question her imprisonment. But she did know it hadn't done her morale much good.

Shouldn't have happened so soon, she was thinking. I should have had time to learn to be married to Henry and keeping a house. I should have had a longer chance to fit into this place, to meet all the people and settle myself. This queer little town . . . I don't pertain to it or anyone in it but Henry. Alone. Who is there, now, I could go to for any real thing? There isn't a woman. There's the doctor. This backwoods doctor. Maybe he's ignorant, how can I know? Her mouth trembled.

Come, Libby, stop it. Stop scaring yourself. Other women . . .

The incantation did not help. Across her mind came that haunting phrase, the silly phrase that now obsessed her. She'd read it in some sentimental journal. "And so," it declaimed, "the woman went now for her child, down into the Valley of the Shadow of Death." Libby knew, with her perfectly good mind, that it was sententious and silly, a piece of purple writing, a fairly ridiculous way to say that women had been known to die in childbirth. All the same, her smoke-blue eyes grew round and bright. Her lip shook and she caught it in her fine teeth. She sent out of her brain a

16

frantic call across a thousand miles. "Mother, please come. Oh, please come, mother."

If you went west from the town hall of Thor past the Methodist Church, and did not bear to your right up the long hill out of town, you could continue westward on a gentler slope for one long block. At the top of it you would come to a pair of iron gates and see through them the long sweep of a driveway edged by fine lawns, and the portico of the superintendent's house, the biggest and finest house in Thor. Below it, all along this block to your left, were the next biggest and finest houses set in the next biggest plots of land that ran deep behind them. These houses would have been on the lake shore had it not been for the railroad tracks. As it was, since the tracks ran below a considerable embankment, the trains were heard but not seen, and the upper windows of the houses had, at least, glimpses of the shy water.

The white clapboard of Duncane's house, which was the second one up in this elegant row, did not suggest New England, for the style was midwestern instead, boxy, set a bit too high off the ground with a smattering of wooden scrollwork on the porches. It was a big house with big rooms. They were rather bare.

Libby Duncane, teetering back from the edge of panic, shook off her fit of nerves. She heard Henry's car. She touched her hair.

She thought, to be fair, that Henry was after all as much a bridegroom as she was a bride, and probably he had not looked forward to this exactly. He would not have expected that after nearly a whole year he would still come home to so bleak a dwelling. She hadn't got around to covering the dining-room chair seats in blue as she had planned. She hadn't been able to make the sitting-room draperies or accomplish the colors in here, the browns and yellows she wanted. She had been warned not to try to paint the shelves. They would have been cream, had she been able. But it must all wait now. And she and Henry must keep on using the downstairs bedroom which Libby was bound she'd make into a library one day . . . for the big rooms upstairs were as good as untouched, and she couldn't climb any more now, or sew on the machine, or scrape and paint furniture, or even get the easier flowers to grow in the shabby garden.

Poor Henry, thought Libby ruefully, must be a little less than delighted to come home and find not the dainty vivacious girl he'd married, but this clumsy hag. (Henry was just the same. *His* body was as supple and lean, *his* eyes as clear, *his* hair, except for the high, bare temples, as thick and shining as ever.)

She heard him coming in through the kitchen and heard him say, "Chicken, eh?" One could always hear what Henry said. There would be, she knew, a most humble murmur out of Celestina, who acted in what Libby supposed to be a hangover of a European idea, as if man were master and woman his slave forevermore. She wiggled a little irritable tension out of her shoulders.

Henry always did come in through the kitchen past the steaming pots, past the smells and the debris of preparation, and so he always knew what he was about to be fed.

Libby thought of her father—who never came home at noon but stayed decently downtown all day—coming in gently at the front door as the day faded, and being received as the master of his house, but graciously by the mistress of it, and sitting genteelly in the parlor with perhaps a sip of sherry beside him. He moved decorously, in due time, to a table which, within their means, would be exquisitely appointed, shaking his white napkin out, smiling about him in the faint, pleasurable suspense before he was served what would always be, for him, a delicious surprise.

But, of course, Henry drove a car, as her father did not, and the garage was beside the kitchen door. And that was that.

Henry wasn't going to walk around the house to come in. Henry would always be home for dinner at noon. That she could not get used to.

There were no restaurants, no luncheon places in Thor.

Libby put mind over matter. She made herself radiant. Henry kissed her on the cheek and put his arm around her briefly. The slight pull off her own balance hurt the weak spot in her spine. "How's Libby?"

Libby said she was fine.

"I'd better wash," said Henry. "Here's the mail." He put the pack of letters in her hands and her mother's was on top. She didn't even look at the rest of them. She let them slip away to fall on the floor. Even to feel the paper, on which lay her mother's firm crabbed handwriting, was comforting to her fingers. "From home!" she cried joyously.

Henry was all the way across the front hall into their bedroom, on his way to wash, and he didn't answer. He never answered when there was no real answer required. He never murmured "So I saw," or "Yes, isn't it?" or "Umhum."

Libby ripped the paper. "My dearest girl:"

Disappointment struck her numb.

I know you will be sorry, dear, at what I have to write today. Your father, it seems, must needs have an operation. It is not dangerous, and you must not be concerned about him, but it does mean that I cannot leave him to come to you. Dr. Amory decrees . . .

It went on. She read it all. Her eyes passed over the lines and the words.

Henry said, "Anything the matter?"

She looked up wondering what made him think anything was the matter. She hadn't moved, she hadn't cried. Now she said in a calm, steady voice, "My mother isn't coming at all . . ."

"Why not, dear?"

"Dad has to have an operation."

"Ah, too bad. Is it anything serious?"

"She says not."

"May I read it?" Henry took the letter. "Oh," he said. He read faster than anyone in the world. How could he have read it all so fast? "Well, I doubt if that's anything much to worry about."

"No," she said in a wondering tone.

"You're disappointed . . ."

"Of course I'm disappointed," she said rather brightly.

"You'll be all right, Libby. Your mother must stay with your father, naturally."

"Naturally," said Libby in the bright cheerful voice that surprised her so. "Poor Dad. I must write . . . and say not to worry about me."

Henry's face was grave and kind and watchful. "That's the girl," he said.

She thought: It isn't though. That isn't the girl. I don't know who it is being so gay about it. Not me.

Henry turned her gently toward the dining room. "Go ahead to dinner. I'll pick these up." He bent to gather the other letters that lay on the floor.

Libby moved slowly through the archway into the dining room, talking to herself. Well, that's that. Well, I can manage. I will just go minute by minute. I'm very calm about it really. It's quite amazing how calm I feel.

Celestina was bringing food from the kitchen. Using her hips she batted through the swinging door. She had a platter of fricasseed chicken balanced on her right hand and a white bowl of gravy grasped in the fingers of her left.

Her thumb was in the gravy.

Libby looked at it and screamed.

When she screamed again, Celestina let go the bowl.

It broke on the floor and the gravy began to flow around the pieces with a nasty eagerness to stain the rug. Celestina grabbed for the tilting platter with her left hand, ran crouching to the table, and all the chicken slid off the platter onto the cloth and the silver.

"Oh, oh," screamed Libby. "How can you be so stupid!"

And then Celestina was wailing and bawling, and Henry's strong arms went around his wife from behind. His cool syllables dropped like ice crystals into the cauldron of noise.

"Be quiet, Celestina. Libby, what happened?"

Henry held her strongly and she seemed to herself to be struggling against his strength, and then she fell back sobbing upon it.

"Her thumb . . . her thumb . . . her thumb!"

"Yes . . ." Henry was patient.

But he must see the enormity! How it was not to be borne! Libby tried to speak quietly, for surely this news would convey its own horror. Surely when Henry knew he would share her revulsion.

"Her thumb was in the gravy," she said.

Celestina said sullenly, "My thumb's clean."

And Henry laughed.

Libby felt the sting all the way down to the bottom of her heart. Laughed . . . ! She knew he was making her walk into the other room, and she knew when he made her sit down, but it was necessary to show him that this was no laughing matter. And she was pouring out a whole mixed flood of words.

"I can't believe that anyone could be so ignorant! *I* can't tell her every single, solitary, tiny thing, I *have* to depend on her. Oh, I'm glad I haven't any friends and nobody comes. Nothing's right, the way I want it. Nothing's neat, and nothing's pretty."

Henry stood pressing her shoulders with his firm hands, saying nothing. And suddenly she heard her mother's voice in her ear. "This is ridiculous, Libby," her mother said, coldly.

"This is ridiculous," sobbed Libby. "I know I shouldn't have screamed. But Henry! Her thumb in our food! It sickens me!"

"You sit here a minute." Henry put his big handkerchief into her hands.

"Oh, I suppose," wailed Libby, fumbling to recover some reasonable attitude, "she doesn't know any better."

"Knows better now." Some dryness in his tone made Libby turn her face up.

She let one eye escape the cambric and suddenly she, too, saw that it *was* funny. It was out of proportion. "I didn't mean to scream the house down and wreck the whole place, Henry. It's just . . . I couldn't . . . Oh, dear . . ." She began to giggle.

"Last straw, I expect," said Henry calmly. "Sit still. I'll see."

Libby sat sobbing softly and, alternately, choking off soft laughter in the handkerchief. A terrible pressure seemed lifted away. She felt quite surprisingly spry and free. She knew already that she must, of course, apologize to Celestina for the lack of proportion in her behavior. But she didn't

21

mind. She felt so much better. She thought: Maybe it was a *good thing* I blew up.

She could hear Henry. One could always hear him. He was saying with a detached crispness that was not unkind, "All right, Celestina." (Was Celestina crying, too?) "Now wipe up that mess on the floor, quickly. Then take everything off this table. Put on a clean cloth, a pretty one, if you can find it. And make some toast."

She thought: He's doing what mother would do, what I ough to be doing. How strange! Henry is such a man. How very strange this is, me to be having such a fit and Henry housekeeping . . .

She let her head drop back and she lay quietly and even rather dreamily in that chair. She thought: Henry is more grown up than I. When he came back and asked gently, "Will you speak to the girl now, Libby?" she said, "Yes, Henry. Of course."

Her blue eyes, soft and shining, searched his face. Henry had such a finished face, the flesh so firm to the bone. There was no baby fat left on it anywhere. He expected her to have collected herself. Well, she had. She felt quite ready to speak to Celestina now, as a lady should.

Celestina came stumbling and said at once, in Henry's words, as Libby divined, "I'll try to be more careful, Mrs. Duncane. I am very sorry."

Libby smiled with all kindness. "Celestina, you must please forgive me. I'm not feeling quite well just now. I will be better soon. *You* shouldn't have carried the bowl as you were carrying it, Celestina, but I certainly shouldn't have screamed at you. So I do beg your pardon."

Celestina said nothing.

"Can't we forget about it?" Libby prodded. "Please."

"All right," said Celestina uneasily. It meant nothing to her that her pardon was begged. Nothing at all. Her own emotions were not to be curbed by a bit of a phrase. Words didn't drive her. When she said "All right," it was not yet all right in her dark, Mediterranean heart, but Libby Duncane could not know this.

"I do know," said Libby sweetly, "that everything falls on you just now. I understand."

Celestina's dark face seemed to sharpen. Her red lips parted. "When is it?" she blurted.

And Libby's pink lips parted, and she drew a little back in the chair. Why the girl was wild with curiosity! All these weeks the girl must have been speculating and trying to guess. It had never occurred to Libby to confide in her. But the girl was wild to be told. For just one flash Libby saw the two of them as simply two females in the same house, both born to bear children, both fascinated by the incomprehensible wonder of their own bodies. But the vision passed. She drew back from such prying.

"The baby will be born in about ten days," she heard her husband say, quite as a matter of fact, informatively.

"That will do, Celestina," she said quickly, and the girl fled. Then Henry began to help her up and, leaning on him, she let it go, let it pass. It was only one more little sting. She could never explain why one was not always blunt and matter-of-fact, why there was reticence, part instinct, part rule. But let it go.

When she had washed and powdered her face and combed her hair, and she took her place at the table, she was surprised to find it charming. Everything was orderly. The cloth was fresh and the rescued pieces of chicken resting daintily on toast were a delicious surprise, somehow. Her outburst must have blown off a lot of steam. It had certainly done her good. She was hungry and her tongue was light. It was easy to chat.

"Mrs. Gilchrist was in the post office," Henry told her. "Said she would be dropping in to see you."

"Oh, when, Henry?"

"She wasn't definite."

"But she was here only the other day. She's been awfully nice," said Libby, pleased.

"Friendly?" He cocked an eyebrow.

"I shouldn't have said I had no friends," Libby confessed. "At least, it's not exactly true. I suppose what I meant is old friends. People who've known me forever. But I couldn't have *them* anywhere but home." She sipped tea. "Mrs. Gilchrist has really helped me more than anyone . . ."

"Helped you how, Libby?"

23

"Oh, telling me about the town. And who is who, and that sort of thing. Whose husband is important . . ."

Henry was looking at her with a wry expression—maybe he was going to laugh at her again. She hurried to forestall this. "Oh, I know she's a snob, Henry, and I think it's ridiculous, too, bothering to be snobbish way up here in the woods." Libby herself laughed. "But for goodness sakes, I need to know these things, don't I?"

"Whose husbands are important, according to Mrs. G.?" asked Henry. Now he wore an innocent-bystander kind of look.

"You should know," she teased. "But you'd never think to tell me."

"If I were asked, I'd say we are *all* important one way or another," Henry said mildly.

"Oh, that's too *dull*," said Libby merrily. "That's no fun. Why there has to be some kind of pushing and climbing going on, even if you have to make it up, or you'd just be bored." She felt he had no capacity for this kind of affectionate laughter at human nature, for he looked at her quite as if he had never heard such talk in his life. She went on gaily, "And if there is, why, I'd better know about it, so I won't make a mistake."

"What kind of mistake?"

Henry was so literal.

"Well, I'm not going to let a social climber climb on me, for instance, just because *I* don't *realize* . . ."

"Who wants to social climb?"

Was he the solemn puzzled innocent he looked, or was Henry going to laugh any minute?

"Well, I don't know, Henry, but there is that Mrs. Arthur Cole, for instance. You know, she is so nice looking and she goes to our church, so of course I thought . . . But, Mrs. Gilchrist says not to get too chummy . . . You see, *you* are important and that makes *me* important."

She thought, Doesn't he understand, at all? She said sharply, "Henry, do you want me to be a little bit careful, or don't you?"

Henry's eyes were unfathomable. "Use your common sense, Libby," he said gently.

24

She sighed, to reproach him, but she felt happy. Gossip was fun. It was give and take, at least. She read so much that Henry had no time to read, and it wasn't fun just to keep telling him what she had been reading or what she had been fancying, and watch him pare all the whimsy, all the playfulness, away from it.

"Oh, and she told me—" Libby remembered more gossip, and she leaned closer—"Henry, now don't raise your voice because whatever you say goes through the whole house. Mrs. Gilchrist told me that up until just four months ago, our Celestina was thick as thieves with Captain Trezona's boy. But the captain found out, and he stopped the two of them on the street one night and flew into a perfect rage. Because she's Catholic, of course . . . and he forbade them to see each other at all—just like an old tyrant. And the boy is so terrified of his father that he walks on the other side of the road. You heard about it." This was accusing. She knew by his look that he had.

"I hear what everybody else hears, I suppose," he admitted.

"Henry, you could have told me. Of course, I don't suppose . . ."

Libby felt her eyes roll. Quite suddenly, she wondered: Why, one could put Mrs. Gilchrist's story and Celestina's urgent curiosity together and make a scandalous guess out of it.

Libby said, tensely, "If she's that kind of girl, Henry, I don't . . . Do you suppose . . . ?"

Their eyes met.

Henry said, "Ask her."

"What?"

"Ask her," he repeated.

"But Henry . . . I can't ask her such a thing. What do you mean? I only wanted to know what you think."

"I don't think about it," Henry said.

"Well, Henry, I don't suppose you do, but I'd like to *know*."

"Quickest way to find out is to ask someone who has the information. Ask her, Libby. She knows what kind of a girl she is," he grinned.

"Oh, Henry . . . You just *put on* that, that bluntness. You know very well it's impossible. . . ." He just sat there wrapped in his merciless reasonableness. He was a million miles away. "You know I can't insult her. . . ."

Henry's lip twitched.

Libby sat as straight as she could. "If I insulted Celestina before dinner, I've apologized for that," she said stiffly. "And I know I shouldn't listen to gossip, Henry, or jump to conclusions. And you needn't remind me, because I'll try not to. But I don't quite understand this kind of town. And I don't know *what* might be going on. It's such a queer place, with so few people, divided up so sharply. I don't always know what I ought to do, and I wish you would help me a little bit more."

Henry's eyes were softer, but they were thoughtful too. "You don't like it here very much, do you, Libby?" he stated.

Well, she didn't. She couldn't lie. "I haven't had a chance . . ." she said impatiently. "It happened too soon, Henry . . ." She wished she hadn't said it. "You know?" she added anxiously.

His lips closed before they opened, as if Henry had been going to offer another thought but now forbore. He said, and rather sadly, too, "Yes, it happened too soon."

Libby was glad he agreed, and a little bit surprised. Henry might have come out with one of those blunt remarks that was always shocking to her sensibilities and undeniably true. She nibbled toast. "Will you always have to live in a town like this one, Henry?" she asked him, suddenly.

"This, or worse. . . ."

"Worse!" She was startled.

"Have to go where the job is," he said lightly, and got up from the table. "I'm late, Libby. Let Celestina do the best she can, will you?"

"Yes, Henry."

"Try not to worry about the house."

"All right."

"There's no need for you to worry," he said, rather awkwardly.

"I know," she lied, absent-mindedly.

"Ring me on the mine phone, in case you want me. I may

26

be going underground for awhile this afternoon, but some-body will find me."

"Oh, yes Henry. All right." She was hardly listening. She was thinking about his word "worse."

"Good-by," said Henry.

Libby, lying on the top blanket with the afghan pulled over her ankles, gratefully let the alien weight go against the bed. The big room was cool and dim. She would close her eyes. She would rest. She would not remember for now that her mother wasn't coming, at all.

But Libby came of people who were in the habit of trying to understand themselves. Lying still, it was revealed to her in the peaceful silence what kind of a woman she had seemed to be during all that dinner hour. A woman who had a tan-trum, who caused an ugly scene with a servant, who wept and complained, who indulged in petty gossip and in cruel speculations. One had only to stop and count to know that, of course, Celestina was not pregnant. Libby Dun-cane, a woman counting! Without a generous thought! She squirmed on the bed. Oh, why had she screamed so?

Then this was revealed to her, also. She had screamed not from the shock of Celestina's thumb, at all, but from the shock of that letter. Because of the news in it. Because of her fear.

Oh, I'm not so small, thought Libby, I'm not so petty. I *am* not. Oh, surely Henry understands. She rubbed her hot cheek on the cool pillow. But I am, she confessed, a woman who is afraid of the Valley of the Shadow of Death. And also afraid to say so.

And she thought, further; Henry Duncane never was afraid in all his life. He's fearless, that's what it is. That's what I feel is so far-away about him.

She bit into the pillow. She thought, I'm afraid, but that doesn't mean I can't be brave. I'll manage—I *will* manage. Everything will be better when this is safely over.

CHAPTER THREE

WHEN Henry Duncane turned off the main road at West Thor Mine and began to climb the crooked hill, his car passed first over the railroad spur, and then ran between the shafthouse and the roaring building across the road which housed the giant hoists. It twisted on around the compressor house, which lay a little higher, and passed, in turn, a very long, low and very narrow wooden building which lay on a shelf of land and was divided like a ruler, of which the inch nearest the crooked road was Captain Trezona's office. (Back of that, other offices—the clerks', the timekeepers', the mining engineer's and his staff, and the chemist's.)

Above this, a footpath snaked and climbed off over the hillside, to the dry. (A change house, for the men who worked underground and of course wore special and necessary costumes to do so.) Highest buildings of all on the hill —the carpenter shop and the machine shop, lay on opposite sides of the road. Duncane's car passed between these two. Here the road ended; the woods came down over the crown of the hill like a cap of curls. There was, however, an upper road, a mere trail that wound off along the hairline above the mine buildings, below the woods on the rim of the sloping meadows that lay to the east and to the west.

On it, Duncane turned his car right and left on a patch of bare ground.

His office bit off this upper corner of the machine shop, and a peaceful north light came in upon his desk and upon the high draftsman's desk where a young man, named Bush, was working.

Henry inspected the drawing in progress and commented. Then he sat at his desk and spoke on the telephone.

28

As chief engineer, Duncane's finger was on the pulse of mechanical power.

He was responsible for everything in the way of machinery that was being erected or operated either on surface or underground. Under him worked the men who erected or operated; among them the electricians, hoisting engineers, pumpmen, the compressor house crew, the machine shop men, and those who tended the steam turbines and the power plant.

Thor mines used electric power. The Company had harnessed for this purpose a fall of the Sturgeon River, about five miles south and east of the town. If and when this source was interrupted, then the steam turbines drew power from coal.

Power there had to be, for mines are wet. Water seeps out of the rock and accumulates. A hole in the ground will fill, and a mine, however vast and complex, is a hole in the ground. The pumps must run. Almost seventy-five per cent of the power generated went, in fact, to do this pumping. (At West Thor, for instance, eighteen hundred gallons of water had to be raised twelve hundred feet every minute, day and night.)

Besides this, of course, the men, mules, timber, and all else, including the ore itself that came up from its deep home, had to be hoisted by power. And besides, power had to compress the air that thereafter ran down through a multitude of pipes to operate the drills that drilled the holes into which they tamped the dynamite that ripped the rock open.

Power there had to be. All the time. Duncane could never put aside his responsibility. Not only because the mine worked day and night shifts, but because the water does not cease to seep out of the rock because night falls and men go home to bed. He was on call, as is a doctor who goes home to bed like other men, but gets up for trouble.

Trouble was a large part of Henry's business.

There was, this Tuesday afternoon, a little trouble at the pumping station on the twelfth level. (So called, because it lay twelve hundred feet below the surface.) So, in mid-afternoon, dressed in oilskins, boots, and a miner's hat, Duncane entered the cage to go down. The cage was no plush elevator.

Henry rang the signal himself—two bells to lower. The engineer sat on a platform in the building across the way with his hands on the tall levers and his eyes on a huge indicator, and could not possibly see who was riding, yet knew it was Duncane and dropped him like a stone. Henry grinned. It was a delicate attention.

Underground, Thomas Thomas, the little Welshman, looking over his shoulder, let the anxiety peel off his face and fall away. The arrival of Duncane had this effect. He never seemed to fumble. If he did not at once perceive the source of trouble and its remedy, he at once began to look for it. And Duncane's groping was so full of purpose; he hunted for cause with such order and clarity, that he was totally reassuring. One felt that Henry Duncane would get to the bottom of a problem if it were humanly possible, and one further felt that it *was* humanly possible, of course.

He was quick to reject a useless idea a split second after he saw it was leading nowhere. So he often came to the useful idea so quickly that the whole process of hypothesis, of exploration and discard, was lost to sight, and his men would whistle and wonder by what magic he was able to go, as it seemed, instantaneously to the answer.

He was not quite so quick to blame a human error—but quick enough. And when he did, the man who had made it knew he had better not make the same mistake again. Henry attracted responsibility; it gravitated toward him and he took it and he carried it. But, by the same token, he expected other people to be responsible. Since he knew what he could expect from a metal shape under certain forces, and that, within limits which he recognized, the expectation was reliable, he tended also to expect obedience and accuracy from his men, within limits that were a trifle rigid, for they did not reckon with the soft blobs of formless personal emotion that fog and impede the functioning of the human organism.

Nevertheless, his men were always relieved to see him. For characteristically, Henry's severity was perfectly reliable. If a man mended his ways he was not nagged, and all came to be imbued with Henry's simple idea: Look for the trouble and eliminate it, wherever it lies. So the worry fell off the Welshman's face, and he began to tell Henry eagerly all he'd known, all he'd done and not done.

The pumping station was well lighted—although the dark was not far off—for darkness here was implacable. Unless it was fought, it fell without a chink or a ray. All around rose the dank and faintly acid smell that prevailed in this deep place.

But the long drifts that were lit, the crosscuts that were not, the high stopes and the raises where men carried their light on their hats, and otherwise had none; all this that lay about and beyond was none of Henry's business.

It was the business of John Erickson, the chief mining engineer, to know the extent of the ore body here. He and his assistant, Gilchrist, and the staff of surveyors plotted and charted the position of the ore, and they directed man's attack upon it.

It was the business of Captain Gideon Trezona to boss, through a hierarchy of assistants and shift bosses, the miners, drillers, muckers, trammers, timbermen, and all who, working underground, got the ore out.

It took Duncane less than an hour to diagnose the trouble and arrange for its cure. That was that.

The cage, going up, stopped at the tenth level. A young surveyor, named Davies, who stepped on, saluted Henry. "My boss is back there feuding with Captain T. I'm getting out ahead before I say something."

"You're not going to make it," Henry said, peering.

In courtesy they waited for the two men who could be seen looming rapidly out of the poorly lit distance.

Captain Gideon Trezona came striding. He was of medium height, but so thin as to seem taller. He had a long, narrow face with a narrow thin-lipped mouth that never quite closed over his long teeth. He had a thin, high-bridged nose and frosty blue eyes. He was fifty-five years old, and in his prime, for he had a cold toughness that showed no sign of diminishing.

Alex Gilchrist was a much younger man. He wore his habitual smile of blended patience and exasperation, a smile that was in its way more arrogant than the captain's cold face altogether, for it implied: I hear you, but you don't understand, and on the whole, your obtuseness amuses me.

After the first murmurs and nods, the four of them rode to the surface without speaking. This silence would have been intolerable to four women in the same circumstances. Four women would have used bright patter to ease the knowledge of tension between two of the party or even the mere accident of being in each others' company. But the four men had no patter.

It wasn't Henry's business. Davies, subordinate, kept his mouth shut. Captain Trezona had said all he intended to say and was in the cage for the purpose of getting above. Gilchrist was glum behind his pitying smile and felt no compulsion to disguise this.

The cagetender's eyes rolled to see such a concentration of authority.

On surface, the captain strode off up the hill with no farewell. Davies grinned and followed him by a few paces. But Gilchrist held Duncane, grumbling, "That son of a gun . . ."

Henry waited to be told why.

"Know what he is going to do now until quitting time?" Gilchrist nodded after the captain's climbing figure. "Sit in his office and read the Bible."

Henry grunted.

"We're taking a second side-slice off a pillar. All of a sudden, he sticks his nose in the air and says he doesn't like it."

"Cousin Jack," shrugged Henry.

"Sometimes I wonder . . ." Gilchrist said. He was a wonderer. For all his air of pitying another's ignorance, Gilchrist himself was carefully what he would call "open minded." He not only saw both sides, but was often *on* both sides of a question.

He and Henry Duncane were classmates and, if not the closest of friends, at least acquaintances of long standing. Gilchrist often told his troubles to Duncane. Duncane rarely told his troubles to anybody.

"Can't figure out whether he's *got* a reason," said Gilchrist impatiently, "or if he just turns stubborn every once in awhile for the fun of it."

"In what way is he being stubborn?" asked Henry. They had begun to walk.

"Oh well, he's going ahead, that's true," Gilchrist said in that exasperated tone. "He won't quit on anything he starts. Never has. But I can't pin him down to why he doesn't like it. When I try, he brings in God. That stops *me*, Henry. How can you talk to a man who brings God into a discussion?"

"I don't know," said Henry, with some sympathy.

"Sometimes, I wonder." Gilchrist shook his head.

"Talked to Erickson or the Old Man, about it?"

"Erickson's on a trip; you know that. McKeever says pay no attention."

"Pay no attention then."

But Gilchrist shook his head again, uneasily.

"That old Cousin Jack—got no education—never read a technical book in his life, I suppose. But these, these Cornishmen . . . got it in their bones. . . ."

"Got what?" Henry was not the man for mystic intuitions.

Gilchrist sucked his cheek. "Damned if I know. Knowledge, maybe." His eyes wavered.

"Knowledge doesn't come in the bone, Alex. You mean he might have a hunch, based on experience, that he can't explain? Something like that?"

"It may be," said Gilchrist uneasily. "The timbering looks good. The roof's all right. We've done it before."

They climbed in silence.

"Did he *like* it before?" asked Henry thoughtfully.

"No," said Gilchrist with relief. "That's right, come to think of it, he did not."

Henry laughed, and they parted.

When the whistle blew, Eedie Trezona peered into her oven and then shifted pots on the top of the wood range until they were safe to leave for a few moments. She went into the dining room, where her daughter, Dorothy, was setting table.

"Dickie 'ome?"

"He's down in the field, Ma."

"Call 'im, dearie. I'll just be waking Wesley now."

33

Dorothy went out onto the porch which overlooked a whole fold of the land, almost a private valley, from this high point on the north of it. Eedie gathered her skirts to climb the stairs.

Gideon Trezona had come over from the 'old country' as a very young man. But Edith, his wife, and the children, of course, had been born in Michigan. The Cornish twist to their tongues was graduated accordingly. The children had it hardly at all. Eedie herself dropped her aitches, but not always. Only the captain sometimes abused his pronouns. Yet all of them kept something of the rhythm, a swift anapaest replacing now and then like a little dance step the iambic march of the English.

Eedie climbed swiftly. Her son, Wesley, was asleep in the largest of the three upstairs bedrooms, for he was on night shift this week and must sleep by day.

If anyone had told Edith Trezona that she was a pretty woman, she would have laughed merrily, and in so laughing been prettier than ever. Small and dainty in body, she was not stout, but pleasantly not thin either, with a neat bosom. Although she was forty-five years old, and sought in no way to deny it, her age seemed like a veil, a gauze thrown over her, so that there was only a faint softening of the line of her chin, and a gentle diminishing of her color. Her hair still was light brown in effect and, although she wore it according to her age and station—pulled straight up all around to a matronly knob on the top of her head—the tendrils that escaped around the forehead and lay on the nape of her neck rolled of themselves into shadowy little curls. Her skin was not a young girl's skin any more, but it was fine and fair, even so, and the cast of her face—round, high at the cheekbones —was pretty as a very young girl's face is pretty. She had small and beautifully even teeth and she smiled a great deal of the time.

She had the gift of being happy. This seemed to her a normal condition. She had no idea it was rare. Everything about her inconvenient, high perched, isolated and old-fashioned frame house pleased her very much. The smells of supper now, the long sunbeams lowering towards the day's end, and the sense of the family drawing toward home at

34

an appointed time, were her delight. The sight of her son, asleep with the quilt kicked askew, filled her with tenderness toward him and toward a good God.

She touched him gently.

"Ma?" he stirred.

"Whistle blew, son."

"All right, Ma," he yawned and he burrowed. But just the same as he awakened, he passed increasingly into that state of tension, that strain she sensed was the accompaniment of Wesley's consciousness these days. So Eedie sat down close beside him. Her hand touched his neck.

"Wesley?"

"Ma?"

"Is she mad?" She meant angry. "Are her people mad, do you think?"

"Uh uh . . ." he said in vigorous denial. And Eedie knew she was not on the right track towards discovering what it was that was worrying him. Something was worrying him, she well knew, although he had not said so.

"Are you thinkin' about the girl much, Wesley?" she asked delicately.

"Not much," he said.

He had turned so that his face lay in profile to her. He was looking past his long lashes across the room away. Eedie believed that he did not think much about the girl any more.

"It's all passed over then?" She stroked him.

"Sure, Ma." His mouth went into the pillow. He was not sure.

"I think about the girl sometime," Eedie confessed. "If she liked you, Wesley—now to be cut off might make her feel bad, eh? Or sad. Or mad." She smiled at her own rhyming.

Wesley said, "We had a lot of fun kidding, Ma. I told you."

She stroked him. Her fingers said, yes I remember. I know you did no wrong. There was no wickedness.

"You didn't ever tell 'er what Pa said . . ."

"Pa said I better never see her at all. Best cut it right off. So I did." He squirmed but his voice was calm. "And anyway . . ." he murmured.

"I've been thinkin', Pa would have give you leave to talk to 'er—straight out. Would that been kinder?"

"Oh Ma, no, Ma. No . . ." He rolled. "And I couldn't've. How could I, Ma? We never . . . never got nowhere near thinking about getting married. I told you. Anyhow she knows. It gets to her."

Eedie was trying to imagine what could be troubling him.

"And listen," he said. "Her people wouldn't want her to get married to me, neither."

Eedie said slowly, "I see that. Still it's 'ard."

"Ma, let me up, eh?"

She felt the tension in him now like springs and she rose to release him. "Pa means to watch out for you," she murmured still groping to understand.

"I know." He flung over toward his mirror and rubbed his head.

"I suppose," said Eedie in an intuitive flash, "young people think less of a boy who minds 'is Pa, eh?"

Now she knew that her hunt to understand was getting warm. He stiffened.

"I'm *not* just minding Pa," Wesley said. "You know that, Ma. Pa's right. If I wouldn't want to marry her, I should quit going with her."

"You saw what Pa was getting at," she said thoughtfully, "and Pa and me know that. But maybe there's bound to be a little while before the young people would see you're not just mindin' Pa, eh?"

Wesley didn't answer.

"Well, you've got past that now," she said in hope.

He said, "Ma, I got to change clothes."

It was evasive and Eedie let it be. Wesley was not yet past all of it. In just what way she did not know, but it had something to do with this *kind* of trouble. Maybe his friends were jeering at him for an obedient boy.

How Eedie Trezona, sheltered in her own world as she was, nevertheless knew what this younger generation's attitude might be, she could not have told. But she did know. Youth was beginning to flame even in Thor that year, and she felt it through her children's conflict with it.

Well, if he needed to tell her his trouble, why, he would

tell her. For Wesley knew he could be absolutely sure of her, and she was serenely sure of that.

"I can see that it's 'ard," she said softly. She straightened his bed with a few quick, practiced motions, smiled lovingly upon him and left his room.

She went downstairs, thanking the warm Deity who lived in the house with her (for she was truly pious and spoke to Him often) that Edith Trezona was so blessed among women. Her husband, Gideon, was a fine and a good man, who feared God, and what he had done to her son Wesley was in Eedie's view no more arrogant or cruel, and no less truly loving, than the slap she, herself, would have given to a baby's fingers drawing near a flame.

And her son, Wesley, was a fine, good boy who understood his father's wise concern for his future. And who agreed with the captain's sternly given warning and who now perhaps had to face, on his father's side, an irreverent, rebellious, younger generation at some pain to himself.

Ah that's 'ard, she thought. Everybody saw Pa order 'im 'ome, but never 'eard the talk they 'ad. And that's 'ard. Yes, 'tis.

She knew what the captain would say. "Wesley must do what was right, whatever." But Eedie tried to know what it was costing Wesley to "do right" in this case. And she felt there was no harm in this effort to understand and no harm in her sympathy. Never harm to say, "I can see that it's 'ard, my dear. I can see that it's 'ard." For her, God was no less loving than she. How could He be? And He understood both these good men just as she did, or even better. And He knew it was hard for the boy, the good boy.

When Gideon Trezona, walking on the upper road eastward, came to his back gate and marched through, Dorothy and Dick and Wesley, coming down, felt the impact of his presence in a tiny tightening of their nerves, a faint tensing of their muscles. For their father's God was a God of Wrath, stern against evil.

"Well mither?" they heard him say in the kitchen.

"Well, fayther," said Eedie, merrily, revolving toward him to touch his stern cheek with loving fingers.

37

And the children's faces reflected the little miracle they saw every day. Their mother was not afraid of Gideon Trezona or his God, either.

It was a fact: she had never been able to fear God very much. Did she not love Him? And He her?

Henry Duncane heading home saw, a little late, out of the tail of his eye, young Davies' sturdy figure at the side of the road. He braked abruptly to offer him a lift. Only then did he see that Davies had a companion. They both thanked him and got in.

Arthur Cole leaned on the seat back and poured his breathy voice into Henry's ear. "Thanks a lot, Mr. Duncane. Night shift, tonight. Be glad to get home. Say, what's your opinion of the School of Mines, at Houghton, Mr. Duncane?"

"Davies knows more about it."

"Good school," Davies said promptly.

"I'm thinking of going there," said Arthur rapidly. A lock of dark hair fell on his forehead. "I want to get ahead somehow. If I'm not too old already, I'd like to get a little schooling along engineering lines. Do you think they'd take me?"

"High school, Cole?"

Davies did the talking. Henry was silent as the car slipped swiftly down into town.

"Yeah, sure, and a year at the Normal before the war."

"You were in the war?"

"Yeah, I was in," said Cole as if he just remembered.

"They should take you."

"What about that, Mr. Duncane? Do you think I'd be smart? I'm married and all, but my wife could go back to teaching. I think she would, and if I could get in a couple of years . . ."

"Education never hurt anybody," Henry said.

"They slam it into you," warned Davies in his pleasant, rasping voice. "You'd have to buckle down."

"I could do that. If I care enough about anything, I can buckle down, don't worry. If it isn't too late, that's all. You were in the war, Mr. Duncane, but it hit you when you were

38

farther along. You *had* the stuff. But I guess, even at my age . . ."

"This all right, Cole?" Henry stopped the car at the foot of the hill, preparing to take the sharp-angled turn back toward his own house.

"Yeah sure, thanks very much. Good night, Mr. Duncane. Thanks for the encouragement."

"Sit still," said Henry to Davies.

The car made the acute angle and Henry stopped it again almost immediately, for Davies boarded with Mrs. Trestrial in the gray house on the right, just back of the pie-shaped vacant lot at the corner. He got out.

He wrinkled his nose. "Say, what's the old Cousin Jinny got? Saffron buns again? Do you smell saffron?"

"Smell it all the way to my house," Henry said, "pretty near every day." In his pleasantry there was the note of parting, but the car did not move yet so Davies stood still.

"Did I encourage him?" asked Henry softly of the evening.

"Not that I heard," said Davies in a surprised tone, and then he laughed.

Henry put the car into gear. They saluted each other. He pulled across the street into his own driveway and Davies moved toward the scent of saffron and his supper.

Arthur Cole, proceeding down the block toward the town hall corner, walked with his face turned to look somewhat wistfully back over his shoulder.

CHAPTER FOUR

BEHIND the town hall to the north, the town of Thor spread
up towards the woods in a double row of little frame houses
that had once been all exactly alike. The Company had built
them so. They had grown different, of course. They had
broken into varying colors, for one thing. Some were white
or gray, some tan or yellow, with assorted trim. Pergolas and
porches, stoops and shutters, had sprouted upon them in
differing arrangements and, moreover, where one man had
planted a vine his neighbor had put a tree. The boundaries
of the tiny plots were a wooden fence, a fence of wire, a living hedge, or a border of whitewashed stones, according to
fancy.

But for all of this, it was still immediately apparent that
all these houses were exactly alike in basic design. This design was as simple as could be.

For the Company, which had built them, owned them
and rented them out for a minute amount, was not in the
real estate business. Housing was necessary. Private con-
struction, however, is not profitable in a mining town since
the mines are the only reason for the town's existence and,
therefore, property values cannot rise but instead are bound
someday, when the ore is all gone, to disappear entirely. So
the Company must provide, but the Company saw no reason to be extravagant about it.

The little dwellings were perfectly square boxes with two
windows on each side and a peaked roof for a cover. Inside,
the square floor space was evenly divided into four smaller
squares and—except for a tiny staircase that went up out of
the back room on the right, the dining room, to two small
oblongs under the eaves—that was the house.

There were electric lights, but no gas stoves. There was a sink in each kitchen, but no other plumbing. At the back of the tiny plots, the outhouses stood exactly alike in basic design.

The third house from the corner on the left side of the street was painted white. It had a narrow useless porch all the way across the front and two clumps of straggly lilacs on either side of the steps.

The front door, dead center, opened to face a blank wall (the staircase went up behind it). This made a tiny entry open onto the right front room. The front room at the left, closed off by a door, was Cyril Varker's castle. Crowded into it he had his narrow bed, his wardrobe and his dresser, one chair, and a desk of his own. He sat in the shabby chair which had arms, and a cushioned seat, and was his throne. The one good lamp in the house was at his shoulder although, at the moment, light from the westering sun still came rosily through his south window. On the surface of the desk he had spread his kingdom.

His sister, Madeline, tapped on his door.

"Come."

She opened the door. "Suppertime."

He turned his eyes up. He wondered whether she knew why it was that every evening she made sure to alert him to suppertime, made sure to rout him out of his private place and draw him forth into the part of the house that was common ground for the three of them.

"Arthur's not home yet," he protested mechanically.

"Soon be."

She came a step nearer and he could see, back of his elbow, her white fingers interlacing.

The perfect oval of her face was somber and brooding. "You and your dirty little pieces of paper," she said contemptuously.

"Dirty?"

"And mean."

"Oh come, Madeline." His laugh exploded.

Brother and sister, they were opposites. They opposed each other, and the tension between them was the strength of their bond. It was sometimes necessary for one to attack

41

the other, out of a clear sky, to renew the close comfort of their angry polarity.

"What's mean about it?" Cyril asked reasonably. "I'm a convenience. I'm a service. I'm a business."

"It's secret, and it's cruel, and it's heartless," she said flatly.

Cyril was delighted. He tilted his head and his knob-knuckled hand neatened a pile of small pieces of paper. "You're the expert on the heart," he jeered, "as we agree to call it. Now it's one thing to be softhearted—another to be soft in the head."

"You'll get caught someday," she said, "and that won't be so clever."

"Caught."

"When the Company finds out."

"The Company won't find out," said Cyril calmly, "for the reason that anyone desperate enough to borrow money from me on my terms is in no state to make his position known to the Company. I see to that naturally. I'm not accessible to everyone, you know. I pick and choose."

"You choose the ones you can frighten," she said. "You like that. That's why you'll lose your position when they do find out."

"I doubt if I'll lose my position unless I so choose," said Cyril airily. "I am a more or less valuable employee. The Company will pretend that perhaps I knew no better. So that I can pretend, too. And they won't lose my services. So you see what would happen? I would be warned—oh, very strongly perhaps—that this sort of thing won't do. Very well then, at such time that I am warned, I can decide how I wish to continue."

"How you wish to continue," she mocked his smug language.

"What makes you think the Company would take as sentimental a view as you do?" he taunted. "Do you know what would really infuriate the dear Company?" he said.

"All the money I've made. That would be the outrage," and he laughed again.

"What good is the money . . ." her fingers intertwined. She did not finish the sentence, but he did:

". . . to such as me, eh? What good is anything else?" he said, savagely. He looked up sideways.

"Come to supper," she murmured. It was as if she had drawn blood and was satisfied. But it was his turn now.

"What good is your soft heart?" he inquired. "It got you a child for a husband. It got you Arthur Cole. Why? Because he was red-eyed about you a year ago, and you didn't have the head to see he goes red-eyed after one thing and then another. *You* thought it was a deathless passion, eh, Madeline? Tristan and a somewhat fake Isolde."

"Oh don't . . ." she said somewhat wearily.

"Your heart was soft. He would kill himself if he couldn't have you. Last year, that is. So, in your womanly pity, you conferred his heart's fondest wish upon him. In your soft head you assumed that you would of course be forever cradled in his devotion. Now he's red-eyed with ambition. And I could have told you he was red-eyed to be a military hero, before *you*. So he *was* a hero for a few months while that was hot in his head. Where are his medals now? Kicking around the house somewhere. Tarnished. Dusty. Half-forgotten. That's you too, Madeline."

"If it is," she said listlessly, "what do you care?"

"I had quite an investment in you, if you remember?" he said brutally.

"Did you want me to marry for your profit? How could I do that? You have nothing to complain about. You get along well enough with Arthur."

"I make a nice buffer in this house too, don't I? Which is why you want me to come to supper before the supper's ready."

She looked stung by this perception.

"I do it with my hard head, you know," said Cyril. "After all, it costs me very little to live here."

She said furiously, "That's profit, then. If it saves you money."

He only laughed again. He felt satisfied. No need of any more now. He would keep some things to say another time. He got out of his chair, and for a moment they stood braced tight by their mutual antagonism, leaning on the strong ties

43

of the perpetual conflict that laced them together. She turned and went out and he followed.

Arthur Cole washed his face and hands in the kitchen sink and combed his hair with a wet comb. The long lock that wanted to fall forward was briefly imprisoned by the cohesive moisture, but it stirred as if it were alive, and before he had picked up his fork it was slipping down.

He was twenty-five. He was loose-jointed, tall, a rangy build. His face was thin and attractive although his well-cut lips were pushed forward as if he wore his mouth an inch ahead of where it ought to have been. He was attractive, Cyril thought, because of something restless and pushing, a quality hinting that there would be at least no dull decline into safe routine for Arthur Cole.

The round oak table that nearly filled the tiny dining room was neatly laid, and the food was well-prepared. Madeline seemed to manage the little house with the back of her hand. Keeping house was not her vocation (and of no burning interest to her either) but she seemed able to accomplish it quickly and efficiently out of an overflow of her vitality. She ate daintily with good appetite looking, as always, lovely.

Arthur ate with a bent body and his head too low toward the table. It was the sole defect in his table manners.

"Got a ride home," he said as if this news were a plum he'd been saving, "with Henry Duncane."

Brother and sister sighed. Cyril had long remarked Arthur's habit of fastening on people who interested him, or with whom he wanted to claim intimacy, by a trick of calling them and them only by the full name. He would say George McKeever, for instance, when speaking of the superintendent, where most people said Mr. McKeever or, merely, the Old Man.

"Now there's a man," Arthur continued heartily, "who's got the world by the tail."

"How so?" said Cyril mildly. He was always mild with his brother-in-law. It was a saving of energy. Arthur was going to voice his worship of Henry Duncane again and there was no use resisting.

"There's a man who knows exactly where he's going!"

44

said Arthur vehemently. "And that's the way to be, believe me! I spoke to him about school." He glanced at Madeline's quiet face. "I thought I'd ask because I'd think more of his advice than anybody else's around here."

"Did he advise?" inquired Cyril.

"Yep."

Cyril was amused. He thought Duncane probably had not said much or they'd have it in full flow. "Well?" he prodded.

"Listen, Madeline. Honest, I think I've got to give myself that chance." Arthur raised himself erect in the chair.

"You mean I'm to give you the chance," she said in a tone from which all bitterness was carefully expunged.

"All right," said Arthur, "why not? You don't mind teaching a couple of years."

"Don't I?"

"Well, if afterwards you'll have a lot more. A better place than this shack. Cyril, you don't think that's such a terrible thing to ask her to do? After all, she's got a profession. Lot of women can't earn money, but she can. I'm not asking her to support me, just to support herself for the time it takes. . . ."

"Where will you get the money for your tuition and expenses?" inquired Cyril with malicious smoothness—for he had long known exactly where Arthur hoped to get it.

"Well."

Cyril smiled to himself. Arthur hadn't dared ask outright, yet. It was amusing.

Madeline said, "Oh, Arthur, sometime could we have one meal without . . ."

"But it's important!"

A fountain of energy and enthusiasm seemed to gush out of her husband. "It's my future! I know it is! It's what I *need!* Henry Duncane doesn't think it's impossible. It's not impossible. I don't want to be a miner all my life. I want to know something. I want to get somewhere. You know what's behind Henry Duncane, don't you? You know why it is when *he* shows up, everybody knows something is going to be done, and done right? You do know?"

"No, I don't know," said Madeline, dully passive under his pounding rhetorical questions.

"I do. It's his education. That's what makes him so sure of himself. That's the way to be, too. What I wouldn't give to be sure of myself. It makes all the difference. And when I think all it would take is a little time and money . . . two years even would pull me out of this. What can it cost?"

Madeline shook her head. She didn't speak. They had been here before. Cyril was a little bored by the repetition himself. He said now with malicious intent, "It will cost something certainly. However, I . . . er . . . guess you know I happen to have . . . er . . . a little put by."

He knew the leap of Madeline's startled eyes, but he looked up at Arthur. Arthur's head jerked. His forelock bounced. His brown eyes burned.

"It would be up to my sister, of course," said Cyril demurely. "If this is something she wants very much . . ."

Now he met Madeline's eyes and found them as angry as he had expected.

Cyril hadn't much faith in Arthur's ability to persist in any effort for two whole years. Too red-eyed, he thought. I'd give him six months. Still he might. Cyril didn't care one way or the other. He was watching Madeline to see what she would do now.

She let her lids fall. "Let me think about it awhile longer," she murmured. "Please, Arthur."

"Ah, Maddy, say it now!" Arthur was aflame. "You heard what Cyril said. I'd never forget it. You'd never lose . . ."

"I told you I'd consider," she said, faintly, and pulled her hand out of his grasp. "Don't push me, Arthur."

Arthur simmered in excited hope. Cyril's qualified offer was a step indeed. He was bursting to insist and implore, but he tried to check himself. His eyes roved around the room for another topic—anything. But there was nothing. His whole head was filled with a single idea.

Cyril was aware of this. He glanced to communicate with his sister who would be aware, too, and he saw the pinched places around her beautiful mouth.

"These tomatoes are wonderful," he said, easily finding a topic when he wanted one. "Beauties. Delicious. You were right, Maddy. I thought you put them out too early."

Her hand took one of the perfect red fruits from the bowl,

46

and turned it. "I picked these just an hour ago. They're fresh. And pretty?"

"We've got too many," Arthur said.

"I thought if they all ripen, I might put some of them up."

"Too many," he interrupted. "Say, take a few to Mrs. Duncane, why don't you?"

Under his browbone Cyril's eyes stretched.

"But Arthur," Madeline seemed flustered, "she must have . . ."

"No. No she hasn't. Not a thing in their garden. She's uh . . . you know . . . Didn't get anything in the ground. I think it would be kind of nice for you to do that."

"But I've barely met . . . I hardly know her."

"Nobody hardly knows her. Do it, will you? Do it just because I want you to. Do it now."

"Now!"

"Why not? It's early. You can say we had them for supper and we thought of her. That's true isn't it?"

Cyril said curiously, "What's in your mind, Arthur?"

"I can't see how it could do any harm if my wife's nice to Henry Duncane's wife. After all, they might get friendly. Why not? Madeline's no dumbbell. Mrs. Duncane might enjoy talking to her if they ever got to know each other."

Cyril chewed his lip. Madeline held her head down. He couldn't communicate.

"What are you thinking *that* will do for you?" he mused aloud.

"Why does it have to do anything for me?" said Arthur loudly. "Why do you have to look at it so cold-blooded? Listen, can't Madeline do something decent and friendly?"

Madeline, who still held the tomato, turned her wrist and dropped it. "You want me to do that, Arthur?" she said sharply.

"Yes."

Now her face rippled. A wave of emotion altered it, but in a passage so swift that whatever she felt, whether anger, whether impatience, whether pity for his naïveté, was gone before it could be read.

"If I do, will you please be quiet?"

"Quiet?"

47

"About how crazy you are," she cried, and her fists beat the table so that the china jumped, "to be just like Henry Duncane. Just, just . . ." her voice slipped shrilly, "be quiet, sometimes."

"Gee," said Arthur, "Maddy, listen. . . I . . ."

"No," she said fiercely, and got up. "I get . . . tired." She grasped her plate and her saucer and went into the kitchen.

"What did I *do?*" Dropping his jaw, Arthur turned to his brother-in-law.

"Got on her nerves I suppose," said Cyril mildly.

Arthur immediately shifted and leaned on his elbow. "Listen, Cyril, if you'd see me through I can promise you I'd work like a dog. I'd make it up to you. The thing is . . ."

Cyril settled and appeared to listen with grave interest. For my board and room, he thought cynically. But an inner part of his ears slipped shut against the posturing and passions of the man beside him. He thought the dream in that head, not in itself childish, but dreamed by a child, probably was not going to come true.

CHAPTER FIVE

She put them in a berry basket daintily nested in tissue paper, and she wrapped some of the paper all around. She worked with deft hands, although it was becoming so dim in the kitchen that she could scarcely see what she was doing. For it was late; even the long twilight of this northerly land was fading.

Arthur was not in the house. He had set off up the hill with his dinner pail long ago. But, behind her, she knew Cyril was standing in the dining-room doorway watching, saying nothing.

When the package was ready she left it and, slipping through the doorway without touching him or asking him to move, she ran up the narrow steep stairs to get a coat.

She threw it around her and then looked back at herself in the glass with one long unblinking stare.

When she came downstairs, Cyril had moved out of her way. But he watched her as she picked up the little square basket, as she went through the rooms to the front door. He said nothing. Nor did she.

The arc light at the town hall corner was burning and, at the base of the tall pole, as ever on a fair evening, were gathered the rowdy boys, the restless young men.

It was the central spot, the meeting place, and for an hour or two they would stand or slouch or shuffle there watching for whatever shape the evening might take. There was nothing ordinarily for them to do in Thor. No movie theater, no such thing as a bowling alley, or even an ice cream store.

True, there was a saloon at a crossroads, just beyond the bridge over the railroad, southeast of town. It stood alone, muffled and secret, between main Thor and the eastern set-

49

tlement, isolated from both with empty fields all around. A passer-by, walking on the soft, dusty shoulder of the road, would not hear or see much. The noise and the lights were walled and shaded away within. But if she were a woman, she would step softly and she would hurry with a stirring of the nerves until she was well past, for drunken men in aggressive moods had been known to erupt profanely through those doors.

Sometimes, it is true, a group of the young men, having met at the town hall corner, would make off in the direction of this place, and the bolder might even enter. But in Thor, a boy who lived in his father's house contributed until he left it, and these were the young and unattached. They had very little money at their own disposal. So they had nowhere to go that was within their means. And, anyhow, they were overwhelmed and abashed in the saloon which catered to their elders. So they gathered here and discharged here, under the arc light, what gregarious instincts they had and, meanwhile, observed everything that moved in the heart of the town.

Madeline, wearing her long, light coat, carrying the basket, slipped down her own side of the street and turned the corner. But they saw her and were struck silent. The sudden silence would have been their tribute to any married woman. (Unmarried girls passed at their peril). But for Madeline, after she had gone by, there was further comment; an outburst of loud talk and loud laughter.

Madeline's face was carved and still. She walked with swift grace under the trees where it was growing almost dark.

"Evenin', Miz Cole."

She was startled.

"Made ye jump eh?" Charley Beard, leaning on his gate, pipe in hand, chuckled. His little house was tucked in next to the church, and his yard was a bower. She had not seen him in the shadow of the tall shrubs.

"A little," she said pleasantly. "It's a lovely night, Mr. Beard."

"Yuss," he said, " 'tis." His pipe waved her along.

Now she crossed the road under another arc light and started up the slope.

Duncane's house, like all the others that lined the lakeside, had walks to both the back door and the front door coming in from this same street, for there was no road or even an alley behind them.

Madeline hesitated at the back path which came first. But she did not hesitate long. She turned in and went up a long shadowed walk beside the driveway, around a mass of mock orange, to the kitchen door on the side of this house.

Celestina's apprehensive face appeared in the glass. It was late in Thor for a knock at the back door.

"Good evening," said Madeline brightly as the door cracked. "I have something here for Mrs. Duncane. Would you tell her please that Mrs. Cole thought she might enjoy . . ."

"Just a minute," said Celestina and closed the door in her face. Madeline bit her lip and stared out into the gathering darkness.

When the door opened again behind her, Henry Duncane stood there, Celestina's black head bobbing at his shoulder.

"Why, hello," he said. "Come in."

"I've brought a few of these for Mrs. . . ."

"Come in, Mrs. Cole, please."

She was forced to follow him across the kitchen where Celestina now stood by the sink and frankly stared. She could hear Libby Duncane's voice, within, saying,

"Oh, that girl . . ."

As they came into the sitting room, Libby was struggling to get up.

"Oh, how do you do? Did she leave you standing? I'm so sorry . . ."

"Good evening," said Madeline gravely and almost aloofly. "My husband thought you might enjoy some of our own tomatoes. He asked me to bring them over."

Libby seemed delighted. She took the little basket. She peered under the tissue paper. She exclaimed, "Oh, how very nice of you! And what beauties they are! Do please sit down, Mrs. Cole, won't you?"

"I can't stay."

"Oh, just for a minute . . ."

51

All Libby said was as grateful and friendly as could be, but she was astonished just the same.

Although the sitting room was vast, extending straight through the house, back to front in the center, it seemed cozy at night. The corners lay shadowed. A lamp lit the sofa and Libby's book as it lay open on the cushions beside her. Another lit the newspapers on the floor beside the desk and the chair, and Henry Duncane now walked over to that tall secretary where he had evidently been writing. He picked up his letter, folded it, slipped it into an envelope and licked the flap.

"I'd better walk down to the depot with this, Libby," he said, each syllable precise.

"Oh, Henry, must you really?"

"So if you will excuse me. . . ."

"Of course," said Madeline.

"Well, of course, dear," said Libby Duncane concealing a small dismay.

So the women faced each other. Dark-haired Madeline gracefully erect on the edge of a chair, poised as if to rise again soon—a woman reluctantly polite enough to stay briefly where she did not belong. And the fair-haired Libby with her awkward body resting as best it could against the cushions—a woman polite enough to insist briefly that the intruder stay.

"And you raised them yourself?" she was saying, just on the edge of the false enthusiasm some people use to a child or an inferior.

Henry Duncane went briskly out the back door.

Celestina watched him go by with no comment on her dark handsome face. She finished the last dish and went up the back stairs. She had her own room and bath at the kitchen end. And, of the two, the bathroom was her special shrine and sanctuary. She spent far more time there than in the small, neat bedroom which was nothing so extraordinary. Besides, the bathroom overlooked the street side of the house, and often she would settle at its window in the dark and gaze with vague yearning down toward the arc light at the church corner.

Young girls could no more stand in knots on street corners in Thor than in any other town. They could of course, here, as well as anywhere, make excuses to pass that way between one respectable place and another. Celestina, however, was the Duncane's hired girl and, except on Thursday, a prisoner in their house. She was paid for it. But she was sixteen too. On a soft summer evening any prisoner would yearn through the bars.

Downstairs, Libby said, "Oh, must you go so soon?"

"I'm afraid so," said Madeline who had risen. "Please don't get up, I can just . . ."

"I think Celestina has gone to bed," said Libby listening. "No, please . . . Come this way."

Madeline did not offer to help her as she struggled up. It would not have done. In all their stiff exchange of commonplaces they had broken no ice and were no less strangers than before. Madeline had not tried. She had behaved like a messenger. Libby had remained the gracious recipient of a gift out of the blue, who was too polite to admit how much it surprised her.

Nevertheless Libby was not going to permit this visitor to leave by the back door. Timing her reiteration of thanks to take them just nicely to the point of parting, she switched on the hall light and then the porch light, and let Madeline out herself. It was necessary to linger a moment in the open doorway. Both women caught the rhythm just right. The evening was admired and thanks were finished neatly, and good nights were said in an interval just long enough.

Then Madeline went down the three steps from the porch and Libby, within, held her finger on the switch until her caller's slim back was halfway to the gate. She then flicked it, causing darkness, and she turned thoughtfully back toward her book.

For goodness sakes, she was thinking, that was odd. She paid no attention at all to the tomatoes in their basket on the end table.

Madeline walked quickly till the dark flicked down. Then her feet faltered. The evening was absolutely still.

Then a sound slipped across the lawn and stopped her. It was her name. She turned her head. The whole town was absolutely still.

Her body broke its poised hesitation, and suddenly she ran on the grass; she slipped silently past the tall mock orange.

"I wish you wouldn't come here," said Henry Duncane, in the deep dark.

She felt a flashing triumph like a huzzah in her heart. She swayed toward his sensed presence and fell against him and laid her dark head on his breast.

All the world was absolutely still as his arms came around her.

Directly above them, in the dark, the prisoner pressed her mouth upon her forearm and her forearm on the open window sill. Light burned in Celestina's back bedroom, not here in the bathroom where she was absolutely still.

"Don't do it," Henry said. "Please, Madeline." His voice was clogged and impeded for once, and Madeline, with her ear against his heart, exulted.

Ah, she knew a secret! She alone knew it! This man, this one of the crisp decisions and the cool competence, this admired one with the clear voice, the sharp intelligence; even he wore in his breast a pounding heart, and the heart was just as tempted and torn and bewildered and uncertain as many another.

She rested against him and filled her nostrils with the scent of his clothing and his skin, and felt his arms tremble even as he said sternly, "I won't have it."

"Arthur," she murmured. "His idea . . . he insisted."

"Why?"

"Oh, he—because he admires you."

Henry made his arms hard to hold her away. "I won't have anything to do with him. Or you with Libby."

She was startled. Her fingers closed clinging to his shoulders. She was interpreting that sharp alarm. She said, slowly, "No."

"I won't have *that*," he said.

"Ah, Henry . . ." He would not bend though her fingers pressed the warm flesh of his neck under the ear.

"No," he said quickly, as if now he too caught the feeling behind what he had said and hastened to deny it.

"All right. Yes, Henry. I know what you can't do." Her

54

voice soothed and agreed while her whole body, all its magnetism alive, was slyly saying, "We are together. We are here together."

"I understand," she murmured aloud. "I'll do what you say. But you've got to let me *tell* you . . ."

His arms neither tightened nor did they release her yet.

"Don't tell me anything," he said doggedly.

"I may never speak to you again in all my ife," he said and it silenced him.

"I've told you twice . . . this makes the third time   . three times and out . . . last time I'll tell you . . ."

He said dryly, "I think I remember . . ."

"That I love you. Let me say it *all*." Her breath poured its warm whisper against his chin. "And you love me. You know I am the one for you. Though we met too late."

He said neither yes nor no.

"And that's the way it is, Henry. Oh, I know as well as you how much too late it is."

"No good can . . ."

"It's done. My mistake. Yours, too. You never said it and I don't ask you to say it. Or undo it. But I have to tell you. If you called me, I would come. I would go with you any time, any day, east or west, anywhere—so don't you see that I must get free?" She made her voice pure. "Mustn't I? There is no . . . nothing . . . nobody's health for me to consider. I ought not to stay as I am—loving you."

She listened to his heart surging so mysteriously.

"I don't ask you to get free," he said, and the fine edge was off his voice again. It had a choking sound.

"I know. You can't."

He pushed her at arms length. "I ask you nothing one way or another," he said angrily. "If . . ."

"Ah . . . if . . ."

But he was not going to pursue the 'if' of it.

"I can't tell you what to do," he said quietly, helplessly.

"Only call me," she murmured, "if you ever can."

He was helpless.

She thought now he might be at the breaking point, he might embrace her fiercely and desperately as she wished. He did not embrace her.

55

"The little child," she said softly. "I understand." She knew his breath caught. "But I must ask . . . A divorce is right, for me."

"That's for you to decide," he said. And then in a voice cold with a kind of sorrow, "Don't come here again."

"All right," she agreed forlornly. "I'll never come again. No more." And she let herself go drooping, soft as a flower.

He bent, then. "Madeline, will you please . . . for God's sake . . . keep away . . ." said Henry Duncane somewhat frantically.

So she drew herself away, hurting him and trying him as much as she could with gentleness, with lingering. When she stood free, she snatched up his passive hand and put her lips on the back of it. Then she walked, brushing the bushes as if she were blind, away down the back path to the gate.

Celestina let herself back on her haunches with no sound.

Henry Duncane stood in the shadow with his hand held out from his body. In his cool head he knew that the clean-cutting current of his life was to be, henceforward, somewhat blurred and sullied. He had become obligated. He was entangled in the lives of both women. This being intolerable, he would turn away from one. Now he perceived that, either way, there would be remorse for him. Only a part of him could go the way that he was going and this way—either way—would be clogged and muddied with regret, with guilty sorrow.

He blamed nobody.

From his gate, even at this distance, Madeline could see that the gang on the corner had gone. She was relieved. The arc lights shone down upon the bare deserted corners. The town was still. Her own feet rang too loudly upon the sidewalk. She hurried, crossed quickly, went past the silent church and plunged under the tunnel of branches.

On a stoop a match flared. "Good night, Miz Cole," a voice said.

Her heart jumped. "Oh, good night, Mr. Beard," she called, her breath catching. She almost ran as she rounded the turn toward her own house. She slipped between the lilacs and went inside.

56

There was a light in Cyril's room but his door was shut and his blinds drawn.

She locked the front door behind her and went in darkness through the tiny sitting room, to the dining room and to the stair. She groped up on all fours, using her hands to feel the steps before her.

Her brother, Cyril, had never been known to come upstairs.

In her room she lit the lamp and stood staring at her image, the flushed beauty, the wild triumphant happiness.

She smiled. Arthur was naive.

She crossed her arms on her breast and nodded at herself in the glass. You will see. You will see.

And her mind went back over the few moments she had had with Henry, so far. Her first bold and direct acknowledgment of the state they were in. Ah, how wise she had been, to be so bold. For it had caught him. It was pulling him toward her, a little more, a little more, each day. It was her decisiveness, her quick reading of his shock when he first saw her, so beautiful and desirable, and her direct facing of the fact of her own desire (and now her threatened action which she would take, or not, in her own good time). All this was her charm over him.

If Henry did not find her beautiful and desirable he would have slapped her away long since with some decisive humiliation. But he had not. Not yet. And so powerful is a whisper wrapped in the scent of flesh in the dark, the words would ring desperately honest. Oh, Henry would not think her maudlin or brazen or even unwomanly, but rather a woman as brave and direct as a man.

She smiled. Henry was naive, too, in a way. All men were naive. (Except Cyril. He was not. But she cast her brother out of her thoughts.)

Oh, she could have driven him wild, she thought. But had not. Had drawn so softly away. Well, that was wise, too. Her lips parted. She'd driven him wild enough, she thought, and her heart swelled with what was in it, the sweet sensation of her power.

57

CHAPTER SIX

THE Company's frame building was painted a pinkish tan, and in its long façade there were three entrances unevenly spaced. The one at the east end of the offices was a good forty feet away from the other two sets of double doors that led into the store.

But there was a small grilled window let into this blank wall and through it, on paydays, the people of Thor received their wages. On such days a line of them rambled out over the street—Pollack women with scarves tied under their chins, women in house-dresses, women, some men, some boys.

The westernmost entrance to the store led through the grocery and hardware, the other through the dry goods, jewelry, haberdashery, and miscellaneous. Inside, of course, the store was actually one vast room cut up by half-partitions, counters, cases and aisles, smelling indescribably of all its wares, turpentine and cheese, new cloth and leather, rubber and spice. And far inside, at the back of the dry goods, opposite the rack of cotton clothing, there was another small grilled window.

It sometimes seemed that money came out of the building at the first window, hesitated out of doors perhaps long enough for its owner to count it, and then came in through one of the other entrances and flowed through the second window and the hands of the store cashier right back to where it came from. Or it might be concluded that the Company paid in kind.

There was no other store in the town of Thor.

Wednesday morning, when Cyril Varker opened the pay-window, there was already a group waiting quietly in the hot sun. Wednesday was going to be a scorcher.

Payday began. Each came in his turn up to the window and received a rake of Cyril's upturned eye, his cold recognition, and then waited for the somewhat ceremonial search of his hands for the proper envelope. Cyril rarely spoke. His eye accused. "What, *you* here? What money for *you*?" And his hand gave it finally with an air of having found a trifle somewhere of which he had only just been reminded.

Paydays were happy days. He liked to see the people's faces so often eager and smiling, then nervous and anxious under his stare. Could something have gone wrong? Had there been a misunderstanding? And then on each face the relief as it fell, in the sag of the cheek, the soft downward fold of the eyelid, and finally he would watch for the face to turn to the store and betray, in its tightening, that the battle of old bills versus new desires had only begun all over again.

This was Company business in which he represented the Company. But he sometimes had a little pleasure all his own.

When, as the long line wound by, the face of Wesley Trezona appeared before him, Cyril lifted his lip. The boy's face was pale and sought mercy, was eager for mercy, ready to break into a great full smile for mercy's sake. Cyril held the envelope as if it were soiled and distasteful.

"Mr. Varker," said Wesley in a low, hoarse voice, "keep it all this time? And next time too?"

Cyril, head lowered, brow corrugated, looked up.

"This is too little. Next time's too late."

"I know, but please . . . If you could wait . . ."

"Better bring me the balance by Saturday," said Cyril lightly as if this were easy. He knew it was impossible.

"I . . . please . . ."

"Saturday. My house." Cyril's pale eye stabbed him. "Or must I go to your father? Move on. Get along. Busy today."

The boy moved out of the line in a daze, numb, despairing.

Cyril paid off Mrs. Bettiga, with Mr. Bettiga's envelope, and received a barrage of Italian which he neither understood nor listened to. He hadn't the least intention of going to the boy's father over this debt. *He* was not desperate for the money. No, Wesley should sweat blood for three days and then Cyril would have cruel mercy.

He knew it was cat and mouse, of course. He was neither proud nor ashamed of it. He simply enjoyed it. It was balm of a sort. They were all fools. *This* was his small, secret power and it entertained him. There was a little spice of danger too.

Cyril knew quite well the risk he ran, for his rate of interest was fantastic. But he liked that. As he liked the tension, liked being hated and feared and sought after just the same. Liked the shambling, shuffling, anxious, hesitant appearance of another victim. Who had heard this somewhere . . . ? Somebody had said that Mr. Varker might let him have . . . for a short while . . . Cyril liked the baring of the need, the outpouring of fervent gratitude and, later, the screws tightening.

Cyril liked the exercise of his judgment too. Liked the putting on of utter innocent blank denial.

"No truth whatever in the rumor. I'm a poor man. . . . Where did you hear that?"

Sometimes this was necessary. For such people as that Fred Davies, who was wild to buy himself an automobile, Cyril could do nothing. Nothing at all. No doubt Davies would have paid the principal and the high interest, too, promptly and cheerfully, but money was not everything. Cash profit was not all Cyril cared for.

And besides, once having paid up, Davies was more than likely to talk about it with no particular shame. No, the forthright, the confident, the open-eyed, who were willing to pay a high rate for a legitimate advantage, were not the type.

Wesley Trezona now. There was the type. Guilt-ridden.

Cyril raked the next face with a show of cold suspicion. "*You* are Mrs. Miller?" he said to a girl he knew quite well to be a bride.

A very pleasant day was payday.

At the head of his dinner table, that Wednesday, Captain Trezona dipped into the pudding. His blue eyes were thoughtful.

60

"They asked me to go, too, Pa," Dorothy said. "So can I go?"

She couldn't go. She and her mother and brothers knew this already. She couldn't go to Lark Lake.

The captain said, "Robins' cottage, eh? H'overnight, Darithy?"

"Yes, Pa. Mrs. Robins will be there."

"And 'oo else?"

Dorothy named girls' names.

"Go to our church, do they?"

"Three of them are Catholic, two Episcopal."

The captain disposed of a mouthful thoroughly. "Be going over to that there pavilion, Darithy, h'after dark?"

"I don't know," Dorothy said.

She, of the three children, resembled the captain with her narrow face, her narrow mouth, her high-bridged nose; but the fair, firm, pink-and-white of her young flesh made the cast of her face seem delicate and fine.

"Dancin' there?" the captain asked. "Drinkin'?"

"I dunno, Pa, if they'd go."

But she knew they would go. In the soft evening after all the swimming and sunny play, the girls would make a giggling rowboat full and the boat would drift to the edge of the light cast from that wicked place to linger where the music would wash over them. Oh, they would be drawn; the tides in their young blood would set that way. Enchanted, the boat would drift to the lure.

And if a boy they knew were to hail them, who could promise that the boat might not dip dizzily alongside and at least one bold girl climb up and set her slippers sliding on the polished floor? Or even if a boy they didn't know thought one of them was pretty and began to tease. Josephine Doyle was awfully pretty and a devil, everyone knew. She wasn't scared. And Mrs. Robins on the cottage porch across the bay could not, with her bright lantern burning, see far through the screen.

"They might go," said Dorothy stoically.

"Not you," her father said. "No girl of mine. No boy, either. Dancin', drinkin', spoilin' the Lord's work in their bodies. Temptin' themselves."

61

Dorothy dipped her spoon into the pudding. She hadn't expected his permission.

Eedie said serenely, "Will you 'ave a little more of the custard, fayther?"

"No mither, great plenty, no more."

"Catholics think it's no harm to dance. Do they?" Dickie, the youngest asked abruptly. He was twelve, dark, thin, a tense little boy thinking his own thoughts.

"'Ush," said his mother.

"Wicked things do be done," the captain said sternly, "us can be sure. But the Lord, 'E knows when you do what 'E forbids. Remember that."

"Why doesn't He forbid the Catholics?" Dickie was just asking.

"He's not sassy, Pa," Dorothy said quickly.

Eedie felt a stab of joy, because her daughter loved the little brother.

"'E may not be sassy," Dickie's Pa said, "but 'e's on the wrong track, I see." His frosty eye canceled out the humorous timbre of his voice.

Dickie hid any quailing; his small face was impassive.

"Catholics and some, to be sure, may think it's no 'arm. That makes no difference to the sin." The captain's glance went to his eldest. "They say the Priest 'as wine to 'is table, and there's card playin' goin' on. There's corruption," the captain said, "and they may think it's no 'arm, but they'll answer."

"God must feel kinda sorry for them, though," Dickie said licking his spoon.

Eedie had to fight down her delight. There was a little wickedness of mirth that often lay in ambush, a warm joyous spot at the bottom of her heart. It would surge into her throat and make her want to laugh. Ah, the boy was clever, wasn't 'e, though? 'E was the thoughtful one! Ah, the long thoughts in the little 'ead! It was wicked to feel such pride. She must not laugh, and she had no business, either, to think, as she did momentarily, that the boy was in the right. Well? Did not the loving Father in Heaven *know* how they had thought they did no harm?

". . . Not what a man thinks," the captain said severely,

62

"but what 'e does, lad. And 'e must do God's Will. As the Bible tells us, and as 'e prays to understand it."

Eedie's own head bent with the rebuke which was just. Yes, now she saw.

"If 'e does wrong, the Lord 'Imself may be 'urt and sorry, but He will repay. So be sorry for them, if you must be," the captain went on, "but watch out you do no evil, as you do understand it." His head bent and he went into Scripture. "Thou 'ast said," he intoned, "none seeth Me. Thy wisdom and Thy knowledge 'ast perverted thee. Therefore, shall evil come upon thee; thou shalt not know from whence it riseth. . . ."

He went on mouthing silently the ancient music and Eedie, head bent reverently too, prayed quite cheerfully in her heart, "Deliver us from evil."

When the captain raised his head and cleared his throat, the signal that he had returned to the world of flesh, Wesley mumbled, "Excuse me, Ma? Pa?"

The captain nodded, but Eedie's eye caught the state of Wesley's pudding bowl. " 'Aven't eaten up your . . ."

"Too much for me," Wesley said whitely over his shoulder. "Too hot for pudding . . ." and he went whipping up the stairs.

At once she wondered if he were going to be sick and half rose from the table.

"Pity," the captain said, "a sorry waste there."

"I'd be glad to eat it," said Dickie promptly, theology forgotten.

"God bless 'is appetite. 'E shall 'ave it," said Eedie, sinking back. She had the instinct to cover over her alarm.

Leaving the dinner dishes to Dorothy who would dream over them but eventually get them done, Eedie herself went slowly up the stairs. The long leisurely afternoon lay before her for the morning work was done, Gideon gone to the mine; nought to do now till suppertime but laze in the heat, embroider on the porch, be happy. This afternoon held no such peace, yet.

She stood before her eldest's door. He was not asleep although he ought to have been. She knew he was not. The crunch of his body, thrashing on the bed, came faintly to her ears, and some emanation of trouble was at the same time just as sensible to her heart.

She went in.

"Ma?"

She sat down beside him and touched his head. It was wet with sweat.

"Ma?" he said in anguish.

Her fingers stirred, making little loving strokes at the nape of his neck.

"Ma, I've done some bad things. I got in trouble."

I love you just the same, of course, her fingers said.

"Now it's money, Ma. I owe a man a lot of money. I can't pay. He'll tell Pa. What can I do?"

She attacked her complete bewilderment slowly and carefully.

"You owe money?"

"Ma, it's three hundred dollars. I haven't got it."

This was a shocking sum. Of course he had no such amount. Nor did she. Or ever would.

"'Ow do you come to owe . . . ?"

"I borrowed it. That was O.K. I was to pay interest and all. But now I can't."

"'Oo loaned you it, Wesley?" she asked slowly.

"Mr. Varker."

"'Im! 'E loaned you three hundred dollars!"

"Comes to that now," Wesley rolled and rolled again. "Ma, I'm sorry. I'm sorry. What can I do?"

"What did you do with the money, son?"

"I . . . had to have it." He writhed under her hand. "Listen, Ma, I might as well . . . I took too much to drink one night. A bunch of us . . . but I took the most. Then we took Mr. Olsen's car . . . for a joke, we thought. I was driving. I ran into the bridge. And, and, and . . . there were damages . . ."

Her hand was still.

"I borrowed to pay. And then I . . . Ma, I even lost some of that, playing cards . . ." he choked.

Sins! So many sins! Drinking, stealing, sneaking, gambling. . . . Her fingers were still with shock. But she made them

64

move again as steadily gentle as ever, proclaiming her love, even so.

"You did wrong," she said quietly.

"Ma, I don't know how I came to get into it. I don't know. The kids were all watching me. . . . *You* know."

Sneering at the obedient son? He must prove he was no coward, he must swagger somehow and break over the rules in another place and do some daring deed?

"Ma, I didn't go to get drunk. I . . . I had some beer once before. But this was whiskey. He asked me if I'd have it. Well, I . . . I didn't want to back down."

"Showing off," said Eedie, not reproachfully, but to let him know she understood. (No harm in that, surely.)

"Showing off, that's what it was all right. Showing off. Then, well, we . . . we . . . we . . . thought it was funny to take Mr. Olsen's car and go riding around. But I was too dizzy. First thing I knew, Ma, I *had* to pay Mr. Olsen."

Speedy Olsen he was called. He ran the saloon. A touchy and evil man. Eedie shuddered.

"He said he'd keep quiet if he got paid. He didn't want trouble. So I . . . they told me . . . everybody said Mr. Varker would let you have money business-like, and you could pay it off. And I *had* to pay Mr. Olsen, Ma. I knew I couldn't take as much out of my pay as . . . as they thought, because Pa would know. So it wasn't enough. So I thought I could maybe win enough. Well, I was wrong. Wrong about everything . . . everything. So I quit that," he swallowed, "but I quit too late. I had to get a little more from Mr. Varker . . . and I got Mr. Olsen paid all right . . . but Mr. Varker only loaned it till this Saturday. I gave him all my own money ever since then. But it wasn't enough. It can't ever be enough . . . and he won't wait. He'll tell Pa."

"Your Pa will pay," said Eedie with a stiffening mouth.

This will break Pa's 'eart, she was thinking, break 'is 'eart in two.

Evil had come. They were not to be delivered from it. The good man, the good man would have his heart broken. Oh, the captain would pay the debt. He'd have the money. It was not the money.

But his pain. His pain.

Eedie saw everything at once, all of it. Wesley's temptation, the strain put upon him by the captain's dictum, and how weakly he had given in to the strain and slipped along to this. Oh, she saw it from inside Wesley and she could not blame him. He was a good boy; it had been too hard. Too hard. The others had urged him on, she had no doubt. There had been more pressure than the captain guessed.

Nevertheless, since she saw it from inside the captain too, she did not blame him either, for never guessing how hard it would be.

Ah, if a man is leading those he loves above all others on earth across a narrow bridge that carries from birth to salvation, and if his whole heart is in his task to help them, to keep them safe, to get them past the chasm, and one beloved child slips off into the torrents below, how much will the man suffer? Though it be none of his fault, how much will he grieve?

At least as much as if this were to happen in the world of flesh, on an iron bridge over solid rock and river water. She met her son's eyes and saw that Wesley, exactly as well as she, knew what he had done. He could not bear it. Ah, he was a good loving son to his father, though a sinner.

"Ah, Wesley." It was a groan, a sigh, but a sharing of sorrow. "We must pray."

"If there was only a way to pay him and Pa wouldn't know." Her big son, Wesley, began to weep. "I'll never . . . I'll never . . ."

"I know that. You'll never . . . I know that, Wesley, my dear." And she did know. He would never sin these sins again, but the harm was done all the same. She had no money, no money at all. Nowhere in all the world could she find that much money on her own and Pa not know it.

66

CHAPTER SEVEN

SOME summer nights the town of Thor lay in its woodsy
cup and saw the heat lightning play, the ragged crests of the
hills leap into silhouette against that soundless flickering.
But often the blazing midsummer sky would begin to darken
in the late afternoon and, just about suppertime, the thun-
derheads would roll up in the west and hang over the town
for an hour of threat and tension before they broke.

The heat on Wednesday had such a climax.

About five o'clock, Eedie Trezona stood at her back gate
and looked up at the band of ugly, yellow-green which was
being borne, like a bone, in the teeth of the rolling green-
black cloud.

"Will you make it, Ellen?" Eedie asked her departing
caller, anxiously. "Hadn't you better wait over?"

Mrs. Trestrial was climbing headfirst into her model T
Ford. She set her haunches behind the wheel and turned her
long horsy face. The gray curls bobbled at her temples. "I'll
make it, Eedie, never fear."

She was a cousin on the captain's side, sixty odd, a
long-boned, long-jawed, vigorous and independent Cornish-
woman. She looked like a caricature of a spinster. But she
was a widow, although her husband's memory had faded out
of the people's minds. It was almost as if Mrs. Trestrial had
achieved the Mrs. to her name all by herself, a title of respect
for her years and her personality.

"My young men to think on," she said, "and their supper
to get."

"Be careful, do!"

"Never fear," said Mrs. Trestrial cheerily, and bolt upright,
grasping the wheel fearlessly with her head held high, she

67

set off down the hill. Her driving was a caution. Somehow the skittering little car was given its head as if it had been a horse, and Mrs. Trestrial merely clucked to it or gave it a hint to her desires intermittently by a sudden yank at the wheel. The car careened, now, down around the bend at the bottom of the first slope with a sassy flourish of its hind-quarters.

Eedie turned again to look at the clouds.

From this high house, which lay on the upper road north-west of the town, she had a vast skyscape. The full wicked-ness of the coming storm was visible all the way down to a far horizon.

Eedie counted her chickens. She glanced up the road. Gid-eon would be coming soon. No doubt he'd make it. Dorothy was safe in the kitchen. Dickie was safe in the house, too. Wesley had gone to work early to get under shelter before the storm broke. Wesley would be underground soon and safest of them all.

He had been able to sleep in the afternoon, once some of his burden lay on her shoulders, too. All things being equal, it was his heritage to fall into a state of happiness just as she did. In him, as in her, hope would spring up given any chance at all. So, waking, he had seemed a little easier. For this she was easier and grateful.

So, although Ellen Trestrial's presence had prevented any more talk between them about the trouble he was in, still the unspoken word that passed in a glance and a touch as he left was not woe. It was hope. All might yet be well. The man, Varker, would be merciful and give time. Honest en-deavor to pay, made to the best of one's capacity, would surely be recognized. Hearts were not willingly hard. So there would be kindness and mercy.

Evil hung over the house but, like the cloud in the west, it had not yet broken. And in the ominous yellow light, the breathlessness of the air before the storm, Eedie Trezona even found a root reason to tuck under the hope that already flowered out of nothing more substantial than her own quick and ungrudging forgiveness.

To the grandeur and the beauty of all the world she could see the brilliant greens leaping out in this light, the billowing black coming up, the narrowing margin of blue sky—so calm and clear and high and far—that she knew arched over and would return: to all of this she could not help responding with reverent awe. How glorious and powerful was God! She, so small, need not wonder how He would save the truly repentant loving boy, and the good loving father from the stinging blows that could rebound between them, back and forth. Pain and the pain of giving pain . . . She need not wonder nor ask, but hopefully praise, for His was the Power and the Glory.

Madeline Cole moved nervously to and fro in her tiny kitchen. Arthur was gone—off early because of the impending storm. He had caught a ride up to the mine with someone, so the routine was broken and supper over too early. She was restless, thrown off her stride, and pressed upon by the atmosphere besides.

"Going to be a bad one." Cyril put his head through the door. "Windows closed upstairs?"

She nodded.

"Turn on the light, why don't you?"

"I don't like . . ."

"Superstition," scoffed he. "Have some light in here. Lightning's not going to be attracted by a one hundred watt bulb."

"I suppose you know," she said sullenly.

"I'm no engineer."

She stopped in her tracks. "Turn it on then."

Cyril smiled. But he did not turn on the electric light. The wicked sky, the lowering yellow-lined gloom suited his sister, he thought. He watched her begin again to lash to and fro, turning like a cat, beautiful and savage.

He said speculatively, "Say, we got no college dreams tonight, did we?"

"The storm," she said. "He was in a hurry."

Cyril grunted skeptically. He leaned on the doorjamb. "You and Duncane got together last night?" he asked lightly.

She flashed around and faced him with her fists at her neck. "You . . . !"

"You're a fool, Madeline," he said. "Now what? Now what?"

"None of your . . . !"

"Tristan again, eh? But the same old slightly shopworn Isolde."

"You don't understand . . ."

"Tell me it's love," he jeered. "Go ahead. It's in your department, I'll grant you that. If you'd use your head for one minute . . ."

"You don't own me," she cried. "You keep out . . ."

"No," he said. "No, I don't own you. If I did, you'd act less like a headless chicken; that I'd promise."

She started to rush past him but he caught her arm. "What's going on?"

"Nothing."

"You're pretty good," he said, "but I'm the one person you can never deceive. So don't try. What's going on?"

"Nothing," she said this time eye to eye.

He laughed. "Well, I believe it and I'm the only person who will. You realize? What do you think you're going to do?"

Her gaze flickered.

"Ah, you have plans?"

"Maybe," she defied.

"You're insane," he told her gloomily. "What about Arthur?"

"What about him?"

"It's bad enough," said Cyril with a vicious twist to his mouth, "that you jumped into getting married without looking twice at him. But now you live in the same house, haven't you seen him? Don't you know what he's like?"

"What is he like? A child, *you* say."

"A violent one." Cyril was quite earnest. "Violent, I say. Because he's got room in his head for one idea at a time and only one. No second thought is going to cool Arthur off. Not quick enough. Do you want to get your neck broken?"

"No." She jerked to get out of his grasp but he held her.

"Don't scoff. I'm warning you."

"What can he do?" she said sullenly.

"Break your neck. And be very sorry, of course, five min-

70

utes later. Probably sob all the way to the gallows, pitifully."

"I'm not . . . He won't . . . Let go."

Her gray eyes turned. The yellow light washed her pale face. She looked intently into the pale, cold eyes of her brother. "What do you advise?"

He didn't answer. Her voice grew thin and insolent. "Out of your vast experience in affairs of love . . . Tell me, what would *you* do?"

He let go her arm.

"You'd work and send him to college? Or whatever he wants to do next week? Or leave that out of it. *You'd* even live the rest of your life miserably with the wrong one? Or would *you* ask for a divorce?"

"Ask," he said shortly. "Ask, by all means. Ask pretty."

"What can he do? I *haven't* . . ."

Thunder cracked and then settled to a long deep roar.

"Go a thousand miles and hide and then ask," Cyril said.

Lightning quivered wickedly.

"You might as well ask the lightning, you know, to wait and think a minute before it jumps."

"But," she insisted, "you'd try to get out of it? You wouldn't give up? At least, you'd ask?"

"I?"

"Wouldn't you?"

Cyril realized what she wanted from him. "Will *he*, you mean." He smiled. "Poor Henry Duncane. He'll ask. He'll try. You'll devil him until he does."

Outside the cloud broke and the rain gushed down.

Madeline had relaxed suddenly as if the breaking of the storm relieved her. "Go on, scare me," she challenged. "So you can go on living here cheap." Her voice was saucy.

"It would cost me," snapped Cyril, "to bury you. I'd be the one to pay for it."

"Ah, for your sake I'll be careful," she mocked him.

But when the lightning came again, he saw that her face was thoughtful. He knew she had listened to his warning. She saw that he was satisfied.

So was she. Although he might go very shrewdly about it because his blood was colder, Cyril, too, would try—just as she was trying—to get whatever it was he wanted. Anyone

71

would, thought Madeline, with a shiver of pleasure. Whatever they pretended, everyone did.

Libby Duncane had no appetite. In the lurid light she pecked and pretended. Celestina, serving, moved stiffly. If it had not been for Henry, both women would have abandoned the whole idea of a meal in the tension and threat of the weather.

But Henry sat to his supper just as if the whole sky were not about to crack open and possibly destroy them. His indifference was, to Libby's nerves, both comforting and exasperating in a throbbing alternation.

Already her ears were stretched to hear the fatal phone ring. If only she could know for sure that Henry would be here in the house with her throughout the storm. She might then settle against the comfort of his calm. But she couldn't know any such thing for this time, as so often before, one or other of the phones might ring. If there was trouble and there usually was, if lightning struck at any point along the line between the falls and the mine, and it usually did, then the mine phone would ring. And if the mine phone went dead, as it usually did, then the regular phone would ring just the same. And Henry would stand there with lightning playing around his head (or so it seemed to her) and usually, sooner or later, he would fling out of the house into the very worst of it, leaving her not only alone but, outrageously, to be the one who must still those shrieking phones she was afraid to touch—to say that he had gone.

As for Celestina, she gave neither the slightest comfort nor was she of the slightest use. Once the storm broke Celestina would be immobilized. She would not so much as run to close a window in direst need. She would kiss the cross in some dark corner.

Thunder muttered, mumbled and muttered, lying low. No use to think it was going another way or that it would skip over. They were in for it.

Henry was counting. He had a way of counting seconds and multiplying or something. He would sit there and do arithmetic in his head and then he would say calmly that the storm was so and so many miles away. Libby didn't believe it. To her the thunder was as incalculable and tricky as human fury, and it was malign. It could mutter and fool you, for next time it could just as well crack in the very room. And Henry's arithmetic was a silly, school-born abstraction.

"About five miles," he said now. She didn't believe it. "Finished? Let Celestina get the dishes."

He strode into the sitting room. Libby, hearing the dishes chatter in Celestina's nervous hands, looked back at the girl with compassion.

"Just stack them, Celestina. You may wait and wash them later."

Celestina ducked her head. She gave no thanks. She hardly seemed grateful. She wouldn't have washed the dishes anyway.

Libby thought, she looks like an animal. Well, we are all animals.

Henry was standing in the bay window. But what kind of animal was Henry? thought Libby, his wife, that he could stand and look straight up into the storm's dark face? She couldn't help feeling he tempted it. It might smite his insolence.

"I suppose," she said gloomily, "you'll be out in this sooner or later."

He shrugged and leaned toward the glass to see higher. A lightning bolt seemed to dance on the lawn.

"Henry, why do you go? Why do you always go yourself?"

He looked around at her. Now the thunder answered. Not five miles away, not any more.

"Aren't you the chief engineer? Aren't you a boss?"

He looked rather pleased, she thought. He came away from the windows and sat down. The light was so murky now they might have been under the sea. Henry switched on the lamp over his head and smiled at her.

"Don't you have subordinates?" she insisted.

"Sure do." He was still looking at her as if he were pleased.

"Then why aren't there some things you could get out of?" Her blue eyes were earnest. She meant what she was saying. "The dirty work. The going out at night and getting wet. What good is it to be the boss if *you* have to do all the disagreeable things?"

73

"If there's trouble it's my job," he began, gropingly for Henry. The pleased look had vanished. Something she said had wiped it away.

"You could give orders."

"I do."

"But . . ."

"It's important . .." he said slowly.

"What is?" she said irritably. "That you go personally every single time and run around in the middle of lightning and get soaked? I think, in some weird way, you must like it."

He didn't answer until a long roll of thunder had swelled and died. Then he said, "I don't like getting soaked or being routed out, Lib. But I do like making sure the job's done right. I can't . . ."

"So," she said abruptly, cutting into his struggle to express something. "Then I can look forward to being alone in all the worst weather."

He made no answer. He seemed a little stunned by what she was saying. Her sense of injury swelled.

"And the worse it is the more likely I am to be alone?"

"Thunder storms are going to come up, Libby," he said, patiently, "and if the line goes out, or something happens at the Falls . . ."

"Henry, I don't *like* being alone," she interrupted again, "especially now." (She didn't believe he needed to go. She believed he liked it.)

"You won't be alone," said Henry.

"Celestina," she scoffed. "You should see her. She crawls in a corner and puts something over her head."

He said, "Libby, it makes no difference . . ."

"No difference?"

"Lightning strikes without looking to see whether Celestina's got something over her head or even whether I'm home or not."

Was he grinning? A bolt glittered. An after-image of the wicked prongs shook on the eyeball.

"Oh, pull the shades, please," she cried. "I know it does, Henry." Her hands clasped each other. How could you explain the hideous power of unreason to a reasoning mind?

He went to draw the shades. As he did so, lightning glimmered and outlined his body, and the split air clapped together over the roof.

"Close," he said thoughtfully.

Her mouth shook. "I'm so especially nervous right now." She pressed her lips together. Well that was a whopper, she thought. She lifted her head and threw the truth at him.

"I've always been scared to death in a lightning storm," she said and, so doing, thought she tore up and threw away a whole spring and summer's worth of painful self-control.

"Lots of people are," said Henry, betraying no surprise. Then he added gravely, "There *is* some danger."

Libby's lips fell open. She didn't perceive that he put out a fact to stand as a reasonable excuse for her. It seemed to her to be one of his blunt ineptitudes. A truth told cruelly at the wrong time because there was no sympathy.

"If you're trying to make me feel better," she struggled to think it was funny, "you certainly go a good way about it." She giggled. "Oh, Henry, how can you tell me there's danger! What do you think scares me?"

"The noise, I imagine," said Henry calmly.

A booming shook the whole house and she jumped and flushed. Suddenly the rain rushed down.

He followed the turn of her eye and got up to draw the streetside shades down too. Now the room closed in and seemed to take its risks blind.

"What did you do at home in a storm?" he asked her.

"At home? Oh, *my* home?"

"*Your home*," he said evenly.

Half Libby's mind was busy being thankful that the phones had not rung yet. So she only half-realized she had fallen into a habit that perhaps she ought to break. She said, half-absently, "Oh, Henry, when I say home I only mean my old home, of course. This is my home."

The storm was high now and the rain pounded down on the house that had never seemed less homelike.

Henry merely amended his question precisely. "What did you do at your old home in a storm? Had them, I suppose?"

What had she done at home? She couldn't remember. She

cringed. Surely that had struck in this very street. "Oh worried it through, I guess. Henry, this is a bad one!"

"Pretty bad," he agreed. But she thought there was something hard and far-off about his agreeing. Bad, to him, was volts, she thought, or some measuring, technical thing.

Her small face, that gathered into a small pointed chin, tried to be placid and proud.

The mine phone rang and she jumped again. Two shorts, two longs. Not Henry's ring. (She knew no rings but his.) She was glad it was not for him, and so was surprised and hurt somehow when he went to the phone and picked it up anyway and told somebody to get ready to do something.

"Not for you," she said reproachfully when he had finished.

His eyes went sideways. He came and sat down beside her. His eyes turned sideways again. "May not last much longer." She knew he had guessed that they said things like this to each other at home. He was right, of course. Of course, they did.

"I don't see how it can," she said shortly.

Doom cracked in the sky. The mine phone rang again but it was not Henry's ring. Nor did he go. She could feel that he listened and knew what it meant, but needn't go.

Now he picked up the *Weekly Current* (published in Pinebend, the nearest town of size) that was the nearest thing Thor had to a local newspaper.

Was he actually reading? How in the roar and tumult could eye tell brain!

"Old Man Hooper's got to shoot his dog, I see," drawled Henry.

"What?"

"Dog's been killing chickens . . ."

This too seemed so inept, so fantastically apart, that she almost laughed.

Why, the sky had opened. Water fell out in lumps. There could be no air to breathe outside these walls. Nothing could be less pertinent, less interesting than the trouble about the dog and the chickens.

Still she began to talk very fast with great animation. "But think of the dog," she cried, "poor beast! Don't you suppose he tried to do what the man wanted? He must have thought he understood and *was* understood. He thought he and the man were friends, didn't he?"

Henry was listening.

"Then one day, he does something thoroughly doggy, just what he ought to do, according to his ideas. And the man never told him not to. Never could. And his friend kills him for that. It must be such a shock and a confusion. He didn't know it was in the bargain."

She became aware that Henry was listening very intently indeed. What had she been saying? Some fanciful stuff about a dog's feelings.

"Oh, well, I don't know . . ." she broke off.

"Quite a shock to be shot, certainly," said Henry drolly.

Lightning struck close, and then the instantaneous tearing, cracking, rending came a second time. Left them alive.

"Henry, you don't quite see what I mean."

"You mean a man and a dog can't make a bargain."

"There was no contract," she said, shrilly hanging to a thin cord of communication between mind and mind, a saving thing. "Once I heard a lawyer say . . ."

(The descending water was less solid. Maybe it was lessening, maybe it would soon be over. And the phones were silent. So cling to the thin thread, Libby, and make the brain turn to remember that lean young lawyer, so keen on his calling, extending and expanding against her father's gentle questions that could nudge out a subject as her mother's rolling pin nudged out the piecrust. Oh the talk, the good talk at home.)

"Did you know this, Henry, about the law? If two parties sign a contract and later it develops that they'd misunderstood—they'd had different meanings for words, say, in the contract, or they somehow hadn't meant the same thing or realized what they'd bound themselves to do—well, if they can prove this, why, in law there *is* no contract. Did you know that?"

Henry was still.

"I never did, until he told us. Did you?"

That phone was going to ring, she knew, and the thunder guffawed.

"No I didn't know that," Henry said slowly. "But it seems very fair. I didn't know that."

"So what chance has a poor dog?" she murmured. She was proud to have come back to the dog. It was an intellectual feat, in the circumstances. She thought, I'm doing pretty well. I really am.

Henry stretched out his legs. "*No contract*," he murmured as if he liked that. Libby stared at him. She did not know what he was thinking. Or what she had been saying. The thread was broken. And the phone rang.

Two longs and a short, and Henry was at it in one of his fluid motions.

"Duncane . . . Do you know where? I'll have a crew out right away . . . Stay on, I'll ring Stanley. . . ." So he cranked and he spoke, and cranked and spoke again, and his crisp words began to go out, attacking a problem.

Libby saw only the lightning flashing around his head. Then the phone cracked in his hand and was dead. He raced to the other phone which had not failed yet. Lightning whizzed and the storm shook the whole world in its teeth.

The lights went out. Henry dropped the phone and lit matches. Huddling where she sat, in the dark, she heard him make his way without stumbling to the cellar door, go down, find the switch. He threw it and the lights came on, for this house had two kinds of current, Company current and town current. Not that any light was going to last. Everything was going to go tonight.

Henry thought so too.

"Better find the candles," he warned. He was back already and opening the closet. What he took out was his raincoat.

She wailed.

"You'll be all right." Putting boots on, he looked up. His eyes were surprised, she thought. They seemed to be saying, "Why, Libby, you aren't serious!"

"The baby," she said feebly. "What if the baby starts? Henry, I don't think it's good for me to be alone."

He replied, "Doctor's right next door, easy to call."

"I know but . . . I know but . . ."

His face was blank.

78

"Oh, you can't understand!" she cried. "You just don't! You *never* can."

He looked at her.

There had to be power. Henry knew this but he did not consider how some men's lives and some men's money could hang in the balance for, even if they did not, there would be power if he could manage it. *That* was the job. First came the facts, then the decisions, then the orders. These had to be reconsidered in the light of any new facts, new decisions, and all pushed through until the job was done. He was compelled to go. It was simply necessary. And he was drawn by a deep desire, something she didn't seem to know about. She could afford to huddle and wait. But he must keep his purposes and his functions alive.

Sometimes she didn't seem to know what he was doing. True, he went away each day and came back with money, but that wasn't what he was doing.

For him the storm had no malice. The careless loosening of destruction was not, if he could help it, going to interfere with what he had been doing. That was all. But that was nearly everything.

"I'd please you if I could," he said lightly, stamping foot into boot, "but I guess this is just one of the doggy things I do."

Libby understood him perfectly. She cried out at once, "But you knew I was a woman. I never told you I wasn't a woman."

He took her by the shoulders, "Guessed it, Libby, long ago." He grinned. "Look, you know there's no more real danger if I've gone. Do what you did at home. Worry it through."

"You'll drown," she shrieked.

But he was gone. He had not heard. He was gone.

She was alone. There was no sign of Celestina (who was a heap on the floor of her sanctuary upstairs). The thought of her barely crossed Libby's frantic mind.

She was as good as alone in the dark now. For these lights would go out, too, very soon, and she could never find the candles quickly enough, she could not do anything quickly any more.

She made her way clumsily to the streetside windows and peered around the blind. Henry's car splashed out and tore off in the wet. Yes, he was gone. Were the arc lights burning? She could not tell. The storm roared down. She could see two mellow yellow squares across the street at Mrs. Trestrial's.

She teetered into the hall and to the coat closet to find Henry's big winter coat. The rain might spot it. But it was *big* enough. That was the point. She was going to run away from being alone. It would not do for her to be alone in the dark. Henry was *wrong* to leave her.

Someone must help her to be brave the only way she knew how to be brave. Someone must exchange with her the hopeful fibs and prophecies by which fear was not expunged but tricked and avoided, by which one coaxed oneself to endure it by saying that the worst was past. Soon over now . . . the shower that clears . . . always darkest before dawn.

And she would run away from the telephone, too. It wouldn't be good for her to have a telephone crack in her hand as the one had cracked in Henry's.

She was not going to the Hodges' next door, to the doctor and his medically minded wife, for she was in no mood to be thought of as a bundle of misbehaving glands. She was not going to the Gilchrists' either, so bedraggled and panic-stricken.

Libby had given only neighborly nods to the Cornish landlady across the street, a character in the town. They had never really been introduced. But just the same, she was going straight across to those lights where there was a woman, an eccentric old woman who did as she pleased and didn't care what people said.

She let herself out into the wild wind and whipping rain.

Her heart beat too hard. It couldn't be good for the baby. Henry was *wrong*.

"Land, child," said Mrs. Trestrial, "come you inside."

The arch to Mrs. Trestrial's sitting room was scalloped with velvet. The room itself was a mossy cave dripping with tidies and fringed scarves. A kerosene lamp with a glass chimney was already lit in there as if Fred Davies and young Mr. Weber, the principal of the high school, who were playing checkers there, did not intend to be interrupted when the electric lights invariably went out.

But Mrs. Trestrial whisked Libby past the opening to that cozy scene and the turn of two startled faces with an air of instant decision on the proprieties of the occasion.

"Come you with me."

Libby's soaked feet stumbled into the kitchen.

The kitchen was mossy too. There were calendars everywhere and pot-holders, whisk brooms, fly-swatters—all manner of small objects hanging handy everywhere on the walls. But the blinds were drawn very tight. Another kerosene lamp was burning in readiness and it was a cave, saffron-scented, a deep dry cave and a fortress.

"My husband had to go out," stammered Libby. "I was alone. The house is so big . . . I saw your light . . ."

Mrs. Trestrial clucked in her throat and said the one thing Libby was longing to hear.

"Now you ought not to be alone, child, on such a night, the shape you're in."

Libby sat down. It didn't matter so much any more. She was almost willing to be alone now. Just so somebody recognized that she ought not to be. I was right, she thought. Yes, I *was* right. The tension in all her muscles was dissolving into a kind of buzz.

Mrs. Trestrial made her take off her wet shoes and stockings and dry her feet. She bustled pleasantly. "We'll 'ave a cup of tay," said she, "and this will soon be past."

"I'm so afraid of storms," Libby confessed, tears starting in her eyes. "They scare me all to pieces," she told Mrs. Trestrial. "I ought to be ashamed, but I can't help it."

"We've 'ad some fine storms now, lately," said Mrs. Trestrial with grim relish. "There go the lights, as I expected. Oh, we've 'ad some dandies!"

The storm was not here. No dark came down. The lamp burned quietly. The storm, in its place outside, was a dandy. Libby was pleased to think what a dandy it was.

"You are so good to let me . . ."

81

"Cover your toes," said Mrs. Trestrial. "Now tell me, when does the doctor expect?"

Libby blushed. "The end of next week."

" 'Twill be sooner," said Mrs. Trestrial, bobbing her long face wisely, "or later, either one."

The tea was hot. The rocker creaked.

"Oh, do you think so?"

"Wishin' for a boy? Or a gel, eh?"

Libby began to explain that she could not really care. There was so much to be said for a son—or a daughter. She was quite nobly resolved to leave this to Heaven.

Mrs. Trestrial's long face kept nodding, her chair kept creaking, but she was not fooled. She knew that Libby, so far, cared only for the birth to be safely over. She was not shocked either. "Comes later," she thought, "all the rest."

"And where's yer mother?" said she aloud.

Libby's fingers pushed at her damp hair. She told Mrs. Trestrial how far away her mother must stay.

"But, you see, my father needs her," she finished bravely.

Mrs. Trestrial wasn't fooled. She looked into the girl's big, frightened eyes. "Ah, you'll be surprised."

"I suppose . . ." the eyes shone. "I will?"

Mrs. Trestrial chuckled. "Look ahead if you're a mind to . . ." she said, "but when you're looking back, you'll see . . . 'twas always surprisin'. 'Ard came easy and sometimes easy came 'ard. 'Twasn't what you feared that was on your 'eels. 'Twas another thing. Lies in h'ambush, it do." She sucked a long draught of the tea. She began to tell a tale packed with obstetrical detail.

Libby forgot about the thunder and lightning.

In a little while the storm began to die almost as if it missed the nourishment of anyone's attention.

It was late when Mrs. Trestrial herself walked Libby back across the street. The young men in the parlor—for there was one more turn of two faces—might have volunteered, but Mrs. Trestrial knew what was proper.

Behind the blinds the lights blazed again in Libby's house. Her bare feet cold in her sodden shoes, she stood at her front door in the sparkling fresh night air. As the smell of saffron vanished, so the warm intimacy seemed to blow away, and now her tongue stumbled giving thanks to a stranger. They kept sounding thinner and more false.

Mrs. Trestrial had the old-fashioned habit of holding up her skirts at the side in one hand and so she gathered them.

"No need to speak of it," she said tartly with a shrewd look in her eye. She was not fooled. Girl would feel shame to have run to an old woman, come morning. "I'll just step across 'ome," she announced and she did so.

When Henry came in at last, Libby was tight in bed. The long, gossipy, informative session with Mrs. Trestrial had relaxed her. She felt enlightened but drowsy. Now she knew such a lot she had only been guessing about. Her mind was pried out of its rut of blind apprehension. At the very least, she had new and refreshing things to worry about. She even smiled to think she could worry more knowledgeably tomorrow. But for now, wanting to keep the deliciousness of being so drowsy in the quiet night, the sweet relief and luxury it was, she lay low.

"Libby . . ." she heard him say very softly lest she be asleep. But one could always hear whatever Henry said.

"My coat . . ." It puzzled him, so wet upon the chair.

"I wore it across to Mrs. Trestrial's," she murmured. "Because I *shouldn't* stay alone. So I *didn't!*"

She lay snug in the clean quiet room.

His legs were plastered with mud and water. The road to the Falls had been a slippery nightmare, and he had driven it four times.

Lightning had struck a transformer and it had been burning at the top of its tall pole.

One of his men had picked up one end of a severed and fallen wire and enough voltage had arced through the moisture alone to knock him twenty feet.

But power was flowing. No one hurt. Damage repaired. Trouble licked. Henry home before dawn.

After what seemed to her, and to him, too, a long silence, he said, "You're all right, then?" The syllables seemed to fall mercilessly.

"Yes, I'm all right. Good night, Henry."

She heard him moving about into the bathroom—undress-

ing, washing, returning. She lay low. His precise light syllables fell again on her ear.

"Is Celestina all right?"

"I suppose so," she mumbled.

Silence.

Libby said sharply, "There was no more real danger
because *I* went out."

Silence.

Henry said gravely, "No. Of course not."

She buried her head.

CHAPTER EIGHT

THURSDAY was a pretty day, the sunshine so spanking hot, the shade so sharply cool, colors so clean. The pretty little town had never looked more charming. There was some traffic of white clouds, benevolent and mild as sheep across a crisp blue sky. On the damp earth remained the patterns of rivulets meeting and parting, but the flood was gone. Birds sang. There was no dust. The trees shone, every leaf was polished.

Libby Duncane through her bay window could remark the shimmer of gold over the green of her lawn, winking off and on again as the cloud shadows chased across.

"Oh, no more, my dear," said Mrs. Gilchrist.

Libby went right on pouring tea.

"Really, although it is delicious . . ."

"One and cream?" said Libby, being dainty with the sugar tongs.

"Well," Mrs. Gilchrist succumbed and loosed her easy soprano laughter. She had something to say, yet. A new subject had come up. Her handsome face was animated. She narrowed her bright blue eyes.

"Odd that she brought them to *you*, you mean?"

"Because I've met her only the one time," said Libby. "At church, you know. But I suppose she just happened to think of my empty garden. It does look so bad . . . right on the street. Everyone can see I have no tomato vines."

"Well," said Mrs. Gilchrist and drank tea. She then leaned. "Elizabeth, do you mind if I say something?"

Libby thought, I won't know until you say it. She hated the gambit. It usually meant that you certainly would mind. Definitely you weren't going to like it at all, as the questioner

85

well knew, but you had to give a blanket promise to suppress this or suffer from thwarted curiosity forever after. So she answered cordially.

"Of course not, Marianne."

"You are a newcomer. That is, the newest comer. . . . You do know what I mean?"

"I think so," said Libby. So new I don't know what it's all about, she translated in her mind.

"And suppose Madeline Cole would . . . er . . . like very much to . . . er . . . be asked to certain places."

"Yes," said Libby impatiently.

"Well, you see, you are the one person who might, if she is very pleasant and friendly, ask her here."

Might be dumb enough to ask her, translated Libby silently.

"Do you see then? If she were seen *here* . . . why . . ."

"I see."

"Now it wouldn't occur to Mrs. McKeever, for instance, to include her. Yet if Mrs. McKeever were to meet her under your auspices . . . for of course, my dear, you will have influence . . ."

"In other words she is trying to use me," said Libby bluntly.

"Well," this was too blunt for Marianne Gilchrist although it was exactly what she meant.

"I don't know about that. I don't think so . . ." said Libby doubtfully. "I don't know why she made such a gesture, but I just can't imagine . . ."

"Well . . ." said Mrs. Gilchrist in another accent entirely. This time it meant: You are young and inexperienced and not on to these dodges.

But Libby kept stubbornly to her own opinion.

"She didn't seem to be making up to me a bit. I just don't think she cares that much about that sort of thing. . . ."

Mrs. Gilchrist's face delicately indicated that everyone, of course, cared a great deal about that sort of thing. What else was there?

Libby, on her part, wanted to know why if Madeline Cole cared to be invited she should not be. But she didn't ask directly. She said, "As a matter of fact Mrs. Cole is very attractive. Don't you think so? Quite beautiful, I think."

"Oh, *yes . . .*" said Mrs. Gilchrist at once. It took the wind out of the compliment and turned it inside out. To be so beautiful was just it. Just the trouble.

"I don't often repeat," lied Marianne Gilchrist cheerfully, "but the story is . . . she was a schoolteacher, you know . . . the story is that never once was she asked to come back a second year . . . Anywhere."

"Is that so?"

"Because by the end of each term there was always some situation, some uproar among the men. D'you see?"

"Do you mean scandal?" asked Libby brightly.

"Oh, no, no—not that ever came out." Mrs. Gilchrist's tongue passed swiftly over her lower lip. "Some women just . . . it's like flies to honey . . ." She nodded vigorously. "Flies to honey . . ." she repeated, and then she turned on that mirthless laughter.

Libby experienced a feeling of revulsion. Well then, Madeline Cole would not do. Women closed ranks against such as she for reasons. Libby herself would go with the majority even though, at the same time, she knew quite clearly that the reasons might be merely jealous and defensive, quite unfair.

She sat still beside the tea table. She thought, What's the matter? She was uneasy. She'd been uneasy in a new and different way all this day. Her panic the night before, now over, seemed to have cut into some foundations. For one thing, she was not sure whether she and Henry had quarreled or not. Or had they agreed in some quite disagreeable way? He had gone off in the morning as aloof and *kind*—she bit at the word angrily in her mind—as ever. If they had quarreled, they seemed to have made a truce not to talk about it. Still she had a feeling that she was lost and strayed. Something was wrong with her. Not her pregnancy and the fear of it, not her loneliness, her lacking her mother, but something else.

"My dear, I must fly. Alex will be home and Veronica is out."

"It was so nice of you to come on Thursday," gushed

Libby. "Celestina's out too, of course, and I do hate being alone."

Mrs. Gilchrist's eyes flickered over her hostess' body. But she said, "How is Celestina working out, dear? Any better?"

"Oh, a little," Libby sighed. "I've rather given up."

In fact there was that truce, too, in the house. Celestina went about stolidly. Libby said little to her. But now and then during these last few days there had been a slant of those dark eyes that was provoking. It was as if she watched Libby—not for instruction or to see whether or not her mistress was pleased and certainly not in fear lest her mistress was angry again—but with an air of pure curiosity, Libby thought. As if she watched to see what Libby was going to do out of curiosity alone! As if her mistress was a vaudeville turn or an entertainment!

"She's exasperating . . ." Libby sighed. "But Henry wants me not to worry, at least just now. So I let it go."

"Why of course, you mustn't fuss, just now." Mrs. Gilchrist struck Libby's shoulder playfully with her gloves. "And you must remember to call on me for anything at all. Mercy what are neighbors for!"

Laughing gaily, Mrs. Gilchrist moved to the door. The lovely afternoon was spread before them. "So fresh after the storm," sighed Mrs. Gilchrist. She smoothed gloves on.

Mrs. Trestrial's Model T came looping around the sharp corner and drove fussing and popping into her driveway.

"Mercy," Mrs. Gilchrist's laughter rang. "Oh, my dear . . . the *hat*."

The hat got out of the Ford and was borne across Mrs. Trestrial's back yard to her kitchen door. It was a purple toque and bore a lopsided wreath of velvet violets. But only the trimming was cocked on her head. The hat sat foursquare across her tall brow and above her lantern face. The effect was droll. One had to smile.

"The other day," gasped Mrs. Gilchrist, "my children were . . . of course they do love to tease her. Do you know . . . Hoo, hoo!" Mrs. Gilchrist hooted twice, "what she called at them? 'Don't you tip your tail at me,' " she quoted. "Hoo, hoo, hoo!"

Libby realized with a little shock that she too was hooting.

In a lower register, a softer tone, but it was the same false, mirthless sound. She stopped abruptly.

" 'Tip your tail,' Hoo, hoo!" Mrs. Gilchrist was merry.

Libby wanted to say quietly, "Mrs. Trestrial has been a nice neighbor," or "a kind neighbor." Some such phrase was forming in her mind but it did not form on her mouth. She did not say it. Nor had she said a word about her panic in the storm. Or her flight. Or the refuge she had found.

"She's a scream, poor old soul . . ." gasped Mrs. Gilchrist. "Oh well, my dear, I must run," (archly). "Do take care of yourself."

"I will," said Libby smiling faintly. Her soft blue eyes were sad and sober.

"The nurse, you say . . . next week?"

"Tuesday," said Libby. "Henry thinks I ought to have her as soon as she is free. We don't want to risk her going on another case. She's so much the best, the only one, I'm afraid . . . who would *do*."

"Tuesday, of course. Ah, so nice . . ." Mrs. Gilchrist's eyes licked at Libby's gross figure once more and then she tripped away.

Libby closed her front door. She felt a little stained and dirty. Something was certainly wrong. There was something going on she didn't like, that made her uneasy. Her mind churned around and fastened on a shrewd little speculation. "I bet Marianne Gilchrist knows exactly how influential I'm likely to be. I'll bet that's why *she* puts herself out to call on me."

But she didn't succeed in pushing all of the meanness off on Marianne Gilchrist. She was still uneasy. She had a hunch that her mother could have told her what it was that was wrong. But her mother wasn't coming. That strong hand would not take hers and balance her with one firm tug and set her straight. She knew she was wandering, somewhat, and lost. Or she had lost something.

But there was no time to think or figure it out. No time. There was a Valley of the Shadow close before her through which she must somehow pass. Next week? How soon?

"I won't try to think about anything until it's over. When

it's over I can think," she told herself and pushed nervously at her hair.

Cyril was amused and very curious too. He had no doubt now that Arthur had suddenly lost all interest in education. He had not said a word about it in two days. So the subject no longer burned in his head. Cyril wondered what did. Perhaps, he reflected, nothing. But something must rush into such a vacuum.

Arthur was silent across the supper table this Thursday. Broody, with eyes cast down. Madeline was no chatterer. So little was said.

It was a relief, of course, that Arthur had stopped his pestering and pleading. Yet Cyril wondered what had stopped it. Why did these flaming interests die and lie cold? What put them out?

In a spirit of experiment he made an attempt to poke at the embers.

"Well, Maddy, back to work?" He threw the question down.

"What?" Her gray eyes were clouded with her private thoughts.

"Going to apply for a teaching job in the fall? If so, better hurry."

Now she looked left and right distractedly. *She* didn't appreciate the experiment. He knew what she was thinking.

"I don't know," she said at last flatly.

Arthur pursued some gravy with a crust.

"Arthur will want to enter himself," Cyril continued, "no later than the fall term, I should imagine."

Arthur was dull-eyed.

"Since this may affect *me*," Cyril kept pushing, "I'd like to *know*."

Nothing happened on Arthur's face.

Brother and sister exchanged looks. Cyril's was mocking, "I told you so." Madeline's was cool and reminding, "Be-still."

"Any news?" said Arthur suddenly.

"News? No . . . ." Cyril said, "but if you want opinion, Harding will win, or so they all say."

"I mean around town," Arthur squirmed.

Cyril looked astonished. "Around *this* town?" His eyes stretched. "Biggest news I know is that Hooper shot that mangy dog of his. Four Hooper kids and four Hooper kid-cousins showed up in the post office with nickels for candy to drown their sorrow, I presume. Form of child blackmail. They never paid any attention to the dog, that I know of, except to kick him."

Arthur didn't even seem to hear this cynical report.

"Henry Duncane's kid get born?" he wanted to know.

Cyril twisted his mouth. "You'd have heard. You'd be telling us."

"Kinda nice having a kid," said Arthur dreamily, and drank tea.

Madeline's knuckles went white on the edge of the table.

"I was thinking maybe Maddy won't want to go back to teaching. I mean, she might not want to." He wasn't looking at his wife.

But Madeline said at once, sharply, "Why not!"

"Well," said Arthur, "you can't tell . . ." A sheepish grin, half leer, formed on his face as now he looked at her.

"No! Don't! Don't go red-eyed about that! Now!" she cried out.

"What?"

"Just don't . . ." She put her hand on her mouth and left the table.

Arthur turned in astonishment, "What did I *do?* What did I say? What does she mean? Are my eyes red?"

"Just a little pinkish, so far," said Cyril cryptically. "Now lean back, Art. You shouldn't spring an idea like that on a woman so abruptly."

"No?" said Arthur. "What's so abrupt? You mean *she* never thought of it before?" His face darkened. He got up.

Cyril put his lower lip under his teeth. He could hear them in the kitchen.

"What's so shocking, Madeline? For gosh sakes, *I* want kids. I always . . ."

"Just because you get a sudden notion—"

"Notion! Listen, any normal husband—"

"Arthur, you'd better think it over."

91

"What's to think over?"

"Arthur, I—"

"What?"

"Wait—"

"Why?"

"Because I . . ."

"Because what? Listen, Madeline. I think it might be the best thing in the world. You got nothing much to keep you busy, and I should think you'd be tickled to death. I don't know what we're waiting for. Why *not* have a kid?"

"I thought you wanted to go to college?" she cried.

"Well, I dunno. I might be a little rusty. I get along, I make enough and, well, a man ought to have a son. Henry Duncane . . ."

"Oh, *stop* it!"

"What's the matter?"

"I'm not going to imitate the people you admire . . . to that extent! Now, just *don't* . . . !"

"Imitate! Listen, I was only going to say he got married just about when we did. I was going to point out . . ."

"*Stop* pointing out!"

"You mean you won't?"

"I mean, I won't . . . won't . . . not just like *this*. Arthur, please."

"I dunno what's the matter with you?"

"Someday, I'll tell you," she cried goaded.

"Tell me what?" His voice leapt at her.

"Nothing. Nothing. You'll be late."

"*Tell me what?*"

"Nothing. Arthur, don't keep nagging at me the way you do. You make me . . . I don't know *why* I said that."

He was standing, crowding her against the sink. She was at bay. She could see in his attractive but sulky boyish face an ugly hint.

"You'd better know." he glowered and in the white of the eye, as it turned, she caught the glint of it again. The violence, as Cyril had suggested.

She was afraid of it.

She said softly, "Arthur, won't you please try to understand. When you just offhand in front of Cyril too, say a thing like that . . ."

"What did I say?"

"That I . . . we, should have a baby."

"I said it would be nice to."

"But . . ."

"It would, wouldn't it?"

"Maybe it would." She swallowed and smiled.

"There's something the matter with you?"

"No, no."

"You don't want to have a baby?"

"I didn't say that. I . . . Arthur, you'll be late."

"No, I won't." But he drew away a little and she breathed.

"I don't get it," he said in a harsh whine. "I don't see why you called me red-eyed, either."

"It's—"

"It's what! Sounds like a dirty name to me. Madeline, if you don't want to have a child by me, you better say so right now."

She could feel the blow coming. The pain of it was waiting on her skin. Now she realized that she had felt one coming times before. She knew how to manage. "It isn't that . . ." she said very wearily, and closed her eyes.

She had spoken wearily and closed her eyes just so many times before. It was a familiar reaction.

"All right," he said. "It isn't that. So then you *do* want to?"

"Of course. Some day." She managed to smile.

He took up his dinner pail. He stood glaring down at her and his eyes seemed to her to be literally red.

"Next time," he said, "don't screech as if you thought it was a fate worse than death to have a kid. For gosh sakes."

"I'm sorry." She'd made a mistake. She *was* sorry.

"Give us a kiss."

He kissed her but without any particular passion. The idea was ballooning, filling his whole mind. A kid. A baby. *That* was the thing he lacked. The thing he wanted. The thing he needed to complete himself.

He went toward the door, he half turned back, "O.K.," he

93

said darkly. He might as well have added, "we'll attend to it then."

She crumpled against the kitchen wall.

Cyril looked in. "Now what?" he inquired with a faint overtone of glee. "What now?"

The evening was as beautiful as the day had been, as fresh and as sweet. While the woods drew on their evening mysteries and the high stars came out, the town drowsed in its cozy valley and there the arc lights bloomed on their tall stalks.

Elders rocked on the porches, children ran breathless with delight in and out of shadows tasting the sweet danger of the dark before bed. The boys gathered on their corner. The young girls found they had to see Helen, who lived west of that corner and see her right tonight. Meantime, Helen must see Lotus who lived east of it.

And Celestina stood in the dark by the Duncane's gate with Angelo, who said Trezona didn't care about anything to do with her but was swaggering around town, as everyone knew . . . so that was proved . . . but she tossed her dark curls and would not answer.

Meanwhile, babies cried above stairs and young mothers threw off their dreams in the fragrance of the evening and went to change a diaper, and grandfathers filled pipes.

Peace was on the town.

Libby Duncane felt it and looked up from her novel. A lovely peaceful night but, because of her great inertia, she must stay inside under the lamp to read. Yet the peace was within the room as well, for Henry was reading at a companionable distance. And that made all safe. The day buttoned down. Its efforts over. The sweet evening waning toward sleep.

"Ten o'clock," she yawned. The mine phone rang.

Three short. Henry's lashes fluttered. "Trezona," he muttered.

Again. Long, long. Henry said out loud, "That's the Old Man." (Who called Mr. McKeever at ten in the evening?)

Again. Another call. Not yet Henry's. And another. Not

94

for Henry at all. Libby said to herself, But the weather's so *fine*. What? She looked over at Henry. He was not even pretending to read. There was some jigging madness in the telephone so that it would not be still.

Then Henry got up deliberately. He took off the receiver and listened in. He said loudly, "This is Duncane . . . Where? . . . Any men? Ah . . ." It was a strange sound that ended his part of the conversation. Like a long sigh.

"What's the matter?" she cried out.

His face was strange. Now began a series of blows to which she chimed like a gong as he struck them.

"Been an accident," he told her.

"Oh, where?"

"West Thor."

"Oh, Henry . . ."

"Looks like some men may be caught underground."

"Caught!"

"Buried!" he said.

"Oh! No!"

She didn't understand at all, but she was appalled.

"Listen." Henry turned the strange quiet of his face. "Ah, there's Celestina now. Good. You won't be alone."

"Alone! Oh . . ."

"I'm going up to the shafthouse, at least. Find out how bad this is." His eyes were hard and steady. It was the hard and steady acceptance on his face that was so strange.

"Henry . . ." she wailed, understanding nothing. "Please . . . don't *you* go into anything bad."

"That's not my job," he said, sounding very angry.

He turned on his heel and called, "Celestina!" Libby could hear him telling the girl rapidly, "Been a cave-in at West Thor. They don't know yet what, or who . . . Stay with Mrs. Duncane, will you, until I'm back?"

He was going. He was gone.

Celestina came slowly into the room.

"But what happened? What does it mean!" Libby cried.

She could see a wild sorrow already changing that dark young face.

The child leaped in her body. Libby Duncane got up and brushed by to look out of the window.

Behind her, Celestina began to murmur, "Mary, Mother of God . . ."

And Libby thought, the girl's not going to be any good whatever it *is*, whatever we have to face now.

"Oh, I don't understand!" she cried aloud.

For there was nothing outside but the peace of the night as it lay on the town.

On the surface.

CHAPTER NINE

As HENRY's car described a swift curve backwards into the
street, there was a clatter and a hail from Mrs. Trestrial's
front stoop. Henry swung open the back door on the driver's
side to let Fred Davies tumble in, but the car lost no time
as it reversed and whipped on around the peaked corner and
up the hill toward West Thor mine.

"What do you know?" asked Davies.

"Not much. Tenth level."

Fred Davies said, "Ee-yah . . . I'd have made Trezona
put up or shut up."

"That what you were trying *not* to say to Gilchrist?"

"Hell, maybe it's not the same spot." (They were both
trained not to go too far on a guess.)

"Where else were they working?"

"On the tenth? No place."

"That's the spot, then. Men in there." It was not a guess
any more.

"Well, you know Gilchrist," Davies said, young, breathless,
and bitter. "Somebody don't agree with him, he gets unhappy. Just unhappy."

"I understand Trezona was pretty vague."

"Yeah, vague and religious. Gilchrist doesn't know how to
handle it."

"There's the Old Man." A big, black car debouched from
a side road and proceeded majestically ahead of them. Henry
bit at its heels a short way and then swung off on the upper
road. They climbed swiftly and ripped past Trezona's high-
standing house in which there were many lights.

"Captain's gone," said Davies.

"He'll be on the job."

97

"Bible and all . . ." Davies snorted.

"You don't want to underestimate that old boy," said Henry.

"What did he know though?" gloomed Davies.

"He either didn't know what he knew or didn't know anything. Obviously he couldn't say."

"I'd have—" Davies stopped. "Well, you get a craving to blame somebody. I suppose the captain will get God into it. And call it the Will of God."

Henry said, "Funny, when we get something else to call it, that's when we seem to think we got God out of it."

"Huh?"

"If He's there, He's always there," Henry said as if this were arithmetic.

"You surprise me," murmured Davies. He was amused.

Mr. McKeever was riding the cage. He was in his fifties, spare, white-haired, a man with a deep drawling voice, poised and deliberate in all he did or said. His face was set now in a mold of grave, but nerveless, concern. Davies and Duncane and others, miners who had been called, made up the descending load. They were all, except possibly Duncane, men who were going down to see what was to be done now. So there was a simplicity about them, something quiet and direct that did not make for excited chatter. The remarks exchanged were all brief and bitten off. Henry Duncane made no remarks at all.

At the tenth level the cage stopped. The group strode off along the drift dividing like beads slipping apart on a string. They plodded between the timbered walls, their feet catching the rhythm of the ties under the narrow track on which the trams, or dump cars, ran. They were going along a passage cut into the iron ore itself which ran the long way through the irregularly shaped ore body. The passage, having been exploratory in the first place, was not straight but bent gently.

The ore lies in the ground, and it is not square nor round nor any strict shape.

Men first go down into the ground in a vertical shaft, a straight line, the first dimension. On this they measure off

98

units of one hundred feet. At each one hundred feet within the ore body a level is established.

Now the exploratory drift goes off, probing, bending, and at irregular intervals crosscuts go in at various angles to probe sideways.

But when the work begins, men imagine and impose another straight line—a second dimension—which they draw the long way of the ore. At right angles to this line—a third dimension—they plot (according to the method used at West Thor) a system of rooms and pillars.

They start at the bottom of each level. They attack from below. They begin to take the ore out of a room, drilling and blasting it down in units called sets. The sets are the measure of the timber that goes in to hold the roof and the walls apart.

A room is from two to four sets wide and it will go into the ore the entire width of the ore body. When this has been done there exists a hole from fifteen to thirty feet wide and as deep as the ore goes, but only nine feet high. It is all timbered and held by the honeycombing of square-set timber, with the lagging placed behind the outermost legs to hold the rock walls there from caving in upon the work. One layer out they begin on a second. A hole is cut upward. They proceed as before, placing the sets of timber directly above those already in place, and dropping this second layer of ore down. It is let fall. It goes down into chutes, down into the cars and down out of the cars and, finally, at the very last, rides up and out of the shaft in the skip. But gravity takes it down first and that is why they begin at the bottom.

Once the second layer of a room is out and the honeycomb of timber is two stories high, they go up yet another layer; and so on until the room is all mined out, the hundred feet of that level. Rooms in a series are simultaneously being mined and exist in various stages, some worked almost to the limit, some barely begun. But between the rooms are left the pillars which are standing masses as wide as the rooms that remain untouched blocks of the earth's own structure to hold the great timber-latticed caves apart. A time comes when, the rooms being emptied, they must take the ore out of the pillars too. To do so they first fill the rooms, dropping

99

into them, from the level above, broken rock from other places. The timber is left and never recovered but the emptiness is filled, and lagging now lies against the same supports, but on the inside to prevent the filled rooms from caving in upon the new work in the pillars.

But sometimes when the pillar is very wide, when no strain appears on the timbers of the rooms at either side, it seems wise to take a side-slice. This means that they proceed, beginning at the bottom, to cut off another set's worth of the ore, thus widening the room by one set and of course narrowing the pillar by the same. Sometimes, indeed, even a second slice is taken.

To leave such a very wide unfilled room, and so narrow a pillar, is somewhat risky. But it can be done and has been done. In fact the entire project carries so much normal and continuing risk that the term loses meaning.

For there are ways that the earth can move. Sometimes timbers cannot withstand pressures coming at them awry. A roof will fall, a wall will crumble. The torn-out places do not remain. The earth closes and they are gone.

The little procession, turning, had come to a place where something had happened. A soft indrawn whistling breath passed through young Davies' lips.

It was not easy to see at once that anything was wrong. The confusion in the pattern was not quickly visible, unless the eye knew the pattern very well.

Here, glistening moist, was the rough rock, the crude timber that was everywhere, but the discipline, the imposition of a mind's plan, was gone. Here where there ought to have been order there was a mess. And there were men, standing or milling, the light from their hats dipping and washing around them. There was Captain Trezona, who came to Mr. McKeever.

The pillar had caved in. The roof was down and a confusion of rock, wood, and human bodies had been spilled sideways and down. There must have been noise as it happened but now all was silent.

It was not good; it was pretty bad. The voices, the captain's tenor, McKeever's soft baritone, began to discuss what was to be done. Captain Trezona, in charge, had already assembled a group of good men, the reliable and the experienced. Most of these were in middle years, shrewd canny old hands. There were a few strong young backs among them, but all were cool heads, all were subdued and resolute, tending to be quiet. This was no place for temperament; this was a nasty, ticklish, dangerous, delicate, difficult job.

For somewhere in that vast mess and tangle someone was alive. This was known.

To find and remove the living human bodies was like playing a gigantic game of jackstraws, with a death penalty.

"Be openin' of the pipe now," the captain said. "See if us can talk."

McKeever nodded. Someone was alive, for there was a way to signal and the signal had come. This, of course, made the job harder.

The captain was getting ready to drive with his picked group and every ounce of experience and skill he had. They would make a way into that confusion and inch by inch, foot by foot, pulling with them, over them, and around them, the shell of a timber shelter, they would go narrowly in to find and extract the living, safe and alive.

They must go slowly and yet be quick. No man must make the slightest error, nor yet hesitate. The direction of their effort had to be exactly right and it was a half-blind guess. The whole mass could quake and shudder and chew down at any moment upon the already desperately imperiled men, and their rescuers as well.

There was not a lot of time for discussion, either.

Now as the men wheeled into the pattern of their attack, Henry Duncane slipped quietly away. McKeever was talking to a pale Gilchrist now and Davies was edging around them. None of this was Henry's business. He had seen all that could be seen. He was not useful here so he began to walk back the way he had come.

Part way along the crosscut a man came running toward him.

"Got the pipe open," he gasped out in passing. "They're a tapping of it, all right. They're alive in there."

"Who is it in there?"

The man threw the answer back over his shoulder as he slogged on, "Don't know; checking. Don't know yet."

At the main drift, a group crouched and huddled over the angle of wall and floor.

"Listen," said one, his smudged face turned up. "Listen to it, Mr. Duncane!"

There was a network of these pipes. The compressed air ran down the shaft, branched off at each level, and branched from the branches. Here was the point at which the small pipe tapped into the main supply and carried the compressed air to feed the drills, the tools the men had been using.

Now men had shut valves and taken the branch pipe out of its fitting, for it was a connection. Wherever the lost men were, the other end of this little pipe was still with them.

Henry went on his knees. Traveling on the pipe that was so thin a connection to the lost men, the thin sound came, distant but clear. Tap, tap, tap. Monotonous but yet irregular, it stopped at odd—deliberately odd—intervals to betray its humanity.

The man with the dirty face put his mouth down and hollered: "Are you all right, in there?"

Tap, tap, tap.

No code to that.

"It looks like they can't hear shoutin'," the man said, "but listen—" He picked up a piece of rock and tapped briskly on the pipe. When he stopped, at once the far-distant tapping responded with a frenzied acceleration.

"They hear that, see." He bawled again, "You all right, hey! Helloo—"

Tap, tap, tap.

Henry Duncane said with angry sarcasm, "What do you expect them to answer? 'Oh yes, certainly, we're fine, thank you.' Give them something they *can* answer. Get away, let me try that!"

He lay his mouth close and after summoning his composure somehow and his breath, he began to speak very, very slowly, without much volume but with a crystal clarity, the sharp, distinct, clean-cut, blurless separation of syllables that was natural to him:

"HOW . . . MANY . . . MEN . . . ALIVE?"

He was heard, for the tapping gave him at once that quickened reaction. "Then you hear me? I hear you! Then you hear me?" the quick taps seemed to say.

He tried it again.

"HOW . . . MANY . . . MEN . . . ALIVE?"

No sound returned. No sound at all.

"HOW . . . MANY . . . MEN . . . ALIVE?" He called it a third time.

Now the answer came, if it was an answer. Tap, tap, tap, tap, tap—and silence.

The men around Duncane looked at him with rolling eyes. He repeated the question and got the same answer, five.

"Five men alive," said Duncane into the pipe.

It answered: "Five."

He moistened his lips. "HOW . . . MANY . . . HURT?"

It took time. At last there seemed to return an answer to this too.

Tap, tap, tap, and silence. Three.

"WE'LL . . . GET . . . YOU . . . OUT."

And to this the taps danced urgency. Tap, tap, tatatatap, tatatap, tatap, tap. They seemed to say: Good, good, but hurry up, hurry up about it.

"They seem to hear *you*, Mr. Duncane!" said the dirty-faced man in awe.

"Five in there. I'll tell Captain." A man began to run.

"Wonder who 'tis, though," said another.

For several minutes, Henry Duncane kept calling to the lost that they would be found.

It was a matter of record, of course. Sooner or later the timekeeper would be able to say. It would be known which five men were buried in West Thor mine.

Mabel Marcom was in bed. The knocking woke her. "Middle of the night." Grumbling, she cracked the door and saw the sharp, thin face of her niece, Milly.

"Oh, Aunt! Ma's coming right over. They're saying five men's down the cave-in alive. Aunt, Ma said I was to tell you. They say Uncle's down there. But he's alive, see!"

"Eh?" Mrs. Marcom rocked on her heels. "Caved in? eh?"

"West Thor. Oh, Aunt!" Milly's face was reddening to weep.

" 'Oo says Elisha's in it?" said Elisha's wife tartly.

"Everybody, and Ma, and all. But he's alive. Were you sleeping? Oh Aunt . . ."

Mrs. Marcom reached up and began to pull the metal curlers off her hair. "No need for you to be running out in your night clothes," she snapped. "Go 'ome."

"Oh, Aunt . . ."

"And I'll believe it when somebody tells me 'oo knows what 'e's talking about." She closed the door. Never liked that Milly. Never had.

She pulled five curlers off, clink, clink, clink, clink, clink—they dropped in a china dish. Her hand hesitated. She listened. The house was very quiet. Very quiet. She could hear that mouse back of the baseboard. Hear it plain. The house had never been as quiet as this before.

In Benevenuto Pilotti's little plaster house back of the Catholic Church, there was a kind of family party going on. When the news came, Benevenuto's wife, Luella, threw herself on the floor before Jesus' picture. His sister, Marie, and his mother, Anna, fell on their knees beside her. The sister's husband ran out. A neighbor found candles. Somebody hid the wine. The house began to rock with rhythmic sounds of wailing which softened and quieted to the gentler rhythm of prayer. All the children woke up, because the sound of the house was different, and came creeping in. But it was quite a long time before they understood what was the matter.

Alice Beard had been in the kitchen setting bread so she was still up and about when her own mother came to her door. When her mother told her she said, plaintively, "But Charley only went to work yesterday. 'E was 'ome all the week. 'Is cough was that bad." She swallowed. She had a thin throat. "I didn't think he ought to go," she said in a puzzled way. "I told 'im, with 'is cough 'anging on, he didn't ought to go back yet. But yesterday 'e went. And tonight 'e went. 'E was bound 'e'd go."

"I won't leave you," her mother said flouncing in. "I won't leave you, Alice."

"Bound 'e'd go," Alice said shaking her head. "To think, eh?" She began to cry.

That night Eedie Trezona had been praying a long time before the messenger came. She had been begging God to be kind to those in fear and in sorrow. Now when she heard that one of the five lost men was her son, Wesley, she could only go on asking the same of Him in every breath she drew.

The younger children, who had wakened when Pa was called out, could not go to bed again any more than she. So they were beside her.

John Pengilly, who had brought the news, watched her closely a minute or two. But she stood quietly in the kitchen, the children quiet beside her. So he sighed deeply and left them.

When he had gone, Dorothy suddenly took one wild look around the room, and cried out, "Ma . . . isn't Wesley going to come home? Won't he come home?" And she clung to Eedie with both arms.

"Your fayther will 'ave 'im out. Your fayther's there. Your fayther will never come 'ome 'til 'e 'as 'im out."

Eedie knew this was true. Nor would she and the children have one word from Pa, nor one backward thought of his until, one way or another, the boy was out. Pa was not here but they could be sure what he was doing. "You can be sure," she said.

Now Dickie clawed and slapped at his sister.

"You keep still. You stop that. Let Ma be. Ma doesn't need you to cry. Ma isn't crying. You keep still, you big cry-baby."

Dorothy, who was taller, stooped and rubbed her face dry on Eedie's shoulder. "What can I do then, Ma?" she shuddered, pulling herself away.

Eedie could feel the children's eyes, like four burning lights, searing her stiff face. She said, "Build up the stove. Best think of food. There's 'ard work for Pa and the rest."

"'Ard work's nothing to be ascared of," said Dickie. "It's nothing. Wesley's not going to be afraid there, waiting for Pa.

It's nothing." The boy stood like a little cock, his throat working. He flew into the bathroom, which was so awkwardly off the kitchen in this unhandy old house. He shut the door.

Eedie put up her hands and loosened the skin on her face. Every breath was prayer. Dorothy rattled the sticks of wood into the range, all the energy of her anxiety put into the task. But Dick was making strange sounds in there.

Eedie took her hands down, tapped on the bathroom door and went in. He was being a very sick little boy as she had expected. She held his head and soaked a cloth and wiped his forehead and pale cheeks very gently.

"Don't do to imagine," she said quite severely. "We don't know how 'tis, Dick, there where Wesley's to. Now we don't know. It's 'ard to know nothing. That's true. But imagining, that don't do. It's Wesley there. Not *you*. You stay 'ere, where the Lord leaves you."

She gave him one swift spank of her hand on his bottom. "Get busy. Fill that wood box."

Her hands began to squeeze soap and water through the cloth mechanically. "God keep us from imagining," she prayed. "Give us something to do."

Cyril Varker took the message, and thanked the messenger soberly. He said he would tell Mrs. Cole.

CHAPTER TEN

THE dark was absolute. After awhile the eye surrendered and quit straining. Even the memory of light danced only spasmodically on the inside of the eyelid. The ear quickened.

Each other's breathing, every gasp and every sigh, became what they could know of each other, lacking the eye. They were close, they touched and entangled. In the fraction of time before it happened they had swarmed together, and they had been caught together. They dared not now move more than a cautious finger or a chin in a slow arc.

They tried to work out their position first in relation to the world they remembered. But that world was lost and they could not even agree exactly where it had been. Then in relation to each other? Pilotti said someone lay across his legs. Charley Beard said, "That's me, Benno'."

Pilotti knew some warm liquid was flowing near his knee. He guessed it was blood. Whose blood he was not sure so he did not mention it.

Elisha Thomas touched no one, he said. But Arthur Cole insisted that he touched Elisha, and they argued.

Wesley could tell he lay on his back and someone's sharp bone was beneath one shoulder. Arthur said it was his knee and he did not find it comfortable, either.

They discussed all this thoroughly until they began to repeat too much.

Then Arthur remarked that they had air and Elisha snorted. It was obvious that they had air.

"Not going to suffocate, I mean," Arthur insisted. His voice—all that could be known of him—was querulous.

"Nah," said Elisha, wheezing and sawing. "We breathe, boys, till we die. It's not coal, neyther. Gases there. Poisons."

"It's good it's not coal," said Wesley's cheerful tenor.

The rich music of Pilotti's voice began to recite some litany, softly. The others listened. Wesley felt his hair stir in superstitious dismay. It did not seem to be his father's God to whom the Catholic man was pleading. Yet Charley Beard, a staunch Methodist, said "Amen," in his high voice. He had a voice like a woman. A little man, Charley, who had looked more frail than he was in the past time, the long ago, when he could be seen.

Elisha wheezed.

"Don't move," said Arthur alarmed. "Who is moving? What you doing?"

"Feelin' for my pail, bit of that there pie would go good."

"It would," Charley said with a sucking sound.

"You won't find it."

"Found it," rumbled Elisha. " 'Ad it in my 'and. I thought so."

"You got two 'ands?" Charley said tremulously.

"So far," said Elisha. "Two 'ands and a mouth—all that's needful." In the silence came the pop of a tin lid.

"I'd give it you," Elisha said.

"No."

"No."

"No thanks," said Wesley politely.

Couldn't pass a piece of pie without seeing it and nobody knowing where another's hand was.

Elisha's eating was loud and comforting in the black dark.

Pilotti kept on praying. It seemed to Wesley to be a soft patter, a song without a tune. It was not like the soul-searching effort of Captain Trezona, who often led prayer at church, for his voice was good and he was able.

Pilotti must be in pain, Wesley thought with surprise, examining the sound that was all he could know of the other man now—the middle-aged, black-haired Italian he scarcely knew at all.

Arthur Cole's fingers searched carefully around him as far as they could reach. His hand touched Wesley's.

"Who's that?"

"Trezona."

"Don't move."

"I can't much. Timber above me."

"All right." Arthur's cold fingers walked away. "Hey, I'm lying on the pipe."

"Well, then!" Elisha was sharp.

"It'll lead out." Pilotti broke off his prayer and his voice went up an octave. "Hit it—bang on it—make noise—go on —tell 'em we're in here."

"Wait a minute—I will. I will. Wait a minute."

Then, covering their quick excited breathing and the wispy sound of gentle water that was always around them, the only sound in the world became that bang, bang, bang on the pipe. For it was a bang to them. A hard, loud racket. So tremendous a noise it must resound like thunder somewhere.

"My ear! My ear! Right *on* it," gasped Wesley. "You're pounding directly in my ear."

"No help for that. Listen." Cole stopped, but there was nothing. Nothing but breath and that soft, malicious whispering of seeping moisture. Or, if sound, it was so far away that it was hardly sound at all but more like pressure. Something felt on the flesh—soft, blob-like—not reaching the sharp instrument of the ear.

Pilotti tried to believe that blood was water—for it did not stop spreading and soaking—but he knew it was too warm to be water.

Arthur Cole's wrist began to ache, but he kept up the pounding on the pipe stubbornly, doggedly, forever, until, in the clap of silence as he stopped to shift the rock in his cramped fingers, they all heard the answer.

Hearts leaped like five fish swarming up to feed. The fact of communication seemed to legalize the expression of hope.

"They'll 'ave us out of 'ere," Charley chirped, "yet! Captain Trezona, 'e's a smart one . . ." He coughed with excitement.

"Pa'll do it," Wesley said. " 'E'll never quit."

"Nah, never," Elisha said. "Not 'im."

And then Wesley was crying in the dark, his face soaked by the silent tears. "Ah, Pa. Ah, Pa," for his heart swelled and shook to hear Pa praised in this black place. And Pilotti's prayer was a murmuring obbligato to the paean of the heart.

Arthur said, "Shut up! Listen! What's that? Must be pulling this pipe open . . . eh? Don't you say?"

Far away in the world the vibration began but they were well aware of it.

"Somebody's yelling. Listen to that."

"I can hear," gasped Wesley, "but I can't make out what he says."

It was alive. It was a living voice, little they cared what it said. Pain, where there was pain, was forgotten, and Arthur banged merrily. Yet since they lived by the ear alone now, they could not help straining to understand.

When the slow-paced sound of Duncane's voice began to come creeping to them, it was very different. Nothing was left of it but the vowels really and the tune the syllables played. "Ow . . . en . . . ee . . . n . . . a . . . iive . . . ?" They scanned it and at last they read it and they answered.

"Wants to know 'ow many's alive."

"Well, tell 'im! Tell 'im!"

They kept answering.

"Ow . . . en . . . ee . . . urr . . . ?"

"What's 'e after?"

It took them some time.

"*Hurt*," gasped Pilotti. "*Hurt.* He wants to know how many is hurt."

"Well, tell 'im! Tell 'im!"

"Well, 'ow many, then?" asked Elisha solemnly.

"I don't think I'm hurt much," said Wesley, diffidently. "I don't feel anything. Timber on my thigh aches me."

"Nothing wrong with me," said Arthur truculently. "You O.K., Charley?"

"I'm fine," said Charley feebly.

"He ain't fine," groaned Pilotti. "Nor me. That's two of us."

"I been better," said Elisha dryly. "You might say I was 'urt, boys, to be honest . . ."

"Three," tapped Arthur then. It sobered them to know that three of them were hurt.

But when Arthur cried "He got it!" then they were jubilant again.

" 'E's talkin', be still!"

"What now?"

The distance pushed and throbbed but the vowels came on the pipe.

"Says they'll get us out. *Out!* That's what it is! Going to get us out, he says!"

"Ah."

"And they'll do it!"

"Never quit!"

"Be able to hear them soon. . . ."

"Should be."

They were pleased. The pleasure they felt was innocent and satisfying. What was it to lie in the dark awhile? Why nothing much when work was going, men were doing, striving. None of them said he had any doubt. Not one.

In another part of the world, Captain Gideon Trezona bent his head and spoke aloud, beseeching God. The words were his own but they fell into Bible music for the man loved the Book and knew it well. So his words drew on centuries of memories of reverence, and they rang in that cavernous place. No man within the sound of them refused to bow his head or say "Amen."

After that the captain did not so much as turn his face away from the work in progress. His blue eye was keen, his voice quick, his attention sharp on everything. This was no job for anyone but a master. The men went warily but as he sent them, for he was a master.

McKeever said to Gilchrist, "Do you judge they're going in at the best angle?"

"I?" Gilchrist put out his palms. "Leave it to Trezona. Have to." Under his hatbrim his nervous eyes shifted.

Davies said, "I think he's allowing for too much side-slip. After all, they're alive. They couldn't have shifted far. I don't like . . ."

"Then you tell him you don't like it," Gilchrist snapped. "I'm willing to let him alone."

"He should know best," McKeever murmured. "A good man."

"He'll kill himself to get the boy out," Gilchrist said. "If anybody can do it."

Davies said, *"That's* what I don't like."

"What's on your mind?" the Old Man asked.

"Get Captain Jacka's idea." Davies made a gesture. "If Trezona thinks . . ."

"But *does* he?" muttered Davies. "I'd like to see you ask Captain Jacka, who is a good man too."

McKeever said, "Jacka's under Trezona."

"Let Trezona alone," said Gilchrist impatiently. "He'll get that boy out, God willing."

Davies closed his lips. He felt he was being of no use so he left that place.

Henry Duncane was leaving the spot where the pipe had been opened when Davies came along.

"Poor devils," Davies said when he heard. "Well, they'll get out alive or they won't get out alive. Can't see, myself, how the man can think straight when his head's full of begging the Mercy of God to save his own son. . . ."

"Whose son?"

"Trezona's. He's in there. Don't you know? Marcom, Pilotti, Cole, Beard and Trezona."

Henry stopped walking.

"Yeah. It's been checked," Davies assured him.

"Trezona, Beard, Marcom, Pilotti and Arthur Cole?"

"That's right." Davies sounded angry. "Trezona's a smart miner and all that. But *look* at the Will of God. All right. So it's the Will of God, or something, that if a thing isn't held up it falls down. Isn't that so?"

"Seems so," said Henry.

They stepped on the cage to ascend.

"All right," said Davies in a low, rapid voice. "Then the old boy's got the drive and he'd kill himself, as Gilchrist says, to get the boy out. But, by golly, it takes a cold brain and you know it . . . to figure out the Will of God. . . . And where *is* the cold brain?"

"In Trezona's head, as usual," said Henry calmly.

"Aaah," said Davies. "People don't work that way."

"What are you driving at?" Henry seemed distracted.

"Listen . . . if you're too scared or too damned anxious, your brain's not going to work right."

"Why not?"

"It can't, that's all. People make all kinds of fools of themselves. . . ."

"Henry said, "Some people—"

"Well—"

"Is Trezona scared?"

Davies fidgeted. "He's got to be, bound to be, one way or another. It'll do something to him, affect his judgment."

"What it'll do depends on the man."

"Maybe," said Davies gloomily. "But Captain Jacka isn't even down there and I don't know if it's wise to leave the whole thing to Trezona under the circumstances."

They stepped off. The night sky was clear with many stars. They stood and looked up as if someone had pointed.

"What I know about mining," Henry said, "you can put in a thimble. I suppose there is a time factor."

"Quicker the better, that's pretty clear."

"It's a gamble?"

"Yeah, sure. Speed, direction, guessing right. Maybe Trezona can weigh all that, and maybe nobody can. I guess it's if God is willing, as Gilchrist says." Davies was nervous and a little sheepish.

"It's Trezona's job." Henry began to walk up the hill briskly.

"Yeah, poor old devil, to have *that* on his back, too."

"Poor *what!*" Henry broke his stride. He was astonished. "Pity him if it wasn't," he snapped.

Davies tagged at Henry's heels, "Well . . . I don't know. But I still don't see how he can think straight."

"Simple," said Henry. "He's got to."

CHAPTER ELEVEN

THROUGH the darkest part of that night there were houses lit in the town of Thor. Not all. Many households would not know until morning what shadow lay on the town and lay darkest on the houses where the lights were burning.

At the Trezonas' the kitchen was very warm and filled with savory smells. Eedie and Dorothy had worked long and hard baking as many pasties as they could find ingredients to make.

A Cornish pasty ('a' as in man) is a heap of cut-up beef and potatoes, carrots and onions, turnips and parsley, seasoning and suet, all wrapped around in piecrust, folded over and buttoned along a curve by pinching fingers, stabbed with a fork to let the steam out, and baked in the oven. It is a complete meal to hold in the hand. A Cornishman will eat one hot, cold or lukewarm. Many a pasty has gone down a mine.

When Eedie took the pasties hot and fragrant out of the oven, she wrapped them carefully and packed them into a box.

Dickie would deliver them.

He was young to go off at three in the morning by himself on such a night to such a place. But Eedie consented. He was the one to go. It was not so far as it would seem in the night. He would come to no harm. It was a task for him, a good helpful thing that he could do.

She filled as many thermos jugs as she had with strong hot tea and milk. She saw that his jacket was buttoned.

He set off marching with the burden. She saw him begin to scamper before the dimness swallowed him.

She turned back into the house. The kitchen was already

tidy. Nothing to do? The little boy was on his errand but Eedie could not think of anything now to keep her daughter occupied.

Dorothy was not in the kitchen. Eedie peered through and saw that she was sitting on the black leather couch in the dining-room corner. As her mother watched, Dorothy toppled sleepily.

Eedie was thankful. Quietly she waited and when the time came, she laid a coverlet over the sleeping girl. Worn out, she thought tenderly.

Now she was alone.

She made her way into the dark parlor, a room they used only on the most formal occasions. From here a window let her see out to the west. She could distinguish the tip of West Thor shafthouse, and she could see the road to West Thor Mine.

She settled and looked out. The night grew lighter to her sight. The stars were fine.

Eedie Trezona prayed and feared God. She could see the world wheel through space. How small it was, the little world! How vast the heaven! And in simplicity she thought that God must have so much to attend to. If he, in His Wisdom, took Wesley so young, He wouldn't have the time, the need, or any obligation to lay bare before one little, limited, human woman the meaning of this in all His vast eternal purposes.

What He would do, she could not know. And never *why*.

Where the light burned, at the Coles', Madeline sat with her head on her arms, arms on the dining-room table.

"How long will it *be?*" she said through her teeth. "How long will it *take?*"

"Nobody knows." Cyril shrugged.

"How can we hear? Who will call us or tell us?"

"Don't know."

"I'm going."

"Don't go."

"Can't stand waiting here."

"Better wait here."

"No, I don't think so." She rolled her head.

115

"Don't *fuss*," said Cyril.

She lifted her head, sat up and pushed at her hair.

"You're a mess," he told her.

"Naturally." She bit down on her teeth, hard. "If it gets light and we haven't heard anything, I'm going to take your car whether you like it or not." Her lids were puffy, she looked sullen and angry.

Cyril didn't want to play. The old game of baiting each other, of insult and contempt, had no appeal. He shrugged.

"Be a mistake," he said.

He was thinking of the struggle going on under the ground. He was thinking how the townspeople would wake and find this over them. He was thinking there would not remain one living soul, except the youngest of the children, who would not know and be thereafter thinking about the struggle, and he wondered what the concentration of so much attention did. Did it affect anything, or not?

His sister said, "Why? *Why* a mistake just to go nearer? I don't care if it doesn't look dignified. I can't help that."

He looked at her. To bait her was a strong habit and she asked for it. "You'll convince nobody," he told her sourly.

"My husband's down there dying!" she shrieked.

Cyril smiled and turned his cigar.

"You're a monster," his sister said hoarsely. "You're a monster."

"Not I," said Cyril. "I'm only telling you. Better stay here and keep quiet."

She got up and began to walk restlessly nowhere. "What's it like down there?"

"Don't know. Not nice."

"Dark?"

"Probably."

"Cold?"

He shrugged.

"Cyril, how could they be buried and not, not crushed?"

"Miracle." He looked up sideways.

"*Can* they be saved?"

"It's been done."

"I don't suppose you know anything about it," she said wearily. "Who does?"

116

"Don't know."

"What a comfort you are!" She was blazing again.

"Keep it up. Keep snarling. You don't like waiting. You want to know right now, whether you're going to be a widow or not. Go on. Cut your own throat."

"What!"

"Unbecoming," he snapped.

She began to weep.

"That's a little better," he said coldly.

"Monster," she sobbed. "You don't under—"

". . . stand," he mocked. "Don't understand. Cut it out, Maddy. Don't waste it on me. And you've got to wait like everybody else."

She was sobbing, bending over the table again.

"Although it's hard on your nerves, I know," he said nastily.

"Oh . . ." she turned her head sideways and was quiet.

"Cyril," she said in a minute, her wide eyes staring at the wall, "they're all together?"

"I suppose so. Close enough to count themselves."

"All five."

"Must be."

"Benevenuto Pilotti, who is he?" She was frowning.

"Lives in East Thor. Got four kids and a pack of relatives."

"Elisha Marcom?"

"The one with the handle bars. Widest moustache in town. Looks like hay on his lip."

"Poor old man. Poor old man. And who else? The Trezona boy?"

Cyril looked sourly into space. He spit out a piece of tobacco leaf. "Uh huh," he said.

"And Charley Beard? Cyril?"

"What?"

"Is Charley Beard the other one?"

"You know who they are."

She knew well enough.

Something had occurred to her. It was a small worry, unworthy of attention in this crisis of life or death. And yet it nagged her. She let her mind go where it wanted to go. Oh

117

you could not focus on tragedy with no relief. Nobody could. She closed her eyes and imagined looking up the street from Charley Beard's gate, or his porch. Yes, from there one could see the Duncanes' porch light go on. Surely. And see it go off too. But *could* one see, tell, what gate it was from which a caller emerged, quite a lot too much later? And having seen, *would* one call out 'Good night, Miz Cole'?

To make her jump?

"Charley Beard was a dull, kind little man," she murmured dolefully.

"*Is*, as far as we know. The word is that they are alive."

She said without emotion, quietly, "What chance is there that Arthur will come out of that?"

Cyril said, "I can't put your mind at rest. Wait and see." Chin on chest, forehead wrinkled, eyes rolled up to see, he added, "Hope for the best, of course."

"You wicked, cold-blooded monster!" she whispered. "It's not true. I do not . . . I will not be glad. So stop it!"

Cyril yawned.

"Go to bed," she cried, "and get out of my sight!"

". . . behind thee, Satan?" Cyril stood and stretched. "You stay home," he warned her, "where you are understood."

Alice Beard sat in lamplight and was able to watch the strange thing that was happening to her. Slowly, as the hours crept, she was regressing. She was going back. She was becoming what she had not primarily been for four years now, a daughter. Now less and less a wife, mistress of a house, a man's partner, more and more a girl. She was slipping and sliding back to depending. The house gave itself to her mother. The bread in the kitchen would rise, but even if she baked it it would be her mother's bread.

Four Pilotti children, in their one room, fell sadly asleep. In the outer room the light was low, but it burned . . . and the murmuring continued.

At Marcom's the mouse was bold, for although the light burned, nobody was there.

At Duncane's, Libby lay on the couch with the afghan over her. She dozed. She was grateful now that Celestina sat so quietly. But the girl, obeying orders, was there in a chair. And Libby could imagine that she might even stalk into the bedroom on Henry's orders. So she didn't go to bed but she lay down to rest her back, and she covered herself.

Libby had grown cold, stiff and cold and she could get nothing *out* of the girl, absolutely nothing. Nobody had told Libby anything at all. Maybe Henry thought he had told her but she had no background, no points of reference. Men were buried? Well then, she supposed, they had been killed. She could sense suspense in Celestina and she thought it must be a matter of wondering who they were. And she thought: How awful, if it's that! She did not know whether Celestina's people worked down the mine or not. She supposed they must. She tried to ask about this as delicately and kindly as she could. But Celestina wouldn't answer. Either she couldn't understand an indirect question or she did and wouldn't tell. She kept looking at Libby with dark sorrow and a shadow of hostility in her eyes.

When the phone rang it was Celestina who got it. Someone calling to tell Henry.

"Ask him what's *happening!*" Libby cried.

So Celestina had asked . . . and come away reeling.

"Oh, what?"

"Five men!"

"Oh, who?"

"You wouldn't know them." The dark eyes had flashed.

"Ah, Celestina . . . do *you?*" Libby had asked trembling. "Kin, or friends of yours, my dear?"

"No. No. Nobody. No."

The girl crept to the chair, and Libby lay back sighing and pulled up the cover. She watched the girl's face. The girl looked stunned or dreaming.

And Libby thought: she won't talk to me. Well, *I* mustn't think about it. No, I must not. It would do no good and it would not be good. In her mind she said a prayer for the dead, and then she tried to turn her mind away. Her lip trembled.

Celestina didn't know why she felt as if somebody had hit

her hard with a great club. She was as surprised as she could be. But she certainly was glad when the woman on the couch stopped prying and asking questions.

For awhile she had taken a small malicious satisfaction in Libby Duncane's bewilderment. This woman was an outsider from another life. Now she had to quiz Celestina, for she didn't know anything. Celestina could not help cherishing in herself the sensation of having superior knowledge. Why, for days now she had known more about this woman's own life than the woman did. This pale one who was always noticing Celestina's clothes, or her voice, or her manner of opening doors even . . . Well, someday she'd find out she'd been fussing about the unimportant things. Celestina wasn't exactly sorry for her.

A wife who was going to lose her man to another woman was only a poor thing.

Always calling Celestina stupid and ignorant—now, who was ignorant? Celestina knew more about what could happen in a mine than this woman had any idea. Even the questions she asked were stupid.

Celestina had never before gone through the experience of a disaster in these mines. She had heard tales of disaster many times. She knew her father and brothers were safe since they were on day shift, and she didn't fear for them. But she knew the men who were down there had small chance of getting out again. She also knew there was some chance. She knew it would take time.

Miz Duncane didn't know any of this.

Then, on the telephone, Celestina had been told still more.

And the club hit her. The blow sent her staggering.

She didn't tell Miz Duncane. What could *she* say? What could *she* do? What would *she* care?

Celestina sat down again. Wesley Trezona.

She hadn't minded. If he didn't want to go with her, she should worry. There had been some fantasies . . . (One day. Wesley would come into the Church. Then he would come to Celestina. He would say it was for her sake he had defied his people and everything and come into the true Church. But by this time *she* would be involved with some fascinating person who adored her . . . and she would have to say that she was very sorry.)

(Or Wesley would lie very very sick and calling for her. And the old captain himself, yes, even that enemy, that stern infidel . . . would come after her. Oh, she would go. And Wesley's mother that he was so crazy about, she'd be crying. And she'd wish she'd stood against that mean old man before. But Celestina, although gracious and filled with holy pity, would be very sorry . . .)

Behind the fantasies there was the truth. She would never have *married* Wesley Trezona. It would never have come to that, she knew. And behind the fantasy that he would suffer, there was the truth that he did suffer some. (She didn't think he swaggered around because he didn't care.)

(Oh, that was a fantasy! Wesley would become a drunkard and no good, and somebody would tell the mean old man whose fault *that* was.)

Now all the fantasies whirled in her head together and before them there was the truth. He *was* dying! He might be!

And she didn't care for him any more, of course, but the club hit her. And something shook her, and she didn't know what to do.

She couldn't cry. She couldn't think. She couldn't make a fantasy.

She thought that she needed somebody, real bad, because she felt so awful, but she didn't know who could help her. Not her people. They were glad when it broke off. They never liked her getting mixed up with a Methodist. And not the priest then. And none of her generation; she'd tossed her head too high. Then nobody? Nobody. Least of all that woman, whose pale hair lay on the pillow, whose lashes had slipped over those light blue eyes. Confide in *her? She'd* be the last one. Unthinkable to tell her any real thing.

Celestina tried to pray. She didn't know what.

CHAPTER TWELVE

IN THE morning Libby awoke to find herself mysteriously still in her petticoat but in her bed. She only very dimly remembered Henry coming home and guiding her there. She only very dimly remembered her sleepy questions and his murmuring soothing answers that had let her sink deep into sleep again.

Now he was bending over her, dressed and shaved, and it was morning.

"I'm going, Libby. You stay in bed. Celestina's not around. Don't wake her. And you sleep some more, too."

But she was wide awake.

"No, Henry. Don't leave me . . ."

"I've got to go," he interrupted sharply.

". . . without telling me anything?" she cried. "Can't you see? I don't know what to think, or what to do . . . I—"

"Nothing for you to do," he said.

"But I don't even understand."

So he sat on the bed and told her, making clear as he could when he tried, what had happened and what was happening. For the first time, Libby realized that those buried men still lived.

Her whole self shrank away from it. Every fastidious fiber, every feminine ideal of a dainty-pretty-comfortable world, compelled her to recoil from the brutal fact. Men should never have got themselves *into* a situation of such stark horror. Other men should not have to break their hearts in so terrible and futile an effort to get them out again.

She said, "Oh Henry, what can they do? It's impossible! Isn't it? Just impossible!" She thought: Oh they're gone. They *are* gone.

Henry, looking down upon her, could see the wincing

away of her whole soul. He said, "Easy to make sure it's impossible."

"What?"

He got up. "If you don't go ahead as if it were possible," he said bitingly, "it sure won't be."

"Wh-what?" But her mind fled. "Oh, poor Mrs. Cole . . ." she moaned. "Henry, should I . . . could I do anything? Call her, or . . ."

"Better not," he said flatly.

"I wouldn't know what to say."

"No."

She wrung her hands. "How can she stand it?"

Henry shook his head. "Got to," he muttered.

She reached out to hold him back. "*You're* not going . . . down in there?"

He answered quietly, wearily, "No. Might try to help out on that pipe, that's all. They seem to be able to hear me."

She said foolishly and rather fondly, "Everyone can always hear you."

"Otherwise," he put her grasping hand aside rather angrily, "there's nothing I can do. It's not my job."

"Oh Henry, don't . . ." Libby had no end for her sentence. She didn't know what it was she did not want.

But Henry said angrily, "I can't. But I'll tell you this. I wish to hell I could."

She lay on the pillow. She suspected, because Henry did not often speak so angrily, that this was something she ought to try to understand.

But he rubbed his hand over his hair. "Upsets you," he said ruefully, apologetically.

So, because she understood this much, she nodded.

"Meantime, I'd better go do my own job." He patted her. "Take it easy."

She lay abed with her heart roaring. Suddenly she said aloud, "I suppose it doesn't look impossible to those who know, whose job it is. Henry?"

But he had gone.

Morning flooded the little town. Sunshine poured down from a sky which was cloudless and yet not clear, for a heat-haze was forming already. Friday was going to be hot.

Thor Lake lay sparkling, looking more innocent than it was. Nobody bathed in Thor Lake. The rumor was that it had no bottom. The truth was waste water and certain poisons went into it, so it was a wicked, useless little lake except to look at.

Morning flooded the wooded hills. Where the green shadow did not fall on the brown floor, the glades and alleys were aromatic with the warm pine. But the hill was not so solid as it looked and, in its core, held no peace and no perfume.

Very early, Cyril Varker let himself out of the house and walked, in his peculiar gait, to the corner. But he did not cross the street to proceed past the schoolhouses to the office. Instead he turned and settled himself into a pace suitable for a long walk.

His sister, Madeline, was missing this morning. No stir in the kitchen, no sound above. He had ventured part way up the stairs, far enough to see that her bed was empty, and now he knew that his car was gone from the shack on the alley.

He intended to go where she undoubtedly was and try to persuade her back to the privacy of the house. He was very much annoyed with her. Such a fool!

As he proceeded, Cyril took the temper of the town now that it was morning and everyone had heard the news. It looked much as usual. He thought to himself that he was of the very few in Thor whose business was done on paper. Paper could wait. But not the gain or the preparation of food. Women were doing their house chores as usual. And not the loading of the ore, for the shovels were snorting, as usual. Not the turn of the machinery in the town of Thor. It could not wait.

But the children, who had no business but to play, did not run in shouting groups in the yards this morning.

And the town was quiet.

He passed two women talking, or simply standing together in a yard. He passed men who were not on day shift nor were they sleeping.

All those who saw Cyril pass, even the children, were silent until he was by. And they watched him. Ah, he could see a myth in the making. Yes, some day it would be a tale to be told and the town was already creating the story. Already the characters were being picked out. A halo, of belonging to the cast, was weaving around the heads of those involved. He, himself, was in it. He had at least a small supporting part.

Cyril was faintly amused (and ever so slightly pleased too) at this thought.

The five lost men would be the heroes, of course. He could feel that. And if they died, they were martyrs and heroes, and no evil would ever be said of them. If they lived they were heroes indeed, and triumphant ones too. (But with a sequel, he thought, and sequels are so disappointing.)

He plodded on up the hill. Yes, and the wives and mothers and sweethearts were heroines all. How the town would watch them—and they visible on surface—trying to glean from their demeanor dramatic bits for the story!

Morbid curiosity? Cyril mused. Maybe. Maybe not. Maybe just the human longing to be shaken up, to feel, to share and experience something graver or more startling or merely less dull than ordinary. Same thing took people to a play, or made them read a book with a plot they'd never live in their own lives, because they could partially live it and experience it in the story or in the news, he thought.

But news and history becomes partially story because it comes to be told and the telling alters it. Nobody knows what the truth is about any plot, he considered. Nobody has all the facts, and the facts he has go through a filter, for everything is rejected that he is not equipped to see. And then, of course, he is compelled to fit the thing together.

We are all artists, good or bad. We all tell the whole story as we have put it together. But we have touched it and changed it, and filled it in, and smoothed it out, so that the more plausible we have made it, the bigger the chunks of fiction are sure to be.

Hummm, let's see, said Cyril inwardly. Pilotti is going to be the father-hero. Marcom is . . . oh, the elder, the wise old one. Yes, and the Trezona kid is the juvenile. Arthur? Cyril almost chuckled. Arthur could be the lead! Young and ambitious, with a beautiful young wife, not a year wed. Oh, certainly. But Charley Beard, what is he? The clown?

He had come to the top of the first hill and stood at the junction where the main road ran off level and the upper road climbed on. There were no houses here; the cut bank alongside was weedy. The woods crowned it. The upper road would be a steeper, harder way to go.

Yet he swung into it, for it passed behind Trezona's house. Morbid curiosity? He queried himself. Not at all. He wanted to go that way for a practical reason. He felt uneasy. He could see the pattern, the myth in the making, and privately and practically he thought he might have to reckon with it.

His angular distinctive figure climbed.

Eedie saw him from her kitchen where she was, for the moment, alone. Dorothy was in the parlor watching listlessly to the west. Dickie had run away to the shafthouse. He would bring the news, he said. Eedie had not kept him, couldn't have perhaps. The boy thought this was his task.

Ellen Trestrial had called up. Ellen was coming. But not quite yet.

Here was Cyril Varker coming up the hill and Eedie had a minute.

Cyril saw her standing behind her gate.

His feet dragged in the dust. "Morning . . ." he touched his hat.

"Good mornin' . . ." she stopped him. "Mr. Varker?"

He said, twisting his thin mouth in a smile, sad with the required sympathy, "This is not a very good morning for you and me, Mrs. Trezona."

"It is not," she said. "Is your sister well?"

"As well as may be."

"Poor lady," Eedie's hands tightened on the white wooden pickets of the gate. "Mr. Varker, Wesley has a debt to you."

Under his brows Cyril's eyes rolled up. "Ah, he told you?" He was dismayed and a trifle surprised although this was exactly what he had feared. "Now, Mrs. Trezona, you and the captain must not . . ."

"Wesley told *me*," she said quickly. "'Is fayther knows

nought about it. Now the boy will need time, Mr. Varker. You must give the boy time to pay."

"My dear Mrs. Trezona, of course," cried Cyril. "Of course. You cannot think that I . . ."

Eedie said, "Thank you. 'E's a good boy and 'e will pay as best 'e can." Her tired face managed a little radiance. "Ah, I was *sure* you knew that."

"Ah, I do," said Cyril with gallantry. "Don't think of it. Don't let it be on your mind for one moment. I would like to say this . . ." He paused to get it phrased properly.

She stood looking into his face, a little woman not young any more, cruelly marked by the night behind her.

"We've got to keep our courage up," said Cyril with that writhing smile, "and I don't want to discourage either of us. But I want to say this. If . . ."

Her eyes kept on his. "Ah," she said, "yes? What if he dies?"

Cyril looked away. "*Then*," he said quickly, eyes down, "there is no debt. It would be canceled." Her hand lifted. "No, no," he said. "I mean it. I will never mention it again. The least," he muttered, "that I can do. The sum is not a great deal, you understand, to me. And I would wipe it out. Let it go with the—that is, forget it."

"Thank you," said Eedie in a trembling voice. " 'Is pa is proud of the boy."

"And you are, too, I'm sure," said Cyril smoothly to her bent head, to the little wisps of curls that lay on her neck. "So you see," he said, "you mustn't think of the debt at all. Not any more."

She might have been weeping. He couldn't tell. But he felt satisfied.

"I'll go along," he said softly. "Good day, Mrs. Trezona."

She lifted her head and pierced him with a look of perfect gratitude.

Cyril proceeded on his way which was level now along the edge of the woods. He felt braced. He knew that he had done the smart thing.

He wouldn't risk dunning a martyred hero's family for usurious money. No, not he. Be the end of *his* fun all right, in the town of Thor.

Eedie turned her back to the gate and began to break some faded blossoms off a bush. Morning's heat pressed around her, but she shivered.

She was grateful to the man Varker. He would give time. Ah, it would take time. She understood about the interest. It would take a long, long time. But the man was kind and good, kind enough to say . . . She shivered.

No, *she* could not have told how to save the good father from ever knowing that the boy had sinned. But in the vast sweep and flow of God's power, here was a way, then. Let Wesley die, and the debt died and would never be mentioned. Never need it be explained. Then the captain would grieve, but the grief, sweetened by his faith, would be a simple loss. A good boy gone from here to heaven.

For a moment Eedie herself could see how simple it was. For just that moment she breathed without prayer.

As Cyril jolted down the steep, crooked road between the mine buildings, he saw that his Ford (everybody had a Ford in those days, except the rich or the choosey) was parked below the hoisting house and Madeline was in it.

"You fool!" he said to her.

She didn't even look at him.

He glanced around. People were assembled here. Not a great crowd but a gathering. Some stood, some sat in their cars, all kept carefully out of the way. It wasn't a mob. It had no will, no common purpose but to watch and wait and see. As he looked, one Ford came jolting back on the rough ground to park. A man and a woman and three children were in it. In a businesslike way the man took lollypops out of a paper bag and handed them behind him. The children began to lick. They all settled down.

Well, this was the spot. The grandstand and the finish line for the drama of the race below. The entrance to West Thor Mine and the exit from it.

Cyril divined a pattern among these waiting people. Of course it would have five points, like a star.

Over there, sitting on some old timbers in the shade, was Mabel Marcom. She was sandwiched, protected, between her sister, Bess, and her niece, Milly. But the old lady herself had her jaw set, and she stared belligerently before her.

Lower down, across the road, the Pilottis made a knot. There were a lot of them. The knot surged and moved within itself as if its elements were fluid but, as a whole, the group kept to one rough circle. The dust under their churning feet seemed to have shape in the air.

Kate Worthington, mother of Alice Beard, sat in a car looking out and off, but the shallow sides of the little tin tonneau could not quite hide poor Alice Beard lying like a child across her mother's lap.

Madeline made a point of the tragic star, of course, sitting still and composed in the little car. And he, standing with his hat off, the hot sun beating on his scalp, pertained to her.

Five, though. Was there no fifth point? Trezona? Captain Trezona would be underground. Mrs. Trezona he had just seen at her gate. Cyril hunted with his eyes. He wanted the pattern perfect as long as Madeline had been reckless enough to come. With a certain pleasure he saw the little boy Dick sitting quietly on a pile of gravel, all alone.

Well there it was. The onlookers, he reflected, not only saw this pattern, too, but partly created it. Their attention—whatever flavor it had, whether awe or respect, sympathy or curiosity—picked out the people who were related to the lost. In those the watchers saw and, at the same time, imagined the heroism of suspense, endured the dignity of grief, the halo of hope, and a fat part in the drama. Fact plus fiction. Everything the principals did was watched and magnified. Every expression examined and interpreted. Every emotion guessed at. All to be told some day.

"Foolish," he murmured. "You shouldn't be here."

She said, "Be quiet or go away." And her dark head tilted as her chin came up and the lovely line of her throat was lengthened.

Cyril peered suspiciously across the car. Oh well, certainly. Here came Henry Duncane in his Stearns-Knight, dashing up the hill. Oh yes, certainly, they'd want a word or a glance, the two of them. Want it like crazy. He twisted his face. "It's good I'm in time to play chaperone. You need one."

"Be quiet," she said. "Don't snarl. It's not becoming."

He said furiously, "You get that look off. Don't you realize? The whole town's watching this show. And you're on."

In a little while Henry Duncane, sweltering under a miner's coat, walked back down the hill toward the shafthouse. Moving, he caught the eye. He was going somewhere to do something. The people watching felt more bogged down and stickier than ever with their helplessness as he moved in his decisive way and they watched him.

Henry went directly to the boy on the mound of gravel.

"Trezona?" Dickie scrambled up. "How are you?"

"All right, Mr. Duncane." The boy stood like a little cock.

"Is your mother here?"

"Ma's waiting home," said the boy proudly. "Is there anything new?"

"I'm going down now to find out," said Henry gravely. "I'll let you know."

"Thanks."

"Quite welcome."

Henry smiled and swung away and the boy, with dignity, sat down. One word sang in his sore little heart. He felt a good deal bigger and less forlorn, he, Trezona.

Henry stood before old Mrs. Marcom. "I'm going to try to talk to them. Can't promise but I might be able to get them a message."

"No message," she said severely.

"Ah, Aunt," moaned Milly.

"You 'ush." Her eyes glinted at Henry. "Naught I be thinkin' that 'e don't know."

"I guess not," agreed Henry respectfully.

The old lady's face broke into a ragged grin. " 'E knows me. But thankee." She gave a crisp nod dismissing him.

"Quite welcome."

The pattern was set for Henry now. The people had caught on to the figure too and murmured and were pleased when he turned in the next expected direction.

Cyril, who had seen him coming long since, moved

nervously around the car. Now he stood on the driver's side while Madeline slid away from the wheel to the right. So Henry Duncane came to her on the right and Cyril studied the ground.

His voice, for her, changed from crystal to something warmer. "Ah, I'm sorry about this. I wish I could tell you it'll be all right. I can tell you they're working. Doing their best."

The impact of his sincerity, the warmth, the true wish surprised her. Her lips parted. Her eyes turned. She thought: But I've told him and told him—

"Not much more I can say," murmured Henry. His eyes were intent and glowingly sad, and hers fled. She tore at her handkerchief. She snatched at the possibility of a double meaning. (Yes, everyone watched them, of course, and some could hear, and there was nothing he could say.) Dark head bent she mumbled mournfully the first thing that came into her head.

"It's just . . . I hope he isn't hurt. If only he isn't in pain . . . all of this time . . ."

She put the torn handkerchief to her mouth. "I can't bear to think of him suffering," she whimpered. "I'd rather . . ." Her head went lower.

"He may not be in pain." Henry's voice was muted, as if *he* suffered.

She raised her tearless eyes. "It's so terrible, waiting. Will it be much longer?"

"Can't say." He shook his head. He took a step backwards.

"Oh, thanks. Thank you," she blurted, "for all you are doing." And she put out her hand to him. It must be clasped. It hung for all to see. He could not spurn its invitation.

So she tried to send, as their hands met, a tingling magnetism, a caress, a secret cry down through her fingers.

"Nothing to thank me for. Not doing anything. Believe me, I wish . . ." His hand was dry and firm and it pressed hers strongly and fell away and his face was darkened with something like anger. He swung away.

Madeline covered her eyes.

"Bad idea to wait here," growled Cyril abruptly. He

started around the nose of the little car. He and Duncane met shoulder to shoulder.

"I'm trying to get her back down to the house." Cyril said confidentially, "She hardly knows where she is. The strain . . ."

He looked up from under his skull but Duncane's eyes were focused far away. "Yes, tough."

"Tough on us all. Well, good luck." And Cyril put out *his* hand to be clasped for all to see.

Henry clasped it mechanically. Then he moved on in the pattern.

The Pilottis surged around him with questions and cries and messages. All the messages were too long. He could never send them on that thin line, but Henry did not say so.

"Ah, God bless you, Mr. Duncane," Luella Pilotti cried to him. She was a stocky little woman, dark eyed, volatile. Now, in her distress, she could still feel enthusiastic gratitude toward anyone who seemed to fight what she feared so much, for it lifted her quick heart.

"Quite welcome," Henry said gravely.

When he stepped toward the car where Mrs. Beard was, Kate Worthington lifted her hand and said "Sssh . . ." So he nodded and drew back. Poor Alice was asleep and the better for it.

So Henry completed the figure and now went to the shaft to the cage to be lowered. He went in his purposeful way without looking behind him.

The people sighed and like the wind the word blew. "Talk to them . . ." "No!" "Yes, he said . . ." "On the pipe, eh?" "*Talk* to them." "Joe told me he's the only one they can *hear*." "That *so*?"

Henry Duncane was going to get into the legend.

Cyril got in behind the wheel. "We're going home."

She didn't raise her head. "No, don't try, unless you want to struggle with me in front of everyone."

"Listen . . ."

"I'm not going home."

"Oh, by God," raged her brother, "how can you make such a fool of yourself? Thought you were so pious. Butter wouldn't melt, but the truth came out of your mouth just the same. Dear Arthur, *you'd* prefer him dead. That's a thing for you to say."

"I didn't."

"You did, though. And hell or high water, you had to touch Henry Duncane."

"You touched him."

"So it looks like a habit in our family to shake hands, I hope."

She was crying. "I needed to touch him. You don't care what I'm feeling."

"Not I," said Cyril, "but I know. Keep bawling. Looks fine. They'll make up a better reason than you've got."

"Monster," she sobbed. "No heart."

"Oh, cheer up," he said crossly. "You'll be irresistible in black. And let's not play it's your heart any more."

He thought to himself, maybe she's stupid after all.

CHAPTER THIRTEEN

WEST THOR caved in at nine-twenty o'clock on Thursday night. Now, nearly twelve hours later, the rescuers changed shift for the fourth time. The narrow, timber-lined burrowing-in went slowly but it did progress and, so far, safely. Captain Jacka, a quick youngish man, was there now assisting Captain Trezona who remained in charge. For ten minutes out of each hour the older man now went apart to sit silently and rest. These rests he took in icy calculation of his own strength prevented anyone from saying that he ought to quit or be relieved. In fact not many even thought of it. For the sharp concentration of his mind did not diminish nor did his body falter. He was in charge and would be. There was really nothing else to imagine.

In their dark place the men were talking and they had not noticed how the talk limped and dragged or what long pauses fell between their sentences. There was plenty of time to think well before speaking, and the slow sequence of remark and reply was a chain on which each man's private brooding hung, heavy as a nugget.

"Not one of us with kids, but Pilotti," mused Arthur Cole. "Funny thing."

They thought about it. In the soft buffeting silence the minds clung to any suggested idea.

" 'E's got pretty near enough to go around," Marcom wheezed. (The man was only the thin thready wheezing sound.)

"Only one of us got no wife," piped Wesley. His sound was young and unquenchably cheerful.

"You?"

"Me."

"You're slow," said old Marcom. He meant to tease. Someone might smile.

"But that's a funny thing," said Arthur whose sound was restless like the man and seemed to twist and yearn. "How many you got, eh, Benno?"

"Four, 'e's got," Charley answered and fell into a fit of coughing.

Wesley thought dreamily that there seemed to be something missing, but he could not think what it was. His head was heavy. Meantime, Charley seemed to be strangling and there was nothing anyone could do for him. Nobody spoke until the spell was over.

"Pretty bad cold you got there, Charley," Elisha Marcom had said so four times, so far.

"'Ad it three weeks," said Charley, with the same small disgust he'd shown four times already.

Arthur pursued his subject. "When is a woman really a woman though? She *should* have kids."

Marcom said, "Mine 'ad a kid. But it never lived."

"But she's a *mother*," Arthur said argumentatively. "I don't mean just because she has kids to raise. She doesn't even have to . . . Look it, you can kind of see it in them. For instance, take Duncane's wife. She's going to be a mother."

"So I 'eard," said Elisha minutes later.

"No, what I mean . . . Now take May Nepper, works in the store," (May was a rosy red-head) . . . "So is she."

"'Oo's the man?" Elisha was skeptical.

"No man. I don't mean now. I mean someday."

"What about Flossie Welch, then?"

(Flossie worked in the store, too. She was a very frail and timid girl with tiny, brittle bones.)

"Not her," said Arthur arbitrarily.

They thought about it. Nobody disagreed. Not even Arthur quite understood the point he was himself making.

But in Wesley's dream, scenes shifted. He saw it clear. Something to do with completion . . . with a woman who began as a girl, needing indulgence and protection, a kitten thing . . . but became a protector in her own right, sweet

135

and strong as a woman ought to be. "My mother is a mother," he murmured and the brooding thought was so thick around the words, no one noticed how absurd they were.

"That's so," said Arthur, excited. He could not express his own half-mystical notion. He could only pound away giving examples. ". . . and that little girl you went with," Arthur said, "that Rossi girl . . ."

"Celestina?"

"She'll be."

The others were pleased to consider. It was pleasant to be saying the women's names, whether they understood or not.

"Celestina," said Wesley, "Celestina."

"Most of them Catholic girls, eh?" Elisha threshed in the dark.

Charley coughed. He said, strangling, "Alice? My Alice?"

They thought about Alice Beard.

"She'll be," said Wesley suddenly when the silence seemed too doubtful and too long.

"But my wife will never . . ." said Arthur pursuing his own subject. "Never," he said like doom.

"Aw," said Charley returning a favor, "yuss, she will be."

"Let her have six," gloomed Arthur, "she'll never be."

They thought. He about Madeline Cole, the others vaguely about women.

"My sister, Dorothy?" asked Wesley.

"She'll be," they chorused.

"How young can you tell?"

"Pretty young, pretty young."

"Annie Dawe?"

"No."

"Yes."

It wasn't a bad game. But something was missing.

"Hey." Arthur seemed to call for silence and they were silent . . . so long that this time they noticed it.

Arthur said, "Benno?"

There was no answer.

"Pilotti! Hey!" No reply. "Did he faint—or what?" Arthur

was petulant as if this were a thoughtless thing for their companion to do to them.

No one said anything.

"Hey!" Arthur alone had the push and the urge to make sure. "Trezona, Marcom, and you, Charley, and me. When I say three, hold your breaths."

They were silent a long time before Arthur finally counted, "One, two, three."

Now they could hear no breathing at all. Just the soft pressures, the tiny trickling of water remained.

Elisha exhaled a long, gusty sigh. "Well."

"I shrived 'im," said Charley, on a high, nervous note. "Bleeding all the while 'e was. I shrived 'im, long ago."

"You can't do that." Arthur sounded shocked.

"I did though. And 'e shrived me as well." There was fever in that high voice, something too shrill.

"You can't do that." Arthur was going to argue. "Takes a priest."

Wesley broke in. "That's it. Long time ago he stopped saying his prayers. I didn't know what it was . . . missing."

Arthur said, "Well, you do now." He turned the piece of rock in his hand and tapped on the pipe four times. Pause. Four times.

"Oh, give over," said Elisha. "What matter?"

A long silent time went by.

Wesley said, "He knew a lot of saints, didn't he though?" (All four of them were Protestant so he went on.) "Pack of saints I never heard of. Why do they have so many saints?"

"They *was*," said Charley feebly.

"Go on," Elisha scoffed.

"How do you know they wasn't?"

"What *is* a saint?" Wesley wondered.

"Go-between," said Elisha. "Between them and the Lord God. So is the Pope a go-between."

" 'E was a fine man," said Charley Beard, ". . . and four kids."

They brooded.

"Hey . . ." The syllable quavered, for Wesley had noticed something missing. "Cole! Cole!"

"I'm here," said Arthur's querulous whine, "don't worry. Thinking."

The sense of whirling disintegration subsided.

"Speak up now and again," growled Elisha. "Mind."

"Listen, I'm thinking they ought to be told."

"Well, tell 'em. Tell 'em."

"Might make 'em get a move on," said Charley with sudden peevishness. "But I shrived 'im."

Arthur began to bang four taps at a time on the pipe.

CHAPTER FOURTEEN

At eleven o'clock Friday morning Libby Duncane was roaming distractedly around her house when she felt a sudden ripple in her body, a new and different thing.

She stood still until it was gone. Then she called, "Celestina!"

The girl came out of the kitchen dragging her feet. Her hair was untidy. The young flesh of her face bore swollen marks. Her eyes were dull and uninterested. She had a weary air as if to say, What now?

"I think . . ." said Libby breathlessly. "I don't know. I feel . . . Will you try to call the doctor?"

The girl looked perfectly stupid and began to mumble.

"What?" Libby was impatient.

"Don't know the number."

"You can find it, can't you?" Libby was sharp.

Something hostile glittered in the eyes. In the circumstances, Libby thought that pace was either stupidity or insolence, and she was infuriated.

"Oh, never mind. You are so slow." She got to the phone herself quite nimbly, asked for the doctor's number, turned, and lashed out. "Don't you understand?"

Celestina lowered her head.

"Oh, you're just no . . ." Her mistress turned to the phone. "Dr. Hodge, please."

But in a moment, she turned away biting her thumb.

Dr. Hodge was out. Just out. And his wife too. The hired girl who answered the phone did not seem to know where they were. All she could say was that when he got in touch she would have him call Mrs. Duncane. This she said placidly three times.

But *when?* thought Libby frantically. And what am I supposed to do?

"The doctor is out," she said, aloud, wanly.

Celestina said nothing.

"This backwoods!" cried Elizabeth Meadows Duncane. She hunted for that nurse's telephone number. It was written down somewhere. "Do you know where Mr. Duncane put that piece of yellow paper?"

Celestina didn't answer.

"Celestina!"

Celestina didn't know which one she meant.

"Never mind."

It was there neatly in a cubbyhole of Henry's desk and Libby found it. In all her rushing about she'd had no time to listen for that strange sensation in her body.

Just as she reached someone, at last, at the nurse's number, it came again.

"Oh, this is Mrs. Duncane. I'm calling Miss Cidney. Can she come sooner? I think I need her . . ."

"Oh, Mrs. Duncane, oh dear!" The nurse's relative, or whoever spoke, was so sorry, but with a patient in her care she did not think the nurse could oblige. "And it's not likely, Mrs. Duncane, really, and of course, even so, you will be hours yet. As long as the doctor is coming . . . He can suggest something."

The voice was superior and indulgent and Libby hated it.

She hung up. But what am I going to do? she cried to herself.

She rang Henry's call on the mine phone.

Bush answered.

"Not here, Ma'am. He's been gone all morning. I can try to find him."

"Please—"

"What shall I—"

"Just tell him . . ." Libby gulped, slowed her galloping impulse to scream for help. ". . . to come home," she finished primly.

"Well I certainly will, Mrs. Duncane," said Bush's wondering voice. "He's probably underground, but if it is very important . . ."

Libby said tartly, "It's somewhat important," and hung up.

She held her hands to her cheeks, rocking. It hadn't come again. Maybe . . . She took some deep breaths before she called the Gilchrists' number.

"Yes?"

"Marianne? This is Elizabeth Duncane. Are you terribly busy?" This time she would be cool, she would be a lady.

"I am, rather, dear," said Mrs. Gilchrist. The voice was whispery with respect for the disaster. "You must have heard what's happened at the mine?"

"Yes, I know—"

"Alex is home now. So exhausted," breathed the voice. "Poor man. The strain has just been—"

"I hoped—"

"He *feels* it so dreadfully. Takes it right out of him. And of course with Mr. Erickson away—"

"I called the doctor," Libby broke in desperately, "but he isn't there."

"Oh—"

"I'm alone."

Mrs. Gilchrist gasped. "But, my dear, surely not yet!"

"I don't quite know." Libby clung to the wall.

"But won't the doctor call back?" The voice was sharper.

"The girl said he would, of course. I don't know how soon."

"Oh, well," Mrs. Gilchrist hooted. "He'll be in time, my dear. It's rather a long drawn-out procedure. Hoo, hoo!"

Libby, with her face burning, said quietly, "So I've been told. I was going to ask if you couldn't run down and be with me. But you mustn't leave your husband, of course."

"I have never *seen* him so *upset*," said Marianne. "Really, I don't know . . . Isn't Celestina there?"

"Yes."

"Well then you are not alone, after all," the voice smoothed over. "Now you know I *would* come this minute if I thought . . . But you'll be all right, won't you? A little while . . . ?"

Libby said sweetly, "Oh of course. It's so nice to talk to you, Marianne, but I'd better not keep you."

"No, I should really . . . Why don't you call me in a little while? Perhaps after lunch . . . ?"

But Libby had put the receiver on its hook. Mrs. Gilchrist realized she was talking to nobody.

"Nerves," she said. "For heaven's sake! I wonder—"

"Look," said her husband, "I've got to lie down. Can you stay off that phone? Up all night," he grumbled.

"I didn't sleep a wink, either," she reminded him. "Really a wreck. I don't see how . . . but I will have to go down there sometime today. After all, I can't turn her down."

"Just so the house is quiet," he snapped.

"If I left it off the hook," said his lady thoughtfully, "we could both nap. An hour would be such a God-send."

Marianne went into her bedroom. "Nothing can happen to the girl in an hour." She began to loosen her stays. She'll be very glad to see me, she thought nodding. I can look rushed—

Ellen Trestrial turned away from Eedie's telephone, muffling the mouthpiece.

"Now this is a fix," she said.

"What is it, Ellen?"

"Miz Duncane. Mr. Weber told her where I was to. Poor little thing's alone and thinks her time is on her."

"Ah," said Eedie.

"I'll stay 'ere, mind," said Mrs. Trestrial in a threatening tone, "if I'm any good to you."

"Now you're a great good to me, Ellen, but go to 'er, do."

Mrs. Trestrial's shrewd eyes did not like the look of Eedie's face. It was too pale and too haunted. "Doctor's been called," she growled, "and no real 'arm for her to wait on 'im."

Eedie said, "Now you know you're going."

"If you say so," glowered Mrs. Trestrial and then into the telephone, "Now, 'old your 'orses, child. I'll be there directly."

Libby leaned on the wall. Her head was roaring with relief. She thought she might faint. But the anger came up and seemed to keep her conscious. Was Elizabeth Meadows to bear her child with no mother, no husband, no doctor, no

142

nurse, no friend, nobody except perhaps one old Cornish-woman she barely knew?

Am I an Indian squaw? she thought. A cow? An animal? Her eye lit on the girl Celestina who stood in the middle of the rug still. No decent servant!

"You may as well . . ." she began.

The girl muttered.

"Are you saying something?"

"I said the doctor will come before anything happens."

"You think so?" stormed Libby. "Everybody's so sure of it. Well at least Mrs. Trestrial is coming. She's not going to get paid for it either."

Celestina's eyes glittered.

Libby controlled herself. "I'm sorry, Celestina. I'm sorry. Don't mind it. Surely you can see . . ."

She stumbled to the divan and sat down.

"I can see you don't know very much," said Celestina.

"What?"

But something had got loose in the girl and would not go back. "You don't know *anything*," she said.

"Just a minute, Celestina!"

"You make me laugh," said Celestina. "*You* don't know what's going on at all."

"What do you . . . ?"

"You don't even know about your own husband and that Mrs. Cole. Yah. And you don't know they're dying!" Celestina shrieked. "Men dying, right now, and you don't even *know* it! *You're* ignorant! *You're* ignorant!"

"That will do. Be quiet."

"You think it's so much to have a baby. My sister had three already and I was there."

Libby lost her hold on severity. "Oh, please . . ."

"And I was here all the time," yelled Celestina, "but you said you was *alone*. All right. Pay me, then."

A frigid, cutting voice said quietly, "Celestina. Get out of this room!"

The girl wailed, whirled, and fled, banging and wailing, up the backstairs.

Libby looked at her husband.

"Did you call me," he asked coolly, "because there was a row you couldn't handle?"

Her eyes widened. She said quietly, "No, Henry."

He said quietly, "One of the men is dead. That's where I was, sweating to get a code to them."

"Code," she said numbly.

"No good. All they can get now is the question they got when they were fresher." He was hoarse. "Can't get it understood."

"What understood?"

"A code . . . to tell us which man died."

She said, "I don't know what you are talking about."

He said, "No. I know."

Somebody had come in at the back door. "Hoi . . . Your good pan's burnin'. Water boiled away. Hoi!" Mrs. Trestrial called. "Anybody to home?"

Henry turned and just looked at her as, wearing her purple toque and a long shapeless gray summer coat, she came bustling in.

Her canny eyes scanned the sick-faced girl in the chair.

"Way up the 'ill I was," she panted. " 'Ow do you feel, eh?"

"I guess I was foolishly alarmed," Libby said with her face gray. "It's not . . . happening quite yet."

"The baby!" Henry was startled.

Libby was glad. She said in a revengeful monotone, not looking at him, "Nobody would come, not the doctor, not the nurse, not Mrs. Gilchrist," her lip twisted, "not you. I was a little worried. Celestina was absolutely no use to me and I said so. She flew into a rage."

Mrs. Trestrial was grim but silent.

Henry was silent, his whole face listening.

"I thought," Libby said in the same tone, "at a time like this I would have a little bit of attention. But it seems I was foolish. And ignorant," she added revengefully.

Mrs. Trestrial grinned, showing her long teeth. She cast off the gray coat.

"Now, nothing foolish, child. 'Ot drop to drink and a bite to eat will do us all good. Nor do I think 'twill be long either, that's my opinion. Doctor's *been* called, Mr. Duncane."

Henry left the phone, cast one quick unreadable look at his wife and strode to the back stairs.

He bellowed, "Celestina."

No Henry, she thought, no more.

But Libby felt Mrs. Trestrial's calming and restraining hand on her shoulder as if to remind her that a man did as he pleased in his house.

Henry's voice was not itself, but hoarse and tired. Even so, they could hear every word he said.

"There will be no more of these rows." He was cold and strict.

The girl was sobbing.

"Or you must go."

Sobbing.

"Yes you are needed, if you can behave."

Then Libby, listening in a trance of dismay, was astonished to hear him go on quite quietly, "You know the Trezona boy is down there I suppose?"

Wild sobs, but they in the far room could catch no word except his.

"Naturally, you can't help hoping he'll be all right."

Mumble.

"Maybe you don't. But suppose you do? That's nothing scandalous."

Sobbing.

"Why help it?"

Her voice with a questioning rise to it.

"I'm sorry to have this kind of news, but we know now that one of them died."

A cry.

"No, we don't know which one, and we won't know until they are reached. Yes, it's hard."

Silence.

Whimper.

"Of course you can pray," said Henry kindly. "And of course you are worried. But don't take it out on Mrs. Duncane."

Sobbing.

"All right."

Silence.

Then Mrs. Trestrial left the sitting room.

"There you are, gel," Libby heard her say loudly and cheerily. "Well you can get busy and 'elp me, h'if you please. Cups we'll 'ave and saucers, bit of bread, butter. Cream in the 'ouse?"

Henry came in.

Libby said drearily, "Surely I ought not to think of anything but the baby right now."

"Don't even try," he said kindly. "Sorry, Libby. You must have had a bad scare."

"I was—shocked." she said.

"Why?"

"Oh," she evaded. "Because I was so alone. I don't want to try to remember all she said. Not right now."

"No. Don't try. She's pretty upset, and all alone in *her* trouble, you know."

"Oh?" Libby's eyes glittered.

"Maybe the captain broke it up between her and the boy, but you can't legislate the affection away."

She bit her lips.

"If she's drawn to him, she cannot help it, Libby."

"I . . . see that," she said.

"And the poor girl's frantic."

"Yes. So was I."

"Do you feel . . . safer?" He was awkward. "You called the nurse? Well, I'll find one, somewhere."

"If Mrs. Trestrial will only stay . . ."

"Never fear," said that lady briskly. "And 'ere's doctor coming in the gate. Now Mr. Duncane, you're best out of the way. That's my opinion."

"I mind one time," said Mrs. Trestrial, "they took twelve men out of Briar Hill, and not a bruise on a one. Lively as ever, the whole dozen."

She sat in the only rocker in the house, the one in Libby's bedroom, and she rocked while Libby Duncane sat, stood, walked about, and sat again, and the blazing afternoon poured down outside.

"That was a do," said Mrs. Trestrial. "But I mind one time they tapped up into a lake bottom, up by Ishpeming,

146

'twas. Mud and water was sucked down, see, in a rush, and not a one of that lot was ever seen again. Sealed it up, they did, for their tomb. Fifty men or more." She shook her head. "That was not the same as 'ere. There's 'ope 'ere, mind."

"I don't know very much about it," Libby said feebly.

The doctor had come and gone. All was well, he said. He would return. In good time. Later.

Henry had gone, too.

"Best go about your business," Mrs. Trestrial had advised him cheerily. "You'll do no good 'ere, Mr. Duncane. We've a long way to go yet."

But Henry had asked Libby's permission, or so she judged. Work left undone, he explained, and if she was sure . . . ?

She'd said quietly that if Mrs. Trestrial would stay that was all she cared.

Now the house was quiet and it waited. Celestina, swollen-eyed, worked apart in the kitchen. Mrs. Trestrial rocked and told tales, her sharp eyes comfortingly watchful.

Libby Duncane had had quite a fuss made of her, after all.

But she walked, sat, rose, walked.

Her heart was breaking.

No, it wasn't.

The girl had been hysterical, been blindly shouting anything that would hurt. There was no reason to believe *everything* she'd said.

But Libby Duncane believed some of it because she recognized it. She came of people who tended to examine themselves. She knew there was no denying that she was ignorant. She had *not* understood what this thing in the mine amounted to. She had *not* known, either, that Celestina's friend was one of those in danger of their lives in that terrible place. Nobody had told her, of course. But that was not excuse enough. She might have been told if something about herself had not made the barrier between her and plain information.

What pierced her was the memory of Henry's understanding for that girl, as he never seemed to understand Libby who had been, surely, upset and alone in her trouble, too—or so she had thought. Feared. It's the fear, she thought now.

147

It *is* the fear. He just has none. So he *can't*. To him having a baby is like what? Like a thunderstorm. There is some danger. But you discount it according to probability. You just take your chances. That would be his approach and he *expects* it to be mine.

But she was ignorant. Didn't he know the terror of that? How ignorant was she?

Now she remembered the cool, withdrawn beauty of that woman's face, that Madeline Cole. Well, Henry was not a man to be attracted by beauty, all alone. Libby was no beauty. Oh, she was nice looking with a certain charm, dainty and pleasing. No need to be silly. In all modesty, she *was* all that. (In former days and when all this was over.) But there might be, she mused, some stronger, other thing in Madeline Cole, if he was attracted. Fearlessness, perhaps, she thought sadly. Some brave kind of thing. Maybe the woman was brave or strong or serene, or able to calculate her chances so that, between those two, there could be, or was, a contract.

But maybe—she fluttered away from that quickly—there was nothing. Nothing at all. Think of the woman's reputation—flies to honey—and Celestina's anger and wish to hurt, seizing on the accident of the woman's coming here the other night.

Accident?

She wrenched herself up from the edge of her bed and paced again.

"Anything doin'?" inquired Mrs. Trestrial.

"No. Only that funny feeling, now and then."

"Walk about, do," said Mrs. Trestrial. " 'Twon't be h'altogether funny, before it's over."

Someone tapped on the bedroom door.

Celestina said, mush-mouthed, "Mrs. Gilchrist is calling."

"On the phone?"

"No, dear. I'm right here!" trilled the Gilchrist voice, as if this were a plum for some deserving little one.

Libby lifted her head. Mrs. Trestrial's rocker had paused. Libby's eyes turned to that long comical countenance above which the purple toque still rode, forgotten.

148

"I'm so sorry," trilled she, "but I am not receiving, Marianne."

"My dear, you are not *alone* in there?" The voice was flustered. "I came just as soon—"

"I do thank you for coming," said Libby sweetly. "But I am not alone. I have a friend with me."

"But I—I—I can't go without seeing you, if only for a moment . . . I did hurry . . . Please, mayn't I just . . . ?"

Mrs. Gilchrist was anguished with offense and curiosity.

Mrs. Trestrial was rocking gleefully, a grin on her long face. Libby winked at her.

"Celestina," she called so sweetly, "thank Mrs. Gilchrist for me, won't you? And show her to the door, please."

She heard Celestina say, in blunt obedience, "Miz Duncane says 'thanks.' The door's this way."

They listened to soprano babble, and a retreat in confusion.

"Celestina?"

"Yeh."

"Is she gone?"

"She went."

"Good. Thank you."

The girl said with surprising vigor, "You're welcome."

Libby sat down. "My, that was naughty!" she admitted.

"Did you a lot of good," said Mrs. Trestrial promptly.

"I don't trust her. I don't even like her."

"No need pretend you do." Mrs. Trestrial rocked. "You'll be fine," she said suddenly. "I've a mind to use the phone, eh?"

"Why, of course." Libby was startled. "I haven't even tried to thank you for giving up your day—"

"No need," said Mrs. Trestrial severely. "H'i know when the old woman is wanted. Don't h'i?" She tossed her head, became aware of the toque and took it off.

Libby sat with her face burning, staring at that ridiculous hat. She thought, I love that hat. I don't know where I've been. I certainly haven't been *here*.

Through the open door she could now hear Mrs. Trestrial on the telephone.

"Eedie? 'Eard a bit of news. Not good news, eyther.

"Oh, 'e did? 'E told you, eh? Bless the little chap, 'e's a stout one. 'E's a Trezona, eh?"

Libby thought, Trezona! Oh, she's talking to Mrs. Trezona, that boy's poor mother."

"Well, all there is to do," said Mrs. Trestrial, "is 'ang on, 'old on, pray, yes. Is *anyone* with you, Eedie? Oh, good, h'i see."

Libby thought, I called her away from *there* and I'm keeping her away. I *ought* to tell her to go. Her face burned.

Then Mrs. Trestrial said, "Oh, Miz Duncane's getting along fine. Be a while."

Then lower, "She's younger than her years, Eedie, and this 'ere is 'er first-born."

Libby clutched at her own throat.

"Yes, yes," said Mrs. Trestrial with infinite sadness. "Yes, Eedie. Well, God bless . . . Yes, bound to 'ear soon."

When she turned, Libby cried out at her, "That was *cruel!*"

"Eh?"

"The boy in the mine! How could you *say* that? *He* is her first-born! Isn't he? Oh, you shouldn't have—"

Mrs. Trestrial bridled. "I should 'ope Eedie Trezona knows 'oo's 'er first-born," she said sharply. "And she knows where 'e is now. Don't she? None better."

Libby stepped back. In a vision she seemed to see a different world, one in which the brute fact lay still and immovable and there. And since you knew you could not alter it by failing to mention it or by saying "Dark before dawn," or "Showers that clear . . ." you did not bother.

Into Libby's opening mind, into the middle of the vision, there was inserted a small clean-cut conviction, cold and solid. Celestina had known what she was talking about. There was something going on between Henry and Madeline Cole.

There it lay.

CHAPTER FIFTEEN

The Company store was very quiet that day. Not an item was sold except at the grocery counter. The girls in the dry goods side had nothing to do but fidget and dust. Not a woman in town bought a dress to wear or a yard of cloth or a ribbon.

The Company office functioned but under a weight. Faces were solemn. There were no quips exchanged. No one showed temper either. A frozen courtesy prevailed as if all quailed before God the Father, being good children, fearing punishment. Mr. McKeever emerged from his private room late in the morning when the state man came. He returned alone about two o'clock and announced quietly that progress was steady.

Cyril Varker had not been at his desk all day.

Children grew tired early that Friday from doing nothing, for tension, whether they knew it or not, had kept them from running free all day. During the afternoon people avoided being alone. In knots they talked, but they did not talk much about what they were thinking. So, in knots, they were solitary.

The group near the shafthouse at West Thor lost and gained by people coming and going. So all day it slowly revised and renewed itself. But the five points of the pattern were yet constant. And toward the end of the afternoon the crowd was perceptibly larger.

Everyone knew the rescuers must be getting near the lost men. It could not be borne to think one might leave here just before the final news came.

Madeline Cole, like all the rest, refused to go. Cyril was alternately furious and resigned. He threatened to leave her

151

and once he did, and returned with food which she would not touch.

The sad news of one man forever lost had, hours ago, come spiraling up to burst with a soft but explosive penetration here, and then mushroom over the whole town behind them.

(Taps on that pipe. Numbers, only. You could count them and that was all. Four taps and then silence.)

In the afternoon the priest came. There was something like an outdoor mass across the road, and quiet fell upon those people and something serene. Cyril observed this and was briefly envious.

He noticed that the Methodist women did not know what to do when the priest spoke to them. Mrs. Marcom stared straight before her and must have thanked him tartly, as if she conceded that he might mean well. Alice Beard simply shrank and looked terrified. Little Dick Trezona stood up as best he could to the alien and the strange, and so looked right past the odd clothing into the brown eyes of Father Martin. From far away Cyril guessed that those eyes must soften with tender amusement as the boy's lips would part with his surprise. And he thought he could tell that the priest would have touched the boy but wisely refrained.

Madeline Cole turned her wan face to Father Martin and said, "Will you pray, Father? I can't pray."

The priest prayed for men's souls.

But Cyril turned up his eyes and raked over the priest's near face. Very well-fed and complacent on the whole, thought Cyril, now that the eyes were shut and a certain skilled and professional look of peaceful trust lay on it.

But the brown eyes, when they opened, were not complacent, for the man thought he understood the dilemma of prayer now, and the fearful conscience.

(No one knew which four were alive. Did you ask for mercy for your own? That *he* might not be the unlucky one? Did you dare?)

"I can't pray," she murmured distressed. "Pray for me." The priest's glance caught Cyril's and Cyril was not sure that the brown eyes *saw* or the ears heard the weight of Madeline's "me."

152

When Father Martin was gone, Cyril squirmed and puffed air out of his nostrils contemptuously.

"You remind me in reverse of the man who said he didn't know whether he could play the piano. He'd never tried."

She put her arm on the back of the seat and turned and hid her face on it.

"Now listen," said Cyril, with mock patience. "Have sense. Henry Duncane has gone by three times already and not once looked this way. So you might as well go home."

"I'm not thinking of that."

"No."

"I'm not so mean as you think I am. You don't know what I feel."

"You're making a nervous wreck out of yourself because you can't feel anything," he snarled, "although now you know you'd better."

"No," she moaned.

"Oh, yes. Duncane expected it. Didn't he? *That* enlightened you."

She rolled her head.

"And maybe he caught on although he's not too bright."

She sat up. "I'll scream. I'll run."

"All right," he said grudgingly. "All right. But you're such a fool. And I'm tired and I want to go home."

Cyril put his head on his arms on the wheel. They'd guess it was exhaustion. And guess right. Something was exhausting him.

I see too much, he thought. Why can't I sit like a bump on a log and look at the scenery? Why do I always have to see so much? She's not a fool, Madeline, nor stupid. I wish I couldn't see it, but she has no quality."

The rescue tunnel collapsed at ten minutes after four o'clock. The news rolled up like dust rising, and caused a sound, a soughing, a keening, that blew back rapidly over all the town.

Underground, no man had been caught in the squeeze and rattle of the tunnel's closing because Captain Trezona had ordered them out of it, suddenly, with no visible or audible reason whatever. The evil memory of that rumbling roar still bore on the eardrums. The shouts of the men, shocked and confused, had ceased. In the uncertain, diminished, inadequate flicker of a few lights, and the comparative silence filled with men's murmuring, the captain lay on the rock floor, braced on one elbow.

Fred Davies crouched over him with a flask of whiskey in his hand.

"Don't be a fool, Captain. You need it. It's medicine, that's all. Doctor would tell you the same thing." Davies kept pleading. "Nothing bad about medicine. You've got to have it, Captain. Take it. Please."

The captain's eyes were narrowed to slits but not altogether closed. He was motionless.

Now Gilchrist's voice carried to the young man's ears, not loud but high and nervous.

"Must be all over," he was saying. "No need to push on. Not now. When they've rested they can clean the mess up. But it's all over. Too bad. Good try and too bad."

Davies hoped it was his ear alone which picked out among the voices that one so familiar to him, and heard in it the defeat and despair.

Captain Trezona's head lifted and he stirred. Slowly but smoothly he sat up; he got to his feet.

Davies rose with him.

"Believe me. *Good* for you. Give you a lift. Don't tell me you call it a sin to take a little whiskey, under the circumstances." Davies was young and he felt like crying. "Medicine, can't you see that?"

The captain's eyes were hidden by the hat's shadows. "H'if you'll excuse me," he said courteously.

And Gilchrist said, far away, protesting to someone, "I'm not placing blame. Nothing *like* that. It was impossible, but they tried."

Now Captain Jacka materialized at Davies' elbow.

"Well, sir?" said he to his superior.

"'Ave to go in to the left," said Captain Trezona. "Eh?" Jacka nodded.

"Medicine," begged Davies. "Tonic. Help you."

The captain put his hand against the dancing flask.

"No, thankee, Mr. Davies. I know you mean it well."

"But you're sick."

"H'i'm not aware of it," said the captain. "Boys, while us are waiting on 'er to quiet down . . ." He took a long stride into the thick of the confusion.

Davies walked away. When he came to where Gilchrist stood, he said, "Come on out of here."

"What?"

"It happened," said Davies and jerked his head. "Let them alone."

The older man wavered and stumbled. "Can't ask for miracles."

Davies put a hand under his arm. "Might. You can *ask*."

"I'm sick," said Gilchrist.

"Care for some whiskey?" The young man's voice was aloof and flat.

Now a man was pelting towards them. "Alive!" he shouted.

"What?"

"Two of 'em! Two alive!"

"What?"

The man rushed by.

"Come on," snapped Davies. "Let him alone. It's only a miracle."

"Trezona shouldn't . . . can't . . ."

"Will," said Davies.

"That boy's not alive. That boy's gone. The chances are—"

"Makes no difference what the chances are," said Davies. He strode on. Suddenly he turned his face back. "Listen, I've seen something! I've seen something! That damned, unbeatable old man! He's never going to quit. Don't you know that?"

"He'll kill himself," said Gilchrist whitely.

And Davies shouted, "*He* won't care. He believes in God."

"Don't get hysterical," said the older man mildly, in a minute, as if he had been restored to equilibrium by the other's outburst.

Davies didn't answer. He had a strange feeling that from this moment he, Fred Davies, would not be the same. Would not be so sure, would doubt the usefulness of his doubt, be unable to believe in the advantage of his disbelief.

Arthur said, "Marcom?"

"He said he couldn't wait."

"Charley?"

"Long gone."

"Trezona?"

"You and me," said Wesley. "They were close, though. They nearly had us."

"Who's that banging with the rock on the pipe?"

"That's me."

"I thought it was my ghost," said Arthur light-headedly. Something rose up in Wesley Trezona. "There's no such thing," he said calmly. He lost his aitches. He said, as his father might, " 'Old on now. Us'll 'ave to wait awhile."

Arthur said, "I'm proud to be in the same grave with you." Wesley said politely, "Likewise."

And they laughed.

CHAPTER SIXTEEN

Dick Trezona climbed along the path that ran to the dry.
He climbed slowly. The sun was fierce enough to burn although the air was so thick that he had to push through it
as if he were climbing through hot velvet hangings. He
seemed to creep past that long building, honeycombed inside with lockers and showers, where the miners changed
their clothes and he almost fell on all fours to make the grade
the path took now, a short cut to the upper road.

The boy had it in his head that he must be a kind of link
in the middle between his father and brother down underground, and his mother and sister at home. But just to stay
watching at the shafthouse meant nothing. When there was
any news he must carry it, or he was no real link at all. But
this news—that the rescue tunnel had caved in too—was so
heavy it pulled him back and down. It was like trying to carry
something he wasn't strong enough to lift.

As he gained the road, a car came up behind him. It
stopped.

"Want a ride?"

Dickie hesitated. He'd rather trudge it alone the remaining
hot and dusty way. It would feel better. But something told
him he must accept. He wasn't getting there fast enough
afoot, weighted as he seemed to be.

So he got into the back because Mrs. Cole was sitting in
the front seat next to her brother. She did not say anything.

It seemed to the boy that they whizzed. The hot wind
scorched his face for not more than a minute and they were
there.

Ma must have seen him in the car, coming, because she
was out at the gate.

"Ma—" he spoke first. (If he didn't the man would tell her.)

But she said briskly, "Go in the 'ouse, Dick. You're to stay 'ome now. They'll be all night, at least, 'aving to start over as they do."

The air lightened all around him.

" 'Op out, now," she said. "Say your thanks to Mr. Varker."

The boy murmured his manners, tumbled through the gate and flew in at the kitchen door.

Cyril was bending forward to see past Madeline, who had not moved or even opened her eyes.

"Ah, you've heard then, Mrs. Trezona?" he said in accents of condolence.

"Yes."

Cyril wondered how. He thought he had got away from the shafthouse as quickly as anyone. For some paralyzed minutes (who could say how many?) everyone had been suspended there in shocked dismay at the news of the rescue tunnel's falling. But he had been among the first to jerk a car into motion.

"That's *enough*," he'd said savagely. "That will be *all*. We go home *now*."

Madeline had not said a word then or yet. Bucking and bouncing, the car had gone into the road and turned up the hill because people starting to leave on foot were taking the easier way and blocking it.

"I was told on the telephone," Mrs. Trezona said. Her head was high. Something about her was refreshed, he thought. Perhaps she had slept or been able to rest.

"Mr. Davies 'twas, called me," Eedie said with color in her cheeks. "The captain'll 'ave them out if it can be done."

Her cheeks were pink with the pride that had come flowing from her heart when that Mr. Davies had said what he'd said about Pa.

Done her good, it had.

The news was bad. The earth had closed and more men gone. But there was good news too. That, in a man, there was something so stubborn and hard and undefeated she could almost close her fist around it. Something real as rock, to be proud of forever.

Madeline opened her eyes and sat up.

"Ah, you didn't 'ear that?" said Eedie quickly. "Two taps, still, so they told me. Captain Trezona 'as already begun again. 'Twill take time per'aps, but they'll not rest."

"They might as well," said Madeline bluntly.

There was an atmosphere of shock between the two women, Madeline's shock at Eedie's hope; Eedie's shock that the other dared say she had none.

Cyril interposed hastily. "I must get my sister home. She hardly knows . . . She's exhausted."

"I'm sorry," said Madeline, wildly. "I never say anything right." She fell back and covered her face.

"Poor lady," said Eedie gently. "Yes, take 'er 'ome, do. That's best. But there's a thing I want to say to you, Mr. Varker, if you'll take one minute."

"Yes?"

Cyril himself was full of nervous resentment. He thought if there had been no more taps on that damned pipe the whole population might have found some peace in a finality. But now he realized one could not even assume it was probably all over. Looking at Eedie Trezona, he knew it only began again.

"I've been thinking," said Eedie, softly, as if she did not wish to disturb poor crumpled Madeline. "And I see now, 'tisn't right."

"What?" He wheeled his attention to her words.

"You loaned the money in good faith, Mr. Varker. And he made 'is promise. Rightfully, you should 'ave it. So 'is fayther will pay the boy's debt, Mr. Varker. 'E would wish to."

Cyril was shocked.

" 'Twas good of you," Eedie went on, cheeks pink, "to say if 'e's gone 'twill be canceled. But 'tisn't right." She nodded.

He licked his lip. He said carefully, "Mrs. Trezona, I thought that the boy's father did not know about this."

She said, "I can tell 'im, you see, for I was told."

"You know how he . . . what the money was for?"

"Yes," she said. " 'E told me all that."

159

Cyril was quite well aware that the captain's fierce and narrow views existed and he knew they had force and pressure on his family. He knew how Wesley had feared them. He had thought this woman feared them, too.

He said, "But it isn't necessary. I wish you wouldn't. I'd much rather let it go." His fist hit the steering wheel.

Eedie said warmly, "Oh no, Mr. Varker, 'tisn't right for you who 'elped the boy in 'is trouble, to lose by it."

And Cyril saw that her eyes were soft and bright with gratitude toward him.

He looked away and gnawed his lip. "But if the boy comes out alive," he blurted, "what then?"

"Then it's 'is own business," she said less vigorously. "Yours and 'is own, 'ow 'e'll pay it back. And I'd say naught without 'is leave." She straightened. "But you will surely 'ave it, Mr. Varker, and the interest as was promised." She smiled and nodded.

"Thank you," said Cyril blankly and then angrily. "Thank you, I'm sure." He put the car in motion.

Eedie watched it go. Her hands came together. She hoped that in this matter she had truly understood Him.

Cyril, rattling down the hill, heard his sister fall into hopeless, dreary weeping. But he was not thinking of her now. He thought: That old Cousin Jack is shrewd enough to understand, if his wife does not, just what kind of deal this was. *He* won't fall all over himself to thank me any. Oh, he'll pay, to the last penny. But if that boy is gone, *I'm* gone from this town.

He didn't like it. He didn't see what he could do about it. In the back of his head moved a loveless conviction that it was stupid to fret, for something's will was going to be done and it probably was not Cyril's. His shoulders twitched. Wait and see, then, he thought glumly.

"Ma—"

"Darithy?"

Dorothy was sitting at the dining-room table, her narrow blonde head bowed. "Ma, I was thinking."

"Sssh," said Mrs. Combes. She was a friend who had come, a woman Eedie's age, plump and kind. But she sat.

And because she was a visitor and sat, the women of the house must, for some obscure compelling reason, sit too.

"Eh Darithy?" Eedie sank down on the black couch. She was thinking of Pa.

"Don't wake your brother," Mrs. Combes warned. "Poor lad." Dick was already asleep on Eedie's bed in the downstairs bedroom.

But Dorothy sat, fingernail drawing lines on the cloth. "If it fell on them *again*," said Dorothy, "surely they're hurt, Ma? How could . . . ?"

Eedie could feel the girl's gaze come up. She ought to meet it. But with all her heart she felt this kind of talk to be wrong. "If Wesley's 'urt," she murmured, "why 'e must bear it."

The girl's whole face quivered. "Maybe he's one that's not alive?"

"I said to 'er," murmured Mrs. Combes piously, "there's no pain then."

Eedie's blue eyes shot a spark. "'E wants to *live*," she said sharply. "Don't forget that! It's not for us to judge. Never, for no reason."

"Ma?"

(Too hard, too hard, for the child.)

"I'm not going to sit 'ere," snapped Eedie, "and talk about 'is aches and pains. Wesley can bear that, as well as you or I or better. For *I'm* not stone and *I'm* in pain, let me tell you. I'm tired to my bones and my 'ead's aching fit to break open."

"Oh Ma, put your feet up." The girl flew into motion. "Let me take your shoes off. It's so hot. Let me get a bit of ice in a towel."

"Tea!" cried Mrs. Combes and jumped up.

The cold cloth came wetly down on Eedie's forehead.

"Ma, can I rub your neck?"

"Rub it, do," said Eedie sighing, "and down my back, Darithy, for it aches to my waist." She turned on her side and closed her eyes. "Ah, there, Darithy."

(Something to do, Lord. Give her something to do.)

"Where do you keep sugar?" Mrs. Combes was calling.

"Blue can."

"Will she take a piece of bread?"

"Ma?"

"If 'twere toasted," said Eedie. Her lashes stirred.

"Mrs. Combes, you'll find bread . . . Wait, I'll show you."

Eedie caught the slipping towel and pulled it down over her eyes. She could hear whispering. Loving excuses for Eedie's weakness. Loving plots for her comfort.

Well then, she must make her mouth droop and not smile from old habit over the good, busy girl.

CHAPTER SEVENTEEN

THE struggle began again. Now, because young Fred Davies had seen something and felt something, although he did not go about deliberately telling it to everyone, his feeling became known. It got around.

It was told and corroborated. Men were enabled to see what he had seen. So much he added to the story.

People were touched and enlarged and encouraged by the rumor of a strong man, who met defeat head on and strode over it and began again. So Captain Trezona grew in the story and became a symbol of men against black odds.

Those who went on working under his direction were spurred and stimulated and filled with hard pride. A setback was magically changed into an opportunity. The rescuers were cheerful.

On the surface the hot day declined to a stifling twilight. No breeze lifted the blanket of heated air that wrapped the town close. There was something mean and cruel in the weather as if the malignant sun hid over the horizon and sent dark blind feelers back. It would not let the town go.

Down at the corner where the arc lights bloomed, three disconsolate youths stood hunched and, from time to time, looked over their shoulders or up into the sky as if they feared something watched them accusingly. They did not stand here long. No girls came by.

Cyril sat in his castle, on his throne, and surveyed his kingdom. It soothed him to put down the figures and add the sums and consider the money. He was glad to be alone.

His sister, Madeline, in a loose gown, roamed the hot little downstairs rooms. The mass of her hair was hot and heavy on her head. She took it down and combed it and swept it up. She was glad to be alone. It was good to be by herself and no need to think how she looked.

But she needed to show someone how she *could* look, to obliterate a false scene, retrieve something lost.

She told herself now that there was no real hope for Arthur, whatever people like Mrs. Trezona chose to pretend.

Oh, Arthur would never come back. Face it, she thought, and she wept for him. Tears squeezed from her eyes. Cyril was wrong. Of course she wept for him, poor Arthur. She had been very fond, very fond, somehow. He had loved her. Of course it had come into her mind what the world would look like if he died. She wagered it had come into the mind of every wife or woman whose man was in this thing. Why it would! It must! There was nothing so wrong just in imagining.

Cyril was heartless. It wouldn't occur to him that the heart could be fond, while the head saw the consequences.

Cyril was cruel. He liked to wound and to harry people. But she knew he was smart, smarter than she, or more sensitive. He often saw things and prophesied correctly. Now she went over and over in her mind the words she had said to Henry Duncane. The way she had said them.

Of course a heart that was fond would think of pain, and hope there was no pain for another. There was nothing so wrong in what she had said. Or how she'd said it. Anyhow, she'd been distracted. Out of her mind with anxiety. Cyril had nearly said so.

To cover up? Had there been need to cover up?

She took her thumb from her teeth and looked at it. The thumbnail had been stripped down to the quick. Well, naturally. Of course she worried. Everyone did. If *her* anxieties were a little different and a little more complicated, so was she!

If she could only see Henry Duncane for two minutes! He had not thought anything wrong. She could *tell* in two minutes. She had *not* given a wrong impression. How could she? For nothing she had thought or felt was really bad.

She remembered her spell over Henry was just the quality of being forthright, and ruthlessly so. Bold and clearheaded. What if she were to say to him . . .

(Now she saw herself, the pure line of her face, the candid simplicity of her gaze, lifted.) "If Arthur dies down there," (her voice would be low, musical and sad.) "I'm sorry for *his* sake. But for mine . . . he was a violent man and I . . ."

No, no.

Anyhow, she did not feel so, no matter what Cyril said. She felt . . .

Why she wept for him! It was terrible, terrible! She had not wanted to get away from Arthur in this fashion. Not her fault the rocks fell down.

If she could only see Henry for one minute, somewhere alone where meanings needn't be double. Alone. But there was no way to manage it. She could not go to his house. That was impossible, and he had forbidden it, besides.

He would never come here.

Unless, when the news came, finally, he came to condole. She dreamed awhile.

But he might not come. She wasn't absolutely sure that he would come.

Wait and see, she supposed drearily. Wait and wait, and months later, and she a widow. . . .

One minute, tonight, and she would know where she was. She didn't know where she was, and it was intolerable!

So hot! She brushed up her hair from her ears with both hands and went to the door. Dark on the porch. She slipped out. No breeze. No stars. The sky was low. This heat after dark was abnormal. She lifted the pure lines of her face and her lovely eyes rolled up.

There might be a storm brewing.

In a minute she felt sure of it.

She went softly upstairs and got her raincoat, she brought it down softly and hid it behind the kitchen door.

A storm? A lightning storm! It meant, to Madeline, a chance, a hope. Something might happen that she could seize upon for her own purposes.

Libby Duncane was disappointed to be able to sit at table for their late supper. It was late because Henry was late. When he came in finally he was surprised that they had waited for him.

Libby still wasn't hungry. She didn't want to talk—especially not about how she was feeling. She was impatient, and already very tired, and it seemed to her that the afternoon had been days long, the night would never come and never end, this baby was never going to be born, it would never leave her. She longed to get on with the ordeal, get into it, and get it over.

She felt as if she had fooled the whole household, that had waited with her all day, to be able to sit to supper. It was anticlimax. It was shabby of her to have held so much attention under false pretenses.

But Mrs. Trestrial would not leave her. She said her hired girl, Ethel, could manage. She had given instructions over the phone. Her young men must make do with a cold supper.

Henry seemed tired. He was taciturn. "Hot night." He eyed the soup.

"Miz Duncane, taste the soup, child. Yes, 'tis 'ot." Mrs. Trestrial's curls quivered. "Getting on, Mr. Duncane, are they? Up to the mine?"

The story had reached them, the collapse of the rescuers' first effort, the deaths and survivals, and the brave new beginning. Libby had heard it all filtered through Mrs. Trestrial's way of telling it which was bald and calm.

"I mind when Gideon Trezona was a youngish man," said his cousin now. " 'E was that stubborn. Or so 'is Ma called 'im. My Auntie Bess—old Miz Trezona, that was—*she* was the stubborn one in that lot. My—a terror, I'll tell you! Ah, she's gone now. Seven boys, she 'ad, and Gideon the one in the middle. 'Twas a lovin' family. Strict, she was, but lovin' always." Mrs. Trestrial sucked soup.

Celestina came in with the chops too soon. Her face was beaded and wan.

"It's so hot," said Libby. Her eyes licked around at the windows. "Henry, are you going back to the mine?"

"Not tonight," he said quickly. "Nothing for me to do there."

"They'll 'ave 'em out before mornin'," said Mrs. Trestrial, her shrewd eye on Celestina. "We'll 'ear soon enough. No need to try pushin' 'em from 'ere. They be pushin'! I mind, one time . . ." She told a tale of a disaster.

It was like reading history, Libby thought. It comforted. This was not the only time that men had been in trouble. Nor am I, she said to herself, the only woman who ever had a baby in thunder, lightning, and in rain. For, all of a sudden, she was perfectly sure that there was going to be a dreadful storm. I *would*, she thought with some amusement, with a faint relish for coming drama.

The storm, however, held off. The house was hot. The evening was cruel. Henry watched her. Mrs. Trestrial watched her. Celestina, when she had a chance, watched out of her dark sly eyes.

About nine o'clock Libby was standing in her bedroom showing Mrs. Trestrial some baby clothes—for the sake of motion, any kind of motion—when something took hold of her body and shook her. She was held in a great invisible paw that would do what it intended to do with her, now. No effort of hers was required whatsoever.

She said, with a sensation of delight, "Oh. Is *that* how it really begins?"

Mrs. Trestrial said, baldly, "Yes. 'Tis."

"Oh, I see! But it's so surprising! But that's not me doing anything!"

"Certain not," Mrs. Trestrial bridled. "You wasn't thinkin' you would 'ave to see to the Lord's work, single 'anded, was you? 'E's about, child. 'E'll attend to it."

"Well!" said Libby Duncane. She thought: I must write to Mother, it's the funniest thing. . . .

She heard Mrs. Trestrial at the phone calling the doctor. Henry came in. It was a strange and awkward moment. They seemed to have absolutely nothing to say to each other.

Thunder said, Remember me?

Libby spoke first. "Henry, it's going to storm. You know it is. And the lights will go out, of course. They always do. So you'd better fetch a lot of candles."

"Just you run across street and fetch my kerosene lamps," said Mrs. Trestrial behind him briskly. "My young men can sit in the dark tonight. Doctor's coming in about ten o'clock, child."

167

"Thank you," said Libby affectionately. Now she felt keyed-up and as pleased as a prima donna moving into her spotlight. "Go get the lamps, Henry, for goodness sakes. There isn't another thing that you can do."

His look became unfathomable as he ducked away.

Libby waited for the big paw to clutch her again.

Mrs. Trestrial said, "Walk about, do. We'll 'ave a baby in the 'ouse, before mornin'.'"

Now she went to draw the shades and transform Libby's bedroom into a fortress against the weather. Now it was battened down, cozied in.

Henry came hurrying back with the lamps, brushing raindrops from his shoulder. Now Libby shuddered again in the grasp of the powerful thing that was attending to its mysterious business. She saw his face.

"Oh, Henry, don't *watch* me!" she cried. "Go away, please. Because," she said with her jaw hard, "if this gets bad and I feel like screaming, I'm darn well going to scream."

His look was funny. He doesn't understand, she thought. This is just necessary. It's all arranged.

"Go and read or something," she said crossly. "This is my job."

"All right," said Henry meekly.

She thought: now, he thinks I'm being brave but it isn't that. It's only necessary.

Thunder rolled over the roof. She thought of something else. "And Henry, listen. If the phone rings for you, and it probably will—it always does—you just go. I'll have the doctor and Mrs. Trestrial, who know what to do . . ."

His lips opened. She was unreasonably annoyed that he should think her remarkably thoughtful of him in these circumstances. It was simply easier to make the matter clear right now. "After all," she snapped, "the baby's going to get born whether you're in the house or not, you know."

"Well, I guess so," he said meekly.

She cocked her tousled head. She thought, I must sound like a shrew, and I must look a perfect fright, and I don't care. But she said, half-apologetically, "Don't I sound bossy?"

"You sure do," said Henry meekly. The blinds were glowing. The thunder cracked. "Close," he said, watching her.

He didn't seem to know. The storm and the thing that had her now were all the same.

"She'll be fine," said Mrs. Trestrial, coming in with things on her arm. "Now—"

Henry put up his hands. "All right, I'm getting out." He grinned. (But she thought his eyes did not.) "I'll be in the sitting room."

Libby thought with grim pleasure, I don't believe he knows what to make of all this.

The storm rolled over the town and the rain drummed down slashing the hot dust. Lightning rived the thick air and cool currents threaded through.

It was all arranged, but it took time. Libby could understand that, now. The house thrust up into the storm, and she, sheltered, was rather pleased with all the tumult outside. Like everybody of any importance in Shakespeare, she mused, this baby gets born with portents.

She said to Mrs. Trestrial, "It will be a boy."

"It will be what it will be," said Mrs. Trestrial, rocking. "That Celestina's got a towel over 'er 'ead."

"She always does."

"Tellin' 'er beads. I told 'er a thing or two."

"Oh, Mrs. Trestrial, if she's scared of the storm she can't help it."

"If she's sweet on Wesley Trezona she'd better 'elp it."

"Why?"

"Never do."

"Why?"

"Never do, is all."

"But if they fell in love . . . ?"

"They can fall h'out," said Mrs. Trestrial.

"But why?" Libby felt, unreasonably at such a time, very sorry for all young things.

"'E's been taught one way, and she another. 'Twouldn't do," said Mrs. Trestrial with authority.

"Oh," said Libby faintly, "there'd be no contract."

"What's that, child?"

Libby began to groan. She enjoyed the noise she made.

169

"Is it bad?"

"Not that bad," she gasped. "I'm glad it's a noisy storm. I can yell all I want."

"No need be quiet," grinned Mrs. Trestrial.

"Mrs. Trestrial, I love you!" (What a delirious thing to say aloud!) "My mother would want me not to yell."

"Expect she believes in puttin' up a good show, eh?"

"Yes," said Libby, eyes widening. "Yes, I suppose. . . ." Her thoughts veered. "I hope the lightning doesn't strike the doctor."

"No matter if it do," said Mrs. Trestrial calmly. "Us'll manage."

The storm was furious. It couldn't get in. The mine phone rang.

Ahha, thought Libby. It wasn't Henry's ring but, as in a vision, she could see a man somewhere needing to tell another about some difference in the way things were going. Strange how she could see the ringing of the phone tonight from the other end of the line instead of here. She thought, I'm getting clairvoyant or something odd. This really is the funniest thing.

There was pain, now and again, but it seemed necessary.

About a quarter of ten Mrs. Trestrial had gone out of the room for a moment and Libby, let off and let rest for one of the intervals between, heard someone near her door.

"Who's there?" she called softly.

"It's me, ma'am."

"Celestina?" With that queer power of seeing things from the other end, Libby felt suddenly a great pity for poor Celestina, so worried about the boy in the mine, so frightened by the storm, so chivvied about by Mrs. Trestrial, and a prisoner in this house. "Come here."

The door opened. "Miz Trestrial went in the kitchen. Said I was to tell her if you called, ma'am."

"Come in."

The girl squeezed through, cowering. "Are you all right, ma'am? Did you want . . . ?"

"Ma'am," said Libby. "Now what makes you . . . ?"

The spasm came and passed while thunder shook the very floor. In the midst of the double uproar Libby thought Celestina might have said, "Mr. Duncane told me to call you ma'am, ma'am."

The girl stood with her shoulders drawn up, tense against thunder and lightning.

"Don't be afraid, Celestina," (What a useless thing that was to say!) "I only wanted to tell you that I'm sorry you and I haven't got along better. I don't want this feeling that you dislike me, and I don't want to dislike you. Can't we improve?"

"Yes, ma'am." The answer was dull and didn't mean much.

"There are many things I didn't know," murmured Libby. "You were right about that. Well, I can only say I'm sorry." (Useless, she was thinking. Well, I've tried.)

But now Celestina's dark eyes turned. She did not like the pale-haired woman in the bed, and never would. But she had a new thing in her heart, now. From a source she had never thought to find it, help had come.

Henry Duncane, by simply listening and then replying, had cleared away the unhappiness of her confusion. It was *all right* for Celestina to feel just the way she did feel. It was *all right* to care and to pray for Wesley Trezona and it did not mean she betrayed herself or her own pride or her loyalties or her people or anything. She felt sure about Wesley now. Of course she liked him and prayed for his safety. But she was less upset about him. She was ready for a quiet sorrow or a quiet rejoicing. Neither would change the course of Celestina's private and personal destiny very much at all.

But her heart was warm toward Henry Duncane. She felt she would do anything—anything—for him. If only she could help him, somehow, someday. She had already made a fantasy or two.

Why, she would even make up with this woman, so she could stay on here and every day cherish the sight and the sound of him. His "Good morning," even. And certainly she wouldn't do anything to trouble him, although maybe she already had. Well, then, she would undo it.

So filled with the best of intentions and impelled by devotion, Celestina drew nearer. "Miz Duncane, I'm sorry. When I said what I said, I was mad at you."

· "I know," said Libby, faintly smiling. She believed she had touched the girl, after all. But she could not give her full attention for, at the same time, she heard the mine phone ring again. This time it was for Henry. Ah yes, she thought, he'll be out in it.

"It wasn't *him*," Celestina was saying passionately. "It was *her*, anyhow. *She's* the one said all about she loved him, he loved her, and she'd get divorced. *He* never said anything like that! He never did! He *wouldn't*, Miz Duncane, and I'm sorry. Honest, all *he* said, he told her not to come here . . ."

"Who?"

"Miz Cole. They was under my window. But he didn't kiss her or anything like that. Ooooooh!"

Lightning blazed and Celestina leapt. A thunderbolt drowned every other sound and the girls arms went around her head. When the noise had rumbled off around the earth and fallen over the horizon, Henry was there in the room with them.

"Do you want her in here, Libby?" he said in his brittle clipped pattering syllables.

Libby looked up at him. Whether he had heard what the girl had been saying or not, his face was cold. "I did call her," Libby said weakly. "No, I don't want her now."

The girl, with her arms still folded over the top of her head, wailed once and turned as if to run, turned back, wild with dismay. "Oh, please, Mr. Duncane. Don't look at me! I never meant anything. I was only . . . I didn't . . ."

"Get your coat, Celestina," Henry said.

"Oh . . . Oh . . ." Wailing and weeping, the girl ran away.

"I'll see that you aren't bothered," Henry said gently. "You mustn't be."

Now Libby was shaken and tossed by the thing that would not be diverted by anything—thunder, lightning, or a piercing of the heart—from what it now proposed to do with the body of Libby Duncane. And when it let her go, she heard Henry say, "You mustn't think about anything but the baby." Her own words, her own decree, now cut her sharply away from knowing, from asking, from being told.

"Henry . . ."

"There's some trouble at the Falls." He evaded—or he did not. She couldn't tell. "I ought to go, Libby. But if you need me . . ."

"I don't need you just now," she said slowly. "I told you so." Ah, no use to ask, she thought, not now. He would not tell her. He would soothe and protect her (as she had, herself, decreed) from any true thing that might offend her delicate sensibilities.

Henry bent. Perhaps he kissed her cheek, she wasn't sure. "I'll be as quick as I can." But he went away and she could tell he was glad to go. She was glad when he was gone.

She wondered whether he had heard how Celestina had let a pretty monstrous cat out of the bag. Maybe he hadn't. Had. Hadn't. Never mind. The cat was out this time.

She thought that she and Henry had married too fast . . . Henry back from the war, bowled over by her daintiness, she by his forcefulness . . . But someone should have said to them a year ago, " 'Twill never do."

She moaned. Mrs. Trestrial came bustling. "That girl's gone," said she, sniffing. "And good riddance, h'i say."

"Gone?"

" 'E asked me if I needed 'er. Land, if she's going to yell and holler, I said, no. So 'e took 'er."

"Henry? Took Celestina with him?"

"Drop 'er off 'ome, 'e said. Just as well." Mrs. Trestrial bristled.

"And she went, in this storm!"

"She went," said Mrs. Trestrial grimly. " 'e wouldn't stand for 'er nonsense."

"No." Libby's mouth grinned of itself.

The phone rang. In a mysterious way, she knew at once it was calling the boilerhouse. Now how did she know? "Trouble. Trouble," she muttered. Thunder boomed. Mrs. Trestrial's warm hand touched her arm. "Do you remember?" gasped Libby Duncane. "You said 'It isn't what you fear that's on your heels, it's some other thing.' "

"Did I say so?"

"You were right, too."

Mrs. Trestrial had pulled a window blind aside. "Thought 'twas about time. 'Ere's Doctor, now . . ."

173

The lights went out.

Libby sighed. As in a vision, she saw the storm-swept roads and Henry's car going toward the trouble in the works, at the Falls. And she saw the deep place where there was no storm, bu where a fight against trouble, trouble and death, was being valiantly fought. And she saw the doctor scooting up her walk, head down in the dark rain, and herself, writhing in this flickering lamplight, with the trouble of birth.

"This town's like a three ring circus tonight," she gasped, as the doctor rubbed the moisture off his ruddy cheerful face. "Is there any news at the mine? Have you heard?"

"I hear," he said soothingly, "they think they're getting very near again."

She was stabbed with pity. What it must be to wait! "So terrible," she said.

Mrs. Trestrial bridled. "She's fine, eh Doctor?"

"Am I?" said Libby, and then, "Gosh . . ."

The doctor laughed and patted her hand.

CHAPTER EIGHTEEN

There was no time to put up any side curtains. Henry made Celestina sit in the center of the tonneau, and still the rain splashed her from both directions. Water gurgled and swooped in the gutters, and the wheels of the car sent hard fans up to roar on the inside of the fenders.

The eye had no defense against the lightning's erratic brilliance. It could not adjust to the feeble effort of the car's headlights or easily learn to discount the silvery slash of light on rain that obscured even this.

Henry drove slowly because he had to.

Celestina, too miserable to be frightened, remembered a fantasy. To be alone in a car at night with such a man . . . ah bliss! But now that it came true it was not bliss, but sickening humiliation. He thought she was a nuisance. Nothing on earth could be worse than that. To be despised, to be hated and feared, to be struck in the face, beaten by the hand, would be better than that.

The car crept down past the first corner where the arc light added its bit to the defeat of any reliable visibility and it crept along the schoolyard in which the tall trees danced grudgingly in the wet wind. As it crept to the next corner a jittering scarecrow, something ragged and nervous in shiny black, flitted into its path.

The car under Henry's quick foot slid to a stop. The phantom had a face. Lightning lit the pale countenance, the wet cheeks, the great gray eyes in the sweet sockets of the beautiful bone of the face of Madeline Cole, and her dark hair lay wet and plastered on the white forehead.

"Henry. Henry." She was on the running board, body bending under the top. Pale insufficient light from the dash came up, weirdly touching the underside of her chin and her nostrils.

He said sharply, "You shouldn't be out in this."

"Take me with you, ah please."

"I can't do that."

He was too staccato quick for Celestina, but the words were in her mouth and they fell out anyway. (She was a nuisance and humiliated to the bottom of her soul, but she could try not to be a nuisance, now, again.) "I can walk," she said shrilly.

The woman had not known she was there. The eyes tore themselves off Henry Duncane. The head turned. The face, in the dark, was a black blank, looking back. Yet neither she nor Mr. Duncane paid any attention to what Celestina had said. (She knew bitterly the idea was fantasy.) The storm whipped at them all.

"Where did you want to go?" asked Henry of Madeline Cole.

"Aren't you . . . going to the mine?" The woman fumbled toward making some sense of this.

"No," shouted Henry in thunder, ". . . going to the Falls. . . got to take Celestina home . . . in a hurry . . ."

"Do you know anything?" Madeline brought her pale hands together like a little steeple. "Oh, I wish this wasn't happening. . . ."

"May be all right," shouted Henry. ". . . don't know any more . . . Doing everything they can."

The woman hung on the car. "Ah, but you understand, don't you? My heart aches. Heart aches. If it only could be as it was before, or if I knew . . ."

Henry said nothing. The storm boiled around them. But now a second scarecrow figure came, angular and floppity, flying through the headlight's beam. "I'll take care of her." It sounded competent. It reached and plucked the woman down.

Henry nodded. "Hurry!" he shouted. Under his hands and feet the car took hold of the slippery road and slewed on around the schoolyard. Celestina looked behind and saw two figures flickering across the street. The car ran to the wide place before the Company store, slipped and clawed

176

to the left, and passed the depot where a dim light burned.

The storm lulled. "I guess she thought you were going to the mine," piped Celestina, bravely. She wanted to please him. Henry gave her no answer at all. Everyone knew West Thor Mine was west, not east. Everyone knew you couldn't get there this way.

Celestina covered her face and wept without sound. Life was too much for her. All her fantasies collapsed. She was a nuisance to Henry Duncane, she didn't know what he wanted, and she couldn't ever help him. Her mother was going to give her the devil, besides, when she got home and, oh Blessed Saint Barbara, turn the lightning from our path.

The car stopped and he said, "You're wet already. You can run home from here, can't you?"

"All right." She got out and stood in the blasting rain. "Mr. Duncane, can I come back?" The dash light would throw up light against her features. Henry didn't even look at her.

"I don't know." Don't care, was in his voice too.

"Please . . ."

But he was gone. His car roared and seemed to slip out of her hand. It splashed around and went, black and glittering, rejecting her as nothing, back to the turn toward the Falls at the saloon corner. She wished she'd get struck by lightning. It would be better.

But she was young and suddenly she began to run; slipping, ducking, dodging, begging Mary, in Her Mercy, not to let Him take her up on that silly wish. The whole world of the Duncanes and all Protestants together (which was a kind of fantasy, anyhow) washed away in reality. She ran to get safe inside the house where the holy pictures hung on the walls and her manners were all they ought to be; into the warm dry place where lingered the scent of all the years of her life, of all she really knew, of home.

Cyril flung the house door open and shoved his sister in. "Middle of town," he growled. His look was disgusted. He had nothing more to say.

She wouldn't have listened, anyhow. She sat down, wet as she was.

Now she reviewed each word and every intonation. "I can't do that." What had he meant? Was it shock, rejection, or a quick warning? Of course he couldn't take her with that Celestina in the car. She thought he might have. She thought of them, close and running free and wild, hidden in the storm. Oh, bad luck!

Nasty little girl saying she could walk. Hinting she understood too much. Well, she didn't matter.

"Where do you want to go?" Had he been helping her, hinting how she was to cover up for that girl's sake? She thrust down the uneasy thought that Henry Duncane was not the man for intrigue. Oh, she couldn't tell . . . didn't know . . . didn't know where she was.

It was all Cyril's fault, actually.

"You," she said bitterly.

"Let it alone." Cyril was wet and disgusted. "Will you ever learn?"

"You!" she said furiously.

"I don't know what you thought you were doing. You don't know either."

"I do. I do. There was something I had to say."

"What?"

She closed her mouth stubbornly.

Cyril said without anger, "A man has, sometimes, other things on his mind besides the swish of your hips, or anybody's hips, dear sister."

She muttered, "Something Charley Beard could know and tell Arthur and if he . . ."

Cyril's laugh was sudden and contemptuous. "Your hips, eh? Even down that mine. Don't be funny."

"Won't be so funny . . ." she said.

"Stay away from Henry Duncane. Don't you know that in a minute he'd have pushed you off that car? The man's busy."

"You forget, he loves me," she flared.

"You never heard of timing? I tell you, other things on his mind important to him . . ."

"I am important to him."

"Not exclusively," said Cyril. "Why don't women know that? I'm telling you and you ought to make a note of it.

178

Don't bother a busy man." He had his coat off and was whipping the water off it.

"What do you know about it? You. You're so wrong about everything. Thinking I want Arthur to die . . ."

"And now you'd rather Duncane didn't realize you'd just as leave Arthur died. All right . . ." he lifted his hand to ward her away. "If you can't see how you are letting yourself open, wider and wider . . ." Cyril wiped his face. "All right," he said. "I don't care."

His eyes rolled up, to see her, and they were sad.

She shrieked, "You!" What she thought was, I have power, I do matter. I will. I can get what I want my own way. "You don't know everything!" she shrieked.

He shook his head. He went into his own room and closed the door.

At the power plant the trouble was serious. Duncane soon knew that repairs would take time. The turbines were ready, and he was in touch on the phone, and they took over. That settled, now there was plenty of time. With power flowing from the auxiliary source, the trouble could be attacked in force and detail, by day, if necessary. Just because it was as serious as this, Henry was able to get away in less than an hour.

The storm was, by this time, nearly spent. It had settled to an aftermath of steady light rain. The road, over hill and dale from the river, was a stew of mud. He could not make time. When, approaching the saloon corner, he hit a harder surface, he put on speed.

He passed the saloon, so shut away that it was hard to believe anyone could be awake inside the drab building in its lonely spot. He skidded badly, turning toward Thor. The bridge, under which the railroad ran in a deep cut, was right before him, low-railed, and narrower than the road.

He entered upon it and picked up speed to fly along the straight stretch that would roll beneath him now. He was a man in a state of urgency toward he knew not what. The dying storm had one more lightning bolt to offer. When it came, his dazzled eyes just saw a movement at the right side of the narrow end of the bridge. Something tottering into his path.

Surprise, coming upon his state of tension, sent his foot down too fast. The car skidded violently on the slick bridge. The back end swung. He fought it and lost. The car hit the rail and tried to mount it. Lights smashed, it quivered in the abrupt darkness and it turned over.

Smashed glass sliced viciously along the arm across Henry's face, but at the same time, something met the back of his head and he lost consciousness before pain.

Now the car's engine coughed, fluttered, and died. Its wheels spun in a wistful fashion as if they sought traction in the soft and empty rain. Underneath, his blood seeped softly, spreading without sound into the dark water on the black road.

CHAPTER NINETEEN

MADELINE COLE was down on her knees. With scarcely a thought for her dress and her stockings, she knelt on the cold, hard, rough, wet ground. The car was tilted. No lightning came to help her see what lay under it. "Henry . . ." her voice trembled. Something pale, upturned, must be his face. "Are you all right? Are you all right?" Her hand touched broken glass. She thought, I must be careful not to cut myself.

He had come along so much sooner than she had expected. She had been startled to recognize his car. It was no wonder she had stirred convulsively from the shelter of the stone at the end of the bridge, where she had thought to spend another hour, at least, escaped from Cyril, hidden from the town, dreaming and waiting in the rain.

Now, she heard a brittle sound like giant soda crackers breaking.

And now somebody's hard hands came, brutally strong, under her armpits and tugged upward. "For God's sake, get out of here!" Her brother Cyril was panting in her very ear. "You fool! You can't stay here! The saloon! Quick! Hurry! You can't be seen!"

He dragged her and she was doubled backwards with her legs folded under her and she scraped her calves, dragging her legs on the road to get them unfolded. He lifted her to her feet and, taking her hand, yanked so violently that she nearly fell.

Now there was a spot of light somewhere in the wet dark world. There, there it was, yards away. She could hear men's quick excited voices. That crackling sound had been a door opening. Men were about to pour out of the saloon. She could sense them peering from their lighted place into the dark and the wet.

"Come away," cried Cyril in her ear. "You little fool!" He was dancing and pulling frantically. "*They*'ll find him. You can't be here when they do. No business . . . Hurry! D'you want that whole bunch from the saloon to find him in your arms, and your husband where he is? Get walking. Get going."

So she began to walk and then to run. Her brother drew her behind a row of bushes. They scurried along the road's margin. There was no lightning to let them be seen. Nor could they be heard because the men's voices were shouting, now. Cyril pulled her violently to the right. Softly, he worked the latch of a gate. There was a dark house on the little ridge that rose opposite the depot. It was the last one in a row of half a dozen. Cyril led her, stepping carefully, up a path and stealthily along the house wall, down through its yard the other side of the low ridge.

Then they were in an alley and well-hidden. They went on to a street that angled in. Between one of Thor's double rows of identical houses, making a duet of her soft sobbing and the sob of his angry breath, they went hurrying northward in the rain. They hurried past the closed and silent town hall and through the circle of light at the corner. At last, soaked, pale and panting, they faced each other inside the little house of Arthur Cole.

"You didn't dream you could get away from *me*," he gasped. "Never. I knew. I was looking out for you."

But now she remembered Henry Duncane. She put her hands to her wet head. She had not screamed yet but in a minute she would begin to scream.

Cyril slapped her. "Was he hurt?"

"I don't know."

"You don't know. Did he see you?"

"I don't know."

"You don't know. Did you speak to him?"

"Yes."

"Did he answer?"

"No."

"Maybe you're lucky."

"Lucky!" she shrieked. Her eyes looked black, not gray.

"All right. Don't even remember it. Never let it get out that you were there. You didn't go anywhere. I'll swear. You'll swear. Ah . . . why do I try?" Cyril fell into a chair. He put his arm across his face. "You made him lose control. You turned that car over."

"Didn't . . ." she swallowed. "How could I?"

"I saw it. How I'd laugh," said Cyril viciously, "if Arthur gets out alive and it's Duncane who dies."

"No!" She recoiled and went staggering backwards away. "Oh, no!"

"What do you think? That isn't possible?"

"You're just . . . You're trying to hurt me," she gasped. "Better call. Be sure. Call the doctor."

"You or I can't call any doctor."

They stared at each other.

Suddenly Cyril raised a clenched fist. "By God, you're no good!" he shouted. "You're rotten! Can't you see you should have stayed there?"

"But . . ."

"You should have stood by him."

"I . . . you . . ."

"Sure. I told you to come away. Sure, I could see what you were in for. Sure. But you shouldn't have listened to me," he raved. "If you had anything to you but a face and a pair of legs . . . Love! That's love for you."

"It was you," she cried. "Why did you *make* me?"

"Nobody could have made you," Cyril raved, "if you were anything."

"There's no pleasing you," she cried. "I can never please you! It was your fault! Your fault!"

Cyril said, "We might as well quit shouting about it and shut up and keep still and wait. . . ."

She sat down, sinking slowly. They stared at each other.

Libby Duncane noticed that the storm was dying, the night was quieting, for, except for the noises she made herself, the big bedroom where the lamp flickered was quiet, now. Mrs. Trestrial rocked nearby with a rhythm that was somehow sensitive and in accord. There was nothing non-

183

chalant about it. There was, instead, calm and reassurance, as if nothing could be wrong while that homely rhythm continued.

The doctor was asleep.

This was not a thing Libby could have foreseen, that she could be where she was and as she was and watch his head lying on his arms on the chair back and hear his breathing and know he was asleep and understand it. He slept while he could and for her sake. And for the sake of other people who might need him yet tonight. It was not indifference and not neglect, but care. Instead of a show of care.

Funniest thing, she thought.

Mrs. Trestrial caught her eye and her comical old face twisted and her curls bounced like a signal or a wink. Libby smiled at her. The doctor stirred. He might almost have had a premonition or, in his sleep, heard the telephone clear its throat, for it rang. Mrs. Trestrial sailed into the sitting room to answer it.

May be Henry, Libby thought. She felt almost positive that it was Henry calling.

"Doctor. They want you." The doctor was awake and on his feet and out of the room without any hesitating transition. It's a skill, thought Libby admiringly, to sleep when you may and wake when you must. It's his work, of course. He had to learn that. The shadows on the high white ceiling made a pretty play.

"I like lamplight," Libby said dreamily. "It's nice and old-fashioned."

"'Tis cozy," murmured Mrs. Trestrial. But her head was turned to look over her shoulder through the door.

"Dr. Hodge, here."

"Say, Doc, this is Turner. Henry Duncane's car turned over on the bridge down by the saloon. Listen, he's under it and he's out and bleeding bad. We're scared to move him. Looks pretty bad. Can you come? We put a lot of towels in there but . . ."

"Don't touch anything," said the doctor sharply, "unless you know what you're doing. What is it? Head?"

184

"No. We don't think so. Looks like the glass . . . Listen, Doc, I dunno but I think you better make it fast."

"Come as quick as I can."

When the doctor came back through the door there was an air of lightning about him, of sharp alarm. He came swiftly close to Libby and said quietly, "Mrs. Duncane, I'm afraid there is an emergency."

Her blue eyes, looking up into his face, opened very wide. "May be a matter of life or death," he said.

"Oh!" She knew, at once, he was going to ask a question.

"The chances are that you will have no trouble," he went on gravely. (He stood as if he would fly. He was poised to go.) "But if I go, I might not get back before the baby comes, although I'd try."

Life or death, she thought. Well, that was the emergency. It always was. Always meant life or death for somebody. That was the question that emerged, that came out of the event, suddenly. "Emergency," she said aloud. "Is it one of the men?" For she thought, at once, of the trouble at the mine.

The doctor, eyes shrewd on her face, merely nodded.

"And you are needed?"

"Yes, right away." (She gasped because she was made to gasp.) "If I go it's got to be now." He bent down, smelling clean. "Can't be two places at once. I can only leave it to you. You are to say. Mrs. Trestrial knows what to do for you, of course. And I'll hurry."

"Of course she knows," said Libby, as the power let her go. "Oh, doctor, I couldn't keep you. I wouldn't dare. Don't let the man die."

He said, "Good girl. I'll hurry." And, as if she had snapped a little thread that lightly held him, now he flew away.

Libby looked at the ceiling. She had taken no thought what she should say. That was in the Bible someplace, wasn't it? Well, just the same, the answer was there. Just there. There was no other.

Mrs. Trestrial, concealing the name with which the doctor had stabbed her as he brushed by, came near and leaned

185

over, and put her strong hand on the girl's brow. "Us'll 'ave to get on with it and surprise 'im," she said gently.

"The three of us, eh?" grinned Libby Duncane. "You know, Mrs. Trestrial—" She stopped and screamed lustily and when it was over she took up the sentence. "—it was my ancestors who said that. Funniest thing."

"I know 'oo 'twas," said Mrs. Trestrial, bridling.

CHAPTER TWENTY

ON SURFACE, when the eye adjusted to the scene at the shaft-house it could discern the shape of the artificially lighted area, the intersecting cones and their limits. Above this it could appreciate the night sky. It could plainly see the framework of the shaft itself, towering, and the outline of the long-legged trestle curling off behind it. The eye could divine when the black cable moved on its massive pulley and see the steel rope vibrating where it crossed the road, like a clothesline, to vanish into the hoisting house where, on the huge symmetry of the great reels, it was wound up or let out.

In the small hours the people waited, and every eye knew when the black shimmer on the cable, that signified motion, began.

Mable Marcom was wrapped in a blanket. She sat on the running board of somebody's car. Her niece, Milly, and her sister, Bess, had not returned after the storm. But her brother-in-law, a big-boned heavy man, leaned on the car beside her. He said nothing to her nor she to him. But he was rooted there. He would not leave her.

Luella Pilotti and Anna and Marie wore coats and scarves, and the three sat, knees high, in a dark row on a low bench of boards. Their men were nearby, restless. One would walk away and light a pipe and stare into the sky. Another would follow and speak and come back to stand behind the women.

A little before three o'clock a car came. Alice Beard was in it. Her father drove it. Her mother was beside him. Alice sat alone in the tonneau, just as she always had ever since Pa got a car. Long ago, when a car was a thrilling excitement and people went riding for its own sake with no destination,

187

she had ridden behind them, an appendage, taken along.

Charley had never been able to afford a car.

Half after three, Dickie Trezona slipped into the light. He was muffled up in a mackinaw and he carried a basket of food. Moving, he caught the eye. After he had given his burden to a miner who promptly sent it underground, Dick settled to wait. He was not going home.

The people murmured. Some wondered what Mrs. Trezona was thinking of to let the young boy out at all in this hour. Tongues clicked. Some guessed he stayed without permission, held by the awful drama and the coming climax. Some thought it a shame. Ought not be here. Ought to be home in bed, boy like that. No time, no place for him. Some, meaning well, went to speak to him.

Dickie said his Ma knew where he was. Ma let him come and yes, Ma knew he'd be staying. He seemed sure.

It made no difference, now, to Eedie herself, to the captain—or to Wesley, God knew—which hour of the twenty-four it happened to be. Day and night were out of joint. Time was not a rolling dial but a stretched line, very straight, from a beginning to some kind of ending. So Eedie looked at her son, Dick, who was twelve, and she could not believe that because he was not yet eighteen, he could not run on family time, too. So the hour did not matter.

Nor did the place. For she could not believe, either, that the long thoughts in the little head would be any easier if the head lay on a pillow, now. He had slept a long time and he could not sleep any more. For herself, she would have liked him under the roof, safe. But he would be safe enough. And, if he had the illusion of helping, she knew that was good for him.

So Dick maintained placidly, to all the kind people who inquired, that his Ma knew. Oh yes. Sure, he was sure.

Cyril Varker was stiff and chilly in body and bone. But now that he was here, he kept watching everything. And he did not suggest that they go home.

Home did not do. The little house could not contain his sister, Madeline, in her agony of guilt and foreboding. The

188

only thing to do was get her out of it, bring her here, where she was on stage, and knew it, and must play a part that required some kind of decorum. And here, where, if there was news, news would be told—whether about the men in the mine or anything else that had happened in Thor tonight.

So he had forced her to change to dry clothing and then they had left the hideous little house that shut them in to wonder and look at each other.

Here it was better, much better. And it looked well, too, he thought, for her to be here with the rest. No one guessed any reason but the wrong reason. Even the way she looked, half out of her head, would go down in the story as a wife's anxious devotion. No one would guess she might have killed a man a while ago.

Dr. Hodge's office, the gray frame building, set in shrubbery in the schoolyard corner, was where all of Thor came to be dosed and diagnosed, for he was all the medicine and all the drugstore, too, there was in town. For attention to their teeth the people must go to Pinebend where there were dentists, drugstores, other doctors, and even a small hospital in that larger place.

But Dr. Hodge belonged to Thor, to the Company and the town and here, in this little building, he probed, prescribed, and dispensed, and held his lonely sector, a front line of defense against death and disease. Among other things, emergency was his business.

A long porch at the side had been glassed in and when, during office hours, the waiting room was full, the overflow of patients sat on a long bench against the porch windows. The waiting room was large and square, lined with shelves, and on the shelves the bottles and boxes were arrayed. The whole place smelled like the doctor himself, of mysteries and cleanliness. The inner room held his desk and some apparatus. In an alcove there was a cot. On this cot, after midnight, they had put Henry Duncane.

"What happened?" said Henry, drowsily, some time later. "Lie still."

He and the doctor were alone. The doctor said, "Lost a lot of blood. Head ache? Lie still." He went toward his desk.

"Don't quite know what to do with you," he said pleasantly. "Wait a minute."

He gave a number into the phone. It was Duncane's own number. "Libby?" said Henry in a sharper voice.

"Just a minute . . . Ah," said the doctor, "Mrs. Trestrial? Ah, yes . . . Yes, I see. . . ." He listened a lengthening time.

Henry had a bewildered look as he felt of his right arm with his left hand.

"Yes, I guessed you wouldn't have answered, otherwise . . . Fine . . . Good . . . Oh yes, he's all right. I was in good time . . . Don't speak of it now. No, I think you'd better not . . . I see . . . I'll tell him . . . Be in as soon as I can make it . . . Yes, all right. Thanks."

The doctor heaved a loud gusty sigh. "You have a son," he announced and watched with perennial pleasure for the smile of foolish delight to spread on the man's mouth. "All's well. Your wife is fine. Mrs. Trestrial, God bless her, has everything in hand. No 'urry, she tells me."

"Libby's fine?"

"Fine."

Henry stirred feebly. "What happened to me?"

"Your car turned over. You don't remember? Knock on the head you had wasn't such a bad one. I should think you could remember."

"It's vague," said Henry. "Skidded on the bridge, didn't I?"

"Yes. What made you do that?"

"I don't know. Something moved. Don't know. Say, I didn't hit anything?"

"Nothing but the rail. No person. Nobody there that I know of."

"Might have been a dog. What time is it now?"

"Nearly one."

"So late?"

"Not too late," said Dr. Hodge and he sat down and let his arms dangle.

"Son," said Henry softly. "Boy."

"I . . . er . . . thought we'd better not mention your accident. Told Mrs. Trestrial so."

"Libby doesn't know I turned over? Who called you?"

"Turner. He was in the saloon. Heard it happen. Used his head, too. If you'd lain there another half hour bleeding like a—"

"Cut?"

"Bad one. I've got you patched together. Don't sit up."

Henry sat up, unsteadily. "Feel pretty fair."

"Take it easy."

"By the way, thanks," said Henry. "I might have bled to death, I suppose."

"You well might have. Good thing you picked a spot next to the only night life around here. Meantime, you managed to have a son."

"Wait a minute," said Henry.

"That's right." The doctor watched the intelligence dawn.

"But . . . who was with her?"

"Mrs. Trestrial." The doctor yawned and snapped his fingers. "Now I knew there was something else. She said your phone's ringing like mad. Mrs. Trestrial wants it stopped. Calling you from the mine, she says."

"Then I'd better . . . *Wait* a minute." Henry rubbed his left hand on his hair. "*You left her?*"

"She sent me."

"To *me?*"

"No, no. I couldn't tell her it was *you*." Henry looked stunned. "Fact," the doctor yawned, "I don't want to tell her now. Not what a close call you had. Not yet. Let her rest and be proud of herself. She earned it." He yawned again.

Henry stood up. "I'll stop that phone from ringing," he muttered.

The electric lights had come back long ago, but there was only one low lamp lit in the bedroom now. Libby was not asleep, although she seemed to be. She lay, limp and quiet, in the shadow. It was over.

You forget, she thought. You *do* forget. I'm beginning to forget already. I feel absolutely wonderful and I have a son. The storm is over, too, and I never had time to be afraid. How queer it all was.

She turned her cheek to the clean pillow feeling a sweet

191

animal comfort. I did all right, she reminded herself. Now wasn't that the funniest thing?

She had a full feeling in her heart for the droll little scrap of life, the fantastically tiny baby that was here in the room. In the house, town, world. A boy. Born to trouble, no doubt. Born to attack some stubborn fact, to work and to do. Born to misunderstand his mother and all women, who misunderstood . . .

But it needn't be so, she thought. Men and women are not as alien as men and dogs. There can be a contract.

About Henry and that rumored something she would not wonder now. She would simply do as Henry would do, ask for the information and then meet it, whatever it was. Deal with it when she *knew*, and not sooner. Learn from him. Henry, she mused, may have been trying to do as he thought Libby would do, slide over. Put up a good temporary show. Hold all in a balance, keep everything steady on the surface until this was over.

Well, it was over.

Not over. Started. Across the room in the crib there was a morsel, a scrap of life. She smiled, dozing, lazy.

In the sitting room, Mrs. Trestrial put down the telephone. She came in. "Awake, eh? I told a fib, then."

"I'm not so very wide awake," said Libby fondly.

"Doctor's coming."

"Oh, did the man live?"

" 'E lived."

"I wonder which one he was."

Mrs. Trestrial said, "Oo knows," carelessly. "Going to brush your 'air, child. In a snarl, 'tis. Land. Your man'll be 'ome soon. You'll want to be neat."

"Mrs. Trestrial, my tongue's loose tonight. Before I lose it again, did I tell you you're a darling?"

"So the old woman came in 'andy," sniffed Mrs. Trestrial. "Now, lift your 'ead. There's a good girl."

Libby thought it was a coincidence that Henry came just as the doctor came. They entered her room together. Henry seemed to whirl toward her in breathless haste. He had a wet coat slung around his right shoulder, the sleeves dangling, and he stopped short, a yard away. "I don't want to touch you, Libby. Too filthy and cold. Are you all right, dear?"

"Right as can be," she beamed. "Oh Henry, look at him!"

She lifted on her elbow to watch the man move toward the baby. She couldn't see his face, only the cords of his neck. Dr. Hodge said, "Well, young lady . . ." She shook her head to hush him.

But when Henry turned back to her, although he was smiling, all he said was, "Awful *little*, isn't he?"

She said defensively, "He isn't very old."

"John?"

"After your father."

"John Samuel."

"And mine."

"Or Samuel John?"

"No. John's prettier."

"Listen," said Dr. Hodge, "if you don't mind . . ."

Libby laughed. "He wants to see whether I survived."

"Looks like you did, all right." Henry's voice was strange. "You must have been pretty scared."

"No," she said. "No, it was funny."

He seemed to totter. He said so quickly that it sounded like pure impatience, "Libby, do you need me now?"

"What?"

"They want me. At the mine."

"Oh," she said, "for heaven's sakes."

"I'm going to throw him out anyway," said Dr. Hodge, "if you please."

"All right, Henry. Don't lose all your sleep."

"You go to sleep."

"All right." Their eyes clung and then drew apart.

"Change those clothes first, Duncane," the doctor said in a voice of threat. "Now, Ma'am . . ."

Henry reeled out of the bedroom and leaned on the stair post. Mrs. Trestrial hurried to support him.

"Doctor doesn't want her to know . . ."

"You're a lucky man, Mr. Duncane."

He gave her a dark look, which she fathomed. She bridled. "Glad I was 'andy."

193

But she was not fooled. Her wise eyes saw a physically weakened, a stunned and confused young man, who was trying to think simply about things that were complicated. He was trying to push on and do what he ought, poor lad, and was more upset about them in the mine than he'd let on and bound he'd help. Not knowing quite where he was on this night when life and death were waltzing around him in the town of Thor.

Oh, he was grateful to Ellen Trestrial, all right, but not because she stayed with the girl in her need. No, for he knew as well as she that there had never been the smallest possibility that she could have done anything else.

Ah, trying to think, simple, poor man, she thought, about the girl, per'aps, who runs from the thunder and 'as squabbles with the 'ired girl, but lets the doctor go, at the last, and makes a joke of survivin'. 'E can't figure out the woman, or any woman, in one of 'is neat written—what do they call 'em?—h'equasions. None but me. I've done naught but what's simple. Been a neighbor and decent. So 'e thinks 'e understands me, poor lad.

Her curls bounced as she nodded wisely. "Get you dry," said she. "I suppose you must go, if you're wanted."

But Libby was thinking with rueful mirth, Isn't that just like Henry? None of this falling on the knees before the miracle. No worshiping tears for the little mother. Not even a kiss. "Little, isn't he? Survived, eh? Well, busy, good-by."

"Doctor," she said, "isn't anything ever what we expected in this world?"

"What's the matter?" He teased her. "Better or worse?"

Libby couldn't say. Could not say.

When the men were gone and the house was quiet, Libby said pensively, "More trouble? Why do they want him at the mine, I wonder?"

"To talk on that there pipe," said Mrs. Trestrial.

"Pipe? Oh, I just about forgot. . . . Oh no, those poor people. Not still buried down there!" Libby was puzzled and not sure why.

Mrs. Trestrial looked at the wall. "They be near, so 'e said. I don't know what 'twas." She shook her curls. Walked to

194

the crib and looked over. "'Is Lordship's sleeping sweet again."

"That poor Mrs. Cole," murmured Libby. "And she has no children."

"Nor 'as Mable Marcom. Nor Alice Beard. Miz Pilotti, though, 'as four."

"She's the lucky one."

"So she is," said Mrs. Trestrial.

"Am I going to pass out?" Henry asked coolly.

"Probably not." The doctor grumbled. "I'd never advise this, mind. I'm taking you up there because you've got no car and I wouldn't let you drive it if you did. But I'm not saying it's the healthiest idea in the world."

"Little enough I can do. It seems they hear me."

"All right," said the doctor testily. He understood, of course. "Don't run around or do any jumping. Try to lean, man. I've had enough trouble with you for one night."

"Will you stay up there, Doctor?"

"No. Home. Sleep."

Henry nodded. He understood perfectly.

People were there around the shafthouse. Now that the storm was over they had come sifting back to stand along the margin of light on the wet ground, in the cool drenched air. Not many. But the drama would not play to an empty house, and those who watched in this uncanny hour were a quality audience, for they did so with double intensity.

The word was that the rescuers were so deep in, now, they must move with a hard-headed, disciplined delicacy that made them slower and slower just when the impulse of the heart most screamed for speed.

It was not yet known whether what they were trying to do was possible.

Henry Duncane got out of the doctor's car and started slowly towards the cage. Moving, he caught the eye. The doctor took it upon himself to lean out and beckon a man who came quickly to listen to him. He was a miner, waiting and hoping to be called to relieve a man below. Smartly, he stepped to a place beside Duncane. "Doc says I should go down with you."

"Thanks, Uren, but I'm all right." Henry was forced to turn, and now he was able to see, across the lighted roadway, a certain Ford where a man and a woman were sitting. For a moment he stood still, peering. Then Henry lifted his left hand, as if some magic had roused him. "Who is that?"

"Miz Cole," said James Uren, "Miz Marcom, she's here too. But they took Miz Beard home."

They could see the woman in that car bend over suddenly as if the lift of Henry's hand had tripped a trigger. Perhaps she burst into weeping. It was hard to tell.

Duncane said in a voice of tight sorrow, "Let's go."

"Pity to see that," said Uren as the cage dropped them. "Miz Trezona don't come here at all. Miz Pilotti went with the priest when it stormed. Pretty hard on the women."

Henry said nothing. His cheek trembled where he was biting it inside. "You don't feel so good, Mr. Duncane?"

"Feel thick-headed," said Henry. "Been a night."

"You don't feel so good," said the man, positively.

Underground, at the pipe-end, the faces lifted. Fred Davies was there.

"Listen," he cried, leaping up. "We can't figure it out. They're tapping, slow. Listen to it, Duncane, will you? What does that mean?"

Henry sank down.

Davies saw the white-wrapped arm under the dangling coat. "What happened to him?"

"Doc brought him, said he lost a lot of blood. Said somebody should get him home soon."

"I'll see he gets a ride home," offered Davies at once.

"Say, if you'll do that . . ." Uren was suddenly on needles to go. "It might be I'm needed."

"Get along, then. I'll take care of him."

Henry said sharply, "Stop that talking, will you?"

On the pipe the sound came. Tap tap tap tap, evenly, monotonously, with no break and no spacing. Just the slow dreary tap tap tap tap, repeating and continuing. "Hear it?" Davies squatted.

Henry said, "Only one thing I can say that they *get*. Wait, I'll try it."

So the long vowels went moaning, "HOW . . . MANY . . . MEN . . . ALIVE?" The group of five or six around the pipe shivered and bent close. They heard the tapping seem to stumble and stutter, and then it stopped.

"HOW . . . MANY . . . MEN . . . ALIVE?"

Tap.

At last Davies looked up into Duncane's face. "Better let them know, eh? I mean those digging."

"I'll go." Somebody went.

Henry leaned on the wall and closed his eyes.

"Say, you better let me get you home." Davies now seemed to dance on coals.

"I'm all right."

"Won't be long, now." Davies looked over his shoulder down the long reaches of the tunnel. "In a minute they ought to be able to hear him from where they've got in. Can tell, then."

"We can wait."

"You feel all right?"

"Fine. I'd like to wait."

"One man left," Davies mourned, "and the old boy's worked so hard."

"Trezona?"

"Him, I mean. Yes."

"Used his brain?"

"Broke his heart, that he's lost four of them."

"Tough."

"Any four of them," Davies insisted, somberly.

"What I said. He's tough." Henry closed his eyes again.

"I . . . can't stay away from it," Davies confessed. "I never saw this before. Listen, if I go back where they are . . ."

"Go ahead."

"Sure you're O.K.?"

"O.K."

"Then I'll come back and help you get home. Don't move."

"Told you, I want to wait."

Davies began to run.

Henry Duncane sat still with his left hand touching the cold gritty pipe as if his fingers lay on that lonely pulse that beat and repeated monotonously. Tap tap tap tap, with no break.

"Captain may 'ave lost 'is boy," somebody said.

"I have a boy."

"No kidding, Mr. Duncane? Say!" A little singing pleasure lifted all their hearts and brightened their voices.

CHAPTER TWENTY-ONE

WHEN the doctor drove up and Henry Duncane got out, alive, and when, turning as he had, he'd seemed to see her and lift his hand, Madeline collapsed. It was pure relief.

Ever since, she had been too relaxed and too cheerful. Cyril had warned her more than once, "All right, you're lucky. He wasn't hurt and he doesn't know and you've skinned out of that one. All right. But take that look off. Remember where you are. Please."

"I know where I am," she caroled.

"Not so *happy*."

"I know, though." She shifted down until her head lay on the seat back. She closed her eyes. It's all right, she thought. Probably Arthur is gone and that means I am free. If he's alive, so much the better for Arthur. It won't make a difference. I'll skin out of that one, too. And if Henry Duncane could not help but wave his hand to me . . . Ah, the rest will go well. The rest will be easy. And she painted the picture on her eyelids: his hand lifting, greeting her alone, indiscreetly, uncontrollably.

How beautiful she must have looked, early in the evening, like an angel in the storm, and all he could know was her longing to be near him. The truth, she thought, complacently. The truth, after all.

"Be a good idea," grumbled Cyril, "if you did lie low. Look asleep, can't you?"

So, dreaming, she looked asleep. And when a man approached with the news that ran so bitterly on that pipe, (One, now. Only one man left, alone, down there.) Cyril had hushed him. He would tell Mrs. Cole, he whispered, all in good time.

"Poor thing."

"Ssh. Been half crazy. Now, let her be."

The man drew off and Cyril sat back. She did not open her eyes. But she had heard the news plainly, and he knew she had heard it. Nothing to say. Cyril peered about. Who prayed for his own, now? Did anyone dare? He thought, if I ever prayed, I'd dare, for Trezona. And then he caught himself wincing superstitiously. No, no. For Arthur, poor pushing Arthur, pushed to this.

Down below the striving men crept, pried, balanced, prayed, and dared not blow breath. Near morning, although they did not know what morning was any more, they heard a voice. And they were led. Delicately they groped. The entrance they were spinning like a thread in the hard dark touched on the place they were seeking and became the exit from it.

The news spiraled and blew upward and, above ground, softly exploded. Cyril saw the explosive rippling outward of the news. It was perfectly visible. "They're through!"

Madeline sat up. "How do you know?"

Now she thought of that one man. Still alive. All of a sudden she knew it was Arthur. Arthur, the stubborn, the single-tracked. Arthur, pounding and nagging at staying alive, would be the one to do it. Why, he would wear death itself out. All of a sudden she saw the look on his forehead and his red eyes, and she heard his whine, and she was certain that he would come up out of the ground, knowing everything. Charley Beard beside him for hours. Things she had said that she shouldn't have said and the time, all this time, to remember them. He would fix on her those terrible eyes . . .

She cried out and in panic hid her face on Cyril's coat. "No! I don't want to know!"

"Ssh." He held her head tightly. "All right. Be quiet. I won't let them tell you. I'll tell you. Don't look, then. Don't look. Don't listen. Take a while."

But Cyril looked, eyes straining from their sockets. His

heart was beating heavily, not fast, but with force. It banged in the flat frail cage of his chest.

He watched everything. Once a man started toward them. Quickly, Cyril motioned him back, nodding, nodding "I understand." For he guessed. He thought he knew.

No man was alive. Not any.

Never mind telling her now. Time enough. He had to see this.

The cage came up. Some weary men got off and were surrounded. Cyril held his sister's dark head and she clung to him, breathing deeply in the dark fold of his coat. The cage went down with more men, fresh men.

The doctor's car came again. The big black car of the superintendent pulled up and stopped in the roadway, and Mr. McKeever himself had come. He went down.

The sky was lighter. After a time all the people saw the cables slipping on the spool again, running in the air. Slowly the cage was coming up, more slowly than it had come yet.

On stretchers the lost men lay. On their biers. Cyril saw everything in the gray and yellow light. Everything was sharp and clear to his staring eyes. He saw Mabel Marcom rise to her feet and cast off the dark blanket. It fell away, and she moved from its warm shell and walked, without shivering, to the bier. He saw her touch old Elisha Marcom's brow in a gesture of infinite tenderness, for a moment—as sweet a sight as a Madonna. Then she threw off the tenderness. It fell away. Sternly, she marshaled her strength and pulled herself high.

He saw Alice Beard get out of the tonneau and fling out both hands to keep her parents behind her, saw her walk alone to the bier where her husband was lying with his boots up beneath the long covering coat. Saw her lift up her face to the hill and the sky and turn and walk back again, where caressing hands would have received her had she not, so steadily, climbed by herself into the little car once more. He saw her sitting there, alone, quiet, looking small, but not childish.

He saw the priest praying and the Pilottis wheel with him away from the body of Benevenuto. Saw the peace fall on them and then fall into the rhythm of their faith and move away in a procession, as if they had music.

And Cyril felt an explosion in his breast. He began to cry. He could not see for the hot gush of his tears.

By God, he cried in his head, they're all licked before they start! All human beings! By God, they'll all die and they know it. By God, how they take it! How they go ahead anyhow. How they *live*, and when death comes they take it and the rest go and *live*. Ah, the poor damned sods, the nervy little bastards, the doomed and indomitable! By God, they deserve something! They can be loved! For the gallant lost, they are, who've got the crust to live as if they were not. And take that. Take *life*, which is lovely and goes, but they have it! They have it!

He licked salt with his tongue. He was sobbing.

After a moment, his astonishment began to prevail and he felt himself mending and drawing together. He could see again and he knew the cage had come up once more.

And they carried off two stretchers. And one was a bier and one was not, for the man who lay on it raised head on neck.

And he saw something fly out of the crowding people. Like thistledown, it flew away. Scarcely touching the hill. Just a boy, running. Dickie Trezona went flying, floating up over the hillside.

Eedie was at the parlor window and when she saw him coming, running as fast as ever he could, her heart leaped and she cried, "Darithy!" And the cry was joyful. For a small boy with very good news has wings to fly home with it.

Cyril said, bluntly, "Madeline, he's dead. I'd better go."

Her shoulders shuddered and seemed to cave down. He put her aside, laid her head down on the leather. And he got out of the car and walked toward the place where poor Arthur lay. The skin of Cyril's face felt brittle where the tears had dried.

"Young Trezona says he was O.K. 'till the rescue tunnel fell. Ah, too bad, Mr. Varker. Trezona says he was real brave."

Cyril kept nodding. Arthur was settled. He was a hero, after all. He would not veer again. Someone drew the coat over the face. Someone now wanted to discuss arrangements. Cyril stood in the pale dawn, hat to his breast, head down, eyes turned up to see, salt in the eye corners.

He saw Captain Trezona coming off the cage, rigid, spare, moving as if he were borne by the crowd around him. They were putting Wesley into an ambulance there, yards away. The doctor was with him. The captain did not look toward his living son.

He was surrounded by miners. Young Davies was there, and a man, not in oilskins, but a suit. Yes, Henry Duncane. All these bent their heads. The surge of people towards this group was stilled, for the captain dragged the miner's hat off his head, looked fiercely at the sky and the first tendrils of morning, and began to speak aloud, as was his habit, to the Lord.

Cyril could hear as well as anyone the melody of faith and sorrow. A lament for the brave dead, a recommendation of souls.

But he did not pray, not he. He was thinking furiously and his eyes were dry. This damned indomitable old man, this towering hero . . . Oh no, if he is told, I'm done! I'm beaten! Little he'll care what people would say, nor will he spare himself anything. He'll never keep it quiet. No, no. He'll ask God and what will his God tell him? Your son, Wesley, is a sinner. *And so is Cyril Varker, the wicked usurer!* He'll run me out of town.

Cyril flung up his head and slipped behind the praying undertaker's man and around the praying people toward that ambulance. The boy lay on the stretcher, pale, young, bubbling, glad to be alive.

"Glad to see you," said Cyril huskily.

"Thanks. Thanks." Every breath was thanks, Cyril could see.

Cyril bent down, achieving privacy. "I don't want you to think about that debt to me," he said in a low voice in the boy's ear. "Forget it, please."

"Pa will pay," said Wesley Trezona.

"No. He doesn't need to know about it."

Wesley looked at him from a place far, far away. "Ma would have told him already, Mr. Varker." The boy smiled. "You'll have it by Saturday, Mr. Varker." The boy tried to be solemn. "Sorry about Cole. He . . . maybe you'd like to tell his wife . . . he was fine."

"Was he?" said Cyril dully. "I'll tell her. Thanks, Trezona." Cyril turned on his heel. It was odd and pathetic that the boy didn't know this was Saturday. It was odd and pathetic that Arthur Cole, in the legend, would be forever fine. It was odd and pathetic, in a way, that he, Cyril, could give no mercy.

He ground his teeth. "She beat me. That woman. Now how did she do it? She'd give me my due. Well, at least I'm bright enough to see it. Made a mistake. Shouldn't have got mixed up with these . . ." He heard the captain's deep Amen.

A woman said sharply, "Look out! He'll fall!"

Cyril turned. The captain was twenty years older in one fading. " 'Twas hard," someone murmured. "Hard, hard."

But Cyril thought: no, not so. How clear and easy everything must be for that old man! It was odd and pathetic, too, that now he prayed . . . or he wished, whatever it was . . . that the old hero, in his honorable fatigue, could be spared the cruel and stinging blow that was to come to him. Who could give mercy, now? Not Cyril. Not he.

The captain put his hat on and then they were helping him toward the ambulance. Cyril kept nodding now, finishing the arrangements. They would take Arthur away. Not to the little house, ever again. Better so. The people, released to motion, churned and hesitated, but would soon disperse. Cyril pushed through them, at last, back to the car.

Madeline Cole had not moved at all, but lay where he'd left her. He peered down at her. "Everything's taken care of," he said heavily. "We can go."

"Not yet," she said. She looked as beautiful as he had ever seen her, lying there. Her eyes were open wide, soft and gray, staring at the sky.

Cyril looked back into the milling crowd and saw among them Henry Duncane.

"He'll come," she said.

CHAPTER TWENTY-TWO

THE day was opening, gold on gray. The sun was rising. The whole town of Thor was released to motion, and had not known, until now, how motionless it had been.

Early as it was, people were astir. Kitchen fires were kindled. Phones rang. Children crept out to dip their feet in the dew and listen to cock's crow, bird's song.

Arrangements were being made. There must be services for the dead. But this was motion.

According to custom, no mining would be done at West Thor mine until after the funerals had taken place. East Thor, of course, continued. And pumps ran. Shovels would rant and snort and carry all day. Repairs got under way at the Falls.

George McKeever, who had come home to shave, to drop into the routine of another day, made ready to descend for his regular breakfast. From his window he could see Thor Lake, dimpling demurely, pale blue beneath the breaking light, pretty and dangerous.

Mrs. McKeever moved quietly, not to disturb his thoughts. His face, she observed, was still and sad. Oh, he felt this.

"Too bad," he sighed, at last. "Still, might have been worse."

"What we can always say," she murmured. "Was there any negligence, George?"

"No. No, none we can see. No one can say so. These things happen," he murmured sadly. "We haven't done too badly in these mines."

For, just as someone must examine and determine whether there was, here, any hint for the future, anything to be learned or used, someone must also consider the record, the long past, and balance the achievement against the losses. Although he knew, and everyone knew the Company was operating to get the ore out and, although there had been many improvements through the years, there was not yet, and might never be such a thing as perfect safety in this job.

"Considering the normal risks," he murmured, "in fact, we haven't done too badly. It's bad when it comes. Well, we'll have to get on." Now, in his head ran the losses. Trouble in terms of time, in terms of money, in terms of production. All these, he thought sadly, were facts, too, and someone must consider them and add them up.

He slipped an arm around her shoulders, and they went downstairs.

Sitting at the table, Mrs. McKeever wondered why. Why must they get on? She thought of the ore that would yet be torn out of the earth, and come up, and fall into the cars, and ride the long water, and meet, in the mills, the fires and the manipulations of men, until it was iron. And then steel, which men demanded, men would have it, so they would get it.

She sighed and picked up a pancake turner to slip under the eggs and the bacon. Its thin steel shaft and its supple blade were strong and handy.

At the Gilchrists' Alex was drinking black coffee. "No. No cereal, Marianne. Couldn't touch it. Not a thing. No."

"So sensitive," she murmured. "Alex, must you go off?"

"Better show up." There was an uneasy question in his glance at her.

"You don't look well," she said promptly.

"I'm not." He was grateful. "You know how it hits me."

"I know."

"Some people," he grumbled, ". . . take Captain Trezona. Man like that doesn't feel it. No physical effect, I mean. Iron stomach." He wore his smile, now, his pitying smile.

"Oh, well," she said, "unintellectual people are lucky, in a way."

He took a piece of toast, after all.

She said, "I wonder what I could take down to Elizabeth

Duncane for the baby." He grunted. Now her eyes were sly and appealing. "I'd like to make it something really nice, Alex. Expensive."

"Well," he said, "why not? Within limits."

Her face cleared and she nodded. Silver, she thought. Maybe gold.

Celestina had been to church, slipping into the holy place before dawn. Now, still very early, she walked slowly around the double corners of the center of Thor and she went up the street to Duncane's.

"My mother said to come," she faltered, as Mrs. Trestrial's long face looked out at the kitchen door, "and ask. We don't know if I'm wanted."

"Come you in. You can wash up 'ere. I see no 'arm in that." The old woman looked weary.

"Miz Trestrial . . ."

"Eh?"

"I'm glad about Wesley." Celestina spoke shyly. "If you see him, maybe you would tell him I am?"

"Tell 'im yourself!" Mrs. Trestrial snapped.

"I probably won't see him," Celestina said placidly.

Mrs. Trestrial's shrewd eyes softened. "Like to see baby, eh?"

"Oh, yeh . . ."

"Come along."

Libby Duncane was awake. She was wearing a dainty bed-jacket and a ribbon, to match, pulled her pale hair back cleanly from her face. She was immaculate. The whole bed-room was fragrant with her bath powder. "Oh, Celestina. Good morning."

"Good morning, ma'am."

"Wants to see baby," said Mrs. Trestrial briskly.

"Of course."

All three women made sounds like purring. The atmos-phere among the three of them was warmer afterwards.

Celestina said, fidgeting, "I didn't know if I was to come back, ma'am. He didn't say." Her eyes implored.

"Mrs. Trestrial must be so tired," Libby said.

Mrs. Trestrial snorted. Tired? Yes, she was. If the girl

would tidy up the kitchen, then, she'd 'ave a nice lie-down till nurse come. She vanished.

"She won't leave me," Libby said fondly. "I'm glad you are here to help her. There is a nurse coming later."

Celestina said, shyly, "You look nice, ma'am."

"Thank you. I suppose you're happy," said Libby gently, "that Wesley Trezona was saved. You were fond of him, I know."

"Yeh." Celestina's dark eyes fell. "Nothing'll come of it, though. I mean . . . nothing . . ."

"Why do you say that, Celestina?"

"Oh, I don't know."

But Libby, looking at her, thought she knew. The church, for one thing, and the blood, and the temperament, and a whole back-log of tradition and mode of thought. As well imagine Mrs. Trestrial with a Latin lover!

"I suppose you're wise," she murmured. "I suppose you couldn't have been in love at all."

"Not *really*," said Celestina, quickly. Their eyes caught and the girl's lips parted. "Nothing comes of it lots of times. I mean, lots of times."

Libby said, quickly and rather sternly, "Now you go help. There must be such a lot to do. Mr. Duncane will want a big breakfast, I imagine."

Where is he? asked Celestina's eyes. Where he is or why, said Libby's, is not for you to ask or tell me. I am willing to try to understand you and even to like you. But we are not pals and never can be. "Quick as you can," she said aloud.

Celestina said, with an air of relief, "Yes, ma'am," and she went quietly away.

Libby lay back. Nothing comes of it, lots of times. What kind of wisdom was that?

Henry had phoned the news half an hour ago. Said he'd be a half an hour yet. He was later than that, already. It was no use. She could not help remarking that Madeline Cole was a widow this morning.

I don't know much about her, Libby mused. She's beautiful, that I've seen. Mrs. Gilchrist says "Flies to honey," but Mrs. Gilchrist is no fountain of truth or discernment. Mrs. Gilchrist is pretty phony.

So have I been.

Maybe Madeline Cole is not. Maybe that's what offends the Gilchrist kind. Henry will know. Maybe, in that, she and Henry are alike. Yet I'm certain, Libby thought. Knowing and granting all the differences, I *am* certain that in some deep and most important way, it's Henry and I who are alike.

As she mused, it came serenely into her mind that Henry would not run out on the baby. And I? she wondered. What must I do?

It didn't occur to her that she might ask her mother.

She lay puzzling, listening for his car. She could hear birds singing, Celestina, distantly, doing dishes, and, from the sitting room, a gentle snore. From the crib a tiny cry tensed her, but soon ceased.

She thought, Henry will do the deciding. I'll have nothing to say about it. He won't expect me to say. He won't even ask me. He thinks no one should ever lean. That's why he throws me to stand on my own feet, but he makes a mistake. He stands too much alone.

Morning crept over the hill. Wesley Trezona, dirty, smelling of the mine, lay on the black couch in the dining room at home. Lay awkwardly, for he was trying to lie on his stomach and the couch was designed with a buffalo hump at one end for the head. But he told the doctor he didn't think he would lie on his back for a year, probably.

Captain Trezona had fallen into his Morris chair. He was stained and reeking of the mine. Dorothy fluttered all around, beaming and beaming. Dick was on the floor and once, quite unknown to himself, he patted his big brother's temple with his grubby hand. Eedie was not conscious of what she did, whether she stood or sat or moved or was still. She was disembodied.

The doctor had just left. Wesley was fine. Black and blue across his thigh. It was nothing.

They would bustle and wash and feed in a moment, but not just yet. Now came the private time. The captain and Eedie, too, had mourned aloud and in their hearts for those lost. But now, in all decency and right, came the family thanksgiving, which was due for the salvation of their own.

The first thing Pa said was, "I'll 'ave the Bible, Darithy."
"Yes, Pa."
Wesley rolled on his side. "Pa . . ."
"Eh?"
"Before you read . . ."
Eedie knew. Now she felt the chair hit the back of her
legs. Well, God had them both in His hands. She sat down
quietly.
"Did Ma tell you?"
She said, "No, Wesley."
Wesley did not hesitate. "Pa, last April I took a drink or
two one night in the saloon. Went joy-riding in Olsen's car.
Car hit the bridge and me driving. Had to pay damages.
Scared to tell you, so borrowed the money. Got in a mess.
Played cards, trying to get money to pay, and lost more. Now
I owe three hundred dollars to Mr. Varker. Will you pay
him, Pa? It's due today. And let me pay you in time?"
The captain's eyes were shocked and very blue in his
smeared face. Eedie prayed. Pa said, brittlely. "If you h'owe
it, it must be paid."
"I got to say this," Wesley went on rapidly. (So different
he sounds, his mother thought, so quick and hard. This was
no frightened, suffering, conscience-sick boy.) "Look, Pa,
before you read . . . Pilotti was Catholic and I heard him
die. Calling on saints and go-betweens. That's all right, too.
I'm sure 'twas the same God, anyhow. But *you* don't need a
go-between. Eh, Pa? And you try to teach us. A day comes,"
Wesley said, "I need no go-between, either. Not even you."
The captain blinked.
"I did wrong and God knows I know it," said Wesley,
stretching and easing his body. Now his voice was fading,
shyly. "Eh, Pa? I've prayed Him to let you take it easy, Pa.
If you can't, then that's the way it is. So . . ." faintly, "Pa,
will you read?"
The children were still. Pa blinked a time or two. Then Pa
took the Bible. His hands trembled. "Worn out," Eedie
thought, tender and indignant. "So long, so 'ard, 'e'd been
working. And then to lose four of them and now to 'ear what
must 'urt 'im so." And she thought, " 'E's the worse off of

the two of them. Lord, give 'im leave to be brief with You this morning. Let me get 'im soon to 'is clean bed."

Pa would do right, of course, whatever he chose to read from the Book, long or short, thunder or sorrow. Eedie bent her head.

"Mither?"

"Yes, Fayther?"

"You 'eard this before?"

" 'E was that troubled about it," she said placidly, " 'e told me."

The captain opened the Book. But he took no time to find the place. He searched in his mind for the Word. When his voice began it was sonorous and reverent, as always.

"And when he cometh 'ome," the captain said, " 'e calleth together 'is friends and neighbors, saying unto them, Rejoice with me; for H'i 'ave found my sheep which was lost.

"H'i say unto you that likewise joy shall be in 'eaven . . ." The voice stopped, although the lips moved on. Not a one of them but knew the passage. Eedie in joy and impatience said, firmly, "Amen. Amen."

"Now that'll do. Surely 'E knows 'ow it goes on." She jumped up. "And now a wash and a bite and a rest for you men, and I'll 'ave no sauce from ayther."

Her face twinkled and sparkled and she saw Wesley's twinkling and sparkling, too, and she knew, thankfully, that so sunny and sweet was his nature, he could bear to be freely forgiven, which is a thing not all natures can bear.

"Eedie, my dear," the captain said, lovingly, for his tired eyes saw, first, that his son had grown and left his hand for God's, and also that his wife, Edith, had forgiven the boy his sins so simply and quickly and easily with the next beat of her heart that she knew nothing whatever about it. "I fear your men's a starvin' weary lot this morning," the captain said.

"And so is Darithy, too." Dick was quite serious. They all looked at him, at first in surprise. Then Eedie cried, in delight, "Now, Darithy must 'elp me see to the *three* of you men, eh? Is that it?"

And so, still laughing, she took the Bible from Pa's torn, tired hands, and Dorothy ran to pour his tea.

CHAPTER TWENTY-THREE

CYRIL stood on the ground answering her questions.

She had rubbed a handkerchief over her face and now she was sitting up, tilting her face to him, making believe she was inquiring what the arrangements were that he had made. He was compelled, pressed into the part, although he knew it was all pretense, this absorbed conversation. It was an excuse for them not to go yet, but to wait until he came.

He was coming.

Cyril could see with his eye's corner young Fred Davies standing, like a footman, by Will Pascoe's car. Will was like a chauffeur, waiting. The whole equipage waited for Henry Duncane, who must first come walking this way.

She turned, gracefully and naturally, and she opened her lovely eyes as if she would let him read to the bottom of her soul.

"I'm sorry about this," he began, with the identical phrase as before. He looked ill. "They did all they could."

She murmured, "Ah, Henry, I know that." Cyril thought, she turns herself on like a light bulb. She sets the current flowing. His knuckles dug into his own side.

"You'll be alone, now," said Henry Duncane.

"Alone," she agreed, flutingly sad. But she put her hand on the car's edge, where his already was, and kept offering him the depth of her eyes.

"Will you tell me one thing?"

She blinked.

"Had you told him?"

"Told him what?" She didn't know what he meant exactly. "About . . . us?" she said.

Cyril shuddered and cast his eyes down.

Henry said, precisely, "Had you told him that you wanted a divorce?"

Her head trembled a negative.

Henry put his left palm to his cheek and pushed the flesh. "I'm glad of that, I suppose." He looked at her piercingly. "Did you change your mind?"

"Ah, no . . . I hadn't . . . couldn't . . . never can . . ." Her dark head went bending and she was swaying a little closer.

"Don't . . ." she said, and her face came up, "don't let this come between . . ."

(Words, hideous enough, whispered in close darkness, now said aloud in the light of morning. Cyril felt sick.)

Henry stepped back. "There's no contract, Mrs. Cole, between you and me." The voice was clear and cold and there was no possible way to misunderstand one syllable of what it was saying. The light, or whatever it was, the magnetism in Madeline flickered.

"I want you to understand that," Henry said crisply, "and I don't mind a witness."

"I understand. I know. You can't."

"Not that I can't," said Henry brutally. "I don't want to."

Cyril heard his own thin angry snarl, "Don't worry, Duncane. My sister and I will be leaving this town."

Duncane said quietly, "Good idea. It may be easier for her somewhere else."

He turned his back to walk away.

Madeline said in a broken murmur, "I can't help it if Arthur died. *I* didn't do it." She began to cry.

Cyril was seething. He darted around the car's nose. There were not many people around, almost none now. He dared catch at Henry Duncane. He said fiercely, "I don't know what was going on but I'm going to know. Duncane, what d'you mean about a contract?"

Henry eyed him steadily. "You want me to tell you what I meant?" His cold eyes bore down.

"I insist on your telling me." Cyril was wild. "If that was a dirty crack you took at my sister . . ."

"No crack," said Henry, distantly.

"Then what was it? What have you been promising?"

"Exactly nothing. That's what I say."

213

"I don't like the insulting way you say it."

Henry said icily, "Let go."

"What d'you mean, easier for *her*? You stuck-up . . ." Cyril didn't understand what had got into him to be breaking all the rules he lived by. ". . . simple-minded prig!" he finished furiously.

"Maybe," said Henry dangerously, "I'd better tell you what I was thinking. In my simple-minded way. She sees life and death for somebody else in terms of herself. And there's something in that that's like an animal. Now I *have* insulted her. Well?"

Cyril took a step back. His thin cheeks burned. "You're wrong. You don't know the facts."

This held Henry listening.

"She would have stayed," said Cyril. "I was the one who dragged her away. I still think I was wise. But you can't blame her for what I chose to do. And no insults of any kind are necessary." Cyril looked as haughty as he could. "Good-by to you, Duncane."

"Stayed where?" said Henry.

"With you, last night."

"Last night? When?"

"When your car turned . . ."

"Then?" said Henry in pure surprise. "Was she there?"

Cyril's face flamed and his tongue stung. "What . . . what do you mean, then? I thought you meant *your* life. We knew, you see . . . we knew you'd be found. It wasn't . . ." He had never been more uncomfortable in all his life.

Henry said, distantly, his eyes on the hills, "Was I the only one thinking about Arthur Cole?"

When his eyes came to Cyril's, Cyril's fell. "She was in a spot," he muttered. "You have to allow . . ."

Henry's voice slashed into that muttering confusion. "I think good-by will cover everything," he said sadly. He walked away.

Fred Davies fretted on the way down the hill. "I should have seen to it that you got out of there a lot sooner. You feel all right?"

"All right. Sure."

"You don't look it. Say, how *did* that happen?"

"This? Skid. Windshield. Glass."

"Pretty slippery last night," called Pascoe over his shoulder. "Bad night."

"I thought I had to avoid something in the road."

"Tried to stop, eh? What was it? Dog?"

"Don't know what it was. Lot I'll never know."

The men did not seek to pry into Henry's mood of sad humility. "Say," Fred thought he changed the subject, "meant to ask you. What was eating Varker, back there?"

"Thought I insulted his sister."

Fred was silent a moment. "Well . . ." he began and stopped. The muscles of Henry's jaw moved. He had a bad taste in his mouth. Had talked too much. Been womanish. He wished he had kept to a simple good-by.

Fred said, mildly, "They're a pair."

The car waltzed around the corner.

"Thanks, Pascoe. Thanks a lot, Fred." Henry got out and drew, a little reluctantly, away from the men.

He was still wearing his coat like a cape, sleeves dangling, which was unlike him, and Libby thought she had never seen him look so wretchedly tired. He said, almost nervously, "You look fine. Sorry I had to be away so long. The whole night, as it turned out."

"Henry, I sent a wire to mother."

"I should have done that," he said, guiltily. "Sorry."

His air of nervous melancholy disturbed her. "I slept," she said. "Henry, I know, you must feel sad."

"Sad?" He straightened his back.

"For those four men. And their families." His eyes flickered as if she surprised him. "I suppose the whole town feels sad," she went on.

"Yes. Although they got the one out. And it's over." He sat down on the bed.

"You look awful. Can you sleep now?"

"I think so." His head moved as if to lead his weary body.

She said clearly, "What will Madeline Cole do, Henry?"

He turned his face. "She's leaving town."

215

"Oh, did you speak to her?" The lace that fell so daintily and frivolously along her throat was quivering.

"I said good-by."

"Henry, did you and she . . ."—stillness fell over him—". . . meet under Celestina's window?"

He said, too weary and sad to play any unnatural game of evasion, "Yes, Libby. And once or twice before."

"She is in love with you?"

"Said so." He rubbed his face. "I don't know."

"You'll have to tell me more about it, Henry." Her voice was calm.

Henry said, blindly, "Whatever you tell yourself, the fact is, you're pretty damned excited. Tempted to think you are responsible. Tempted to think one jump of your pulse makes you guilty and responsible. So then you are obliged . . . to someone so beautiful and honest. Now I don't know how honest it was. I guess I insulted her this morning."

His wife said soberly, "I'll bet you did."

He said, vaguely surprised, "You do?"

But she veered. "Did you fix the trouble?"

"What trouble?"

"The trouble at the Falls?"

"Of course," he said, astonished. She smiled. "What are you smiling at?"

"At what I know about you," she murmured.

He turned toward her so sharply that his coat fell open. "Well . . ." she began in a brisk and practical tone. Then her hand darted. "Henry! What's the matter with your arm?"

He caught her hand before it could touch the dirty bandage. "Nothing to fuss about, Libby. Accident. I kinda smashed up the car, last night."

She looked at him in pure alarm. "Henry! Don't ever not tell me! I can bear to know. Honest, I can! Henry, if I don't know what's going on, how can I be with you? It isn't fair! Don't smile! Henry!"

"I survived," he said lightly. He *was* smiling.

Their eyes met. And, with a kind of click, something opened, something happened. The stiff line of his spine broke and began to relax. Into her mind, at the same time, poured a multitude of urgencies. He must wash. Celestina must be ready to serve his breakfast and he must eat it and go to bed. Must have Celestina make up the bed upstairs so the baby won't disturb him. And they must have something light but nourishing, that can go on a tray, at noon. And for supper something heartier. There's his suit to be cleaned and better order soap—it's nearly out—and get in a laundress on account of the baby and, when the doctor comes, he must look at that arm.

She cried to herself, "This house is a mess!" The current of life roared through her head. "I must get at those chairs just as soon as I can. Oh, I'll make and I'll do. There's the garden and a fenced place for the baby. He must be in the sun. Oh, I can't lie around. There's so much . . ."

"Better get on . . ." Henry sighed, and she nodded.

Cyril's Ford climbed up, it ran along the wood's edge, it passed with busy speed the Trezona house, it rattled down. It began to come into the town of Thor, and they could see the white Methodist Church on the corner.

"Cyril?"

"Yes."

"What did he *say*?" Her face was pinched and rather angry.

"He's got a son," Cyril had heard this in the crowd.

"Oh," she said, inflating, somehow. "That's it, then." Her face smoothed out.

Cyril wouldn't say whether that was it. He would do his best not to repeat or remember what had been said.

"Why did you make that crack about our leaving town?" She roused herself to be belligerent.

"Because it's true. You're not going to hang around deviling Duncane, dear sister. I'm through here and you'll go with me."

"I don't have to go with you," she flared.

"Yes. You have to," he snapped. "I've got money. You haven't."

He could tell that she winced. He was a little sorry for her, not that he loved her, but she was his, after all. "You're through here, too," he said more mildly. "Never were quite right here. Wrong foot, somehow."

"This stupid town!" she said sullenly.

"We'll get away," he promised. "Cheer up. It's not the whole world."

Her shoulders wiggled.

They came to the town hall and turned up to the left. Nowhere to go but the little house. So they went into the alley, into the shack. They got out and came around to the front door. He had the key in his hand.

"This hut," she said. "This God-forsaken stuffy little town! At least I'll be free!" Stormy dreams in her eyes.

Cyril said soothingly, "Neither of us ever did fit in the patterns here." He unlocked the door and she went in. But he stood on the narrow porch and looked down where the big trees swayed over the town's heart. He feared he was wrong.

Because he could see (he saw too much!) how there might be, under the surface patterns, another. How a design, superimposed for show over the fabric, hides but cannot eliminate the real threads that really go in and out and, in simplicity and strength, are both a pattern and the cloth itself.

When the strain comes it is the weave that takes it.

Some of the people in Thor had something that kept them from breaking when the pull came and the stuff was tested, and others had not, they fell apart. In this pattern everyone fits, whether he likes it or no.

And the threads . . . his mind spun and he couldn't stop it . . . the qualities, the ones that hold, are many and different. And yet, *because* they hold, they have a folk name. Oh come . . .

He caught himself beginning to sob in that silly emotional fashion, and he twitched. He sniffed. No need to make a fool of himself! He walked through the door and slammed it.

"We're no good here," he said harshly. "You get upstairs, go to sleep. You need it. You look like hell." That moved her. He knew how to move her. Haggard and beautiful, she turned obediently toward the stairs. "I'm going to lie down myself. Head aches."

"Cyril?"

"What?"

"How much money have you?" Her lovely face was thoughtful.

"Enough, don't worry." His voice was thin and full of re-assuring scorn. But then he added, rather gently, because he had taught her—no one else had taught her anything—"You rest a while."

He did not sound loving. He never had. He never would.

But she turned to look, briefly startled, where he stood with his palms pressed over his sight.

"That was a town?" the motorist said to his wife. "Say, where are we?"

"Thor," she read on the map.

"Mining town."

"What did you say?" The ore train roaring under as they crossed the bridge over the cut was thunderous.

"Said, nothing there. Mining town."